# FOREVER IS NOT JUST TIME

# FOREVER IS NOT JUST TIME

JOE MCKINSTRY

Edited by Don White
Cover Art by Mohammed Omar Arif

ISBN: 978-0-578-28419-4

E-mail: info@joemckinstry.com
Website: https://joemckinstry.com

*For Mrs.* and *Carol*

*because of*

*Paul*

# TABLE OF CONTENTS

*Chapter 1*

# MYTH'D

Magic. Hoodoo. Mojo. Voodoo. They'd only ever heard of those things in books or on TV. But to 18-year-olds Gibbon Mulcahy and Leo Davion, standing outside under a living, breathing April night sky, those exact words may have gotten closest to describing what both of them were seeing and feeling at that very moment.

In silence high above them, the wind drew wispy black clouds across the three-quarter moon like dark curtains, pulling them open to illuminate the world for a few seconds, then yanking them shut again to cast everything back into total darkness. Stars added sparingly to the spectacle, random patch-works of sequins and diamonds winking in and out of sight behind those racing clouds.

Oddly, as wild as the wind was blowing up there in the heavens, Gibb couldn't remember a quieter night down here on the ground. Absolutely nothing and no one made a sound. Until he spoke.

"Why here?" Gibb asked quietly, immediately sorry he'd broken the spellbinding silence.

"Because briars are important to what I'm about to give you," Leo murmured back, his musical Louisiana accent plain.

*Brahrs are impord-ent to wut ahm about to give yoo.*

That's how Gibb had heard it, anyway. He grinned and turned away. The swirling action in the sky was a good distraction from the handsome, upturned face of the young man standing next to him. But as stunning as the sky looked tonight, the show was not enough to keep Gibb from wishing, for at least the thousandth time, that this whole thing wasn't happening.

"Go ahead and stand just over there, on the other side of this briar bush."

Gibb wrinkled his brow, uncertain why he was doing what he was told, but doing it anyway, claiming his spot directly across from Leo on the other side of the gnarled yard-high sticker-bush. Leo reached his hands across the bush toward Gibb. Gibb took them, interlacing his fingers between Leo's, staring at him quizzically.

"Now when I was a little kid," Leo said, staring into Gibb's eyes, "I've told you that the only friend I really had was my sister."

"Which is one more friend than I had," Gibb replied with a self-conscious smirk, suddenly catching himself and frowning as a darker reality dawned on him. "Well, sort of...after a while..."

"Right," Leo said. "But after your cousin died you knew what being friendless felt like, 'cuz you didn't fit in or whatever, right? Meanwhile, other kids were figurin' it out, forming friendships and all that. Some were even, like, blood brothers to each other."

Gibb's eyes widened. Leo wasn't being serious, was he?

"Come on now. We're not standing over this briar bush to prick our fingers and become blood brothers. Are we?" Gibb laughed incredulously. "We're kind of already way more than that at this point."

"No." Leo didn't laugh back. His curt response had a bite, enough to silence Gibb's good-natured sarcasm. "This is something much, much different."

Composing himself, Gibb promised not to interrupt again. Leo, slightly annoyed, continued.

"This all may sound corny to you, but that's only because certain names and symbols associated with this story have become lazy clichés in our every-day life. But it's not the story's fault, OK? The story is the story regardless, and there's nothing I can do to change it. Anyway, what I'm about to give you isn't much, but it's everything, too. Nothing and everything, all at the same time. I hope you'll understand."

Leo pulled his right hand away from Gibb's and reached down into his own jacket pocket. When it returned to grasp Gibb's hand again, Gibb could feel something hard and cold resting between their two palms. He furrowed his brow again.

"The day after I found out I had to leave," Leo began, "I found this in the woods over at Rogers Park. It was sitting smack up against a boulder right there on the edge of Seneca Lake. Sitting there all quiet but conspicuous, like it'd been waitin' on me to come along and pick it up. Maybe so I could have something to give you before I left… something that would help me explain myself to you. But I also need to hear myself say it…out here on this dead-silent night…over top of this daggone briar bush, so the whole unseen Universe can listen in while you hear it. OK?"

✂✂

Gibb had been walking in the dark down the unlit road for a good ten minutes. So far, not a single car had passed him in either direction. He stopped for a moment, just to reach deep into his backpack and feel around. Aha, there it was. The cold scrape of rock against his knuckle was the only assurance he needed. Carefully withdrawing his hand, he zipped the backpack closed as tight as he could and kept walking in the darkness.

That night two long months ago, under the almost-full moon and over a briar bush, Leo had given Gibb a beautiful heart-shaped rose quartz crystal he'd found straddling the edge of the woods and the Seneca Lake beach. There was no mistaking the crystal's beautifully weather-and-water-beaten shape: a rough-hewn heart that fit perfectly in Gibb's palm.

Up until that night, Gibb had never even heard of rose quartz nor did he know or care that it formed in crystals in caves and mines all over the world, even right there where he was in upstate New York. Sure, some rocks were pretty, but a rock was a rock. Pick up the flat ones and skip them across the lake. Who cared about any of the other ones?

But after that night, after every loving thing Leo had said before he finally gave it to him, Gibb cared about *that* rock. He'd fallen asleep grasping onto it every night since Leo left to go back to Louisiana.

That night in April, Leo wanted Gibb to understand *why* a rose quartz crystal was the perfect discovery and the perfect gift. And so he told the story of how rose quartz came to be in Greek mythology.

According to Leo, Adonis, the god of Love, got attacked by a wild boar. Except the boar wasn't a wild animal at all – it was actually Ares, the god of War who was jealous of the goddess Aphrodite's love for Adonis. Ares had taken the form of that boar to kill Adonis by surprise. But from wherever she was hanging out, Aphrodite saw what was happening and hurried down to save her love Adonis from Ares' evil plan. But just as Aphrodite reached Adonis, she got all tangled up in a briar bush. Aphrodite saved Adonis, which was great, but now both of them were injured and bleeding. Apparently, their magical co-mingled blood stained the white quartz crystals lying on the ground around them, turning them pink for all eternity.

Gibb had never seen Leo more serious. At first, he'd wanted to laugh at Leo's solemn tone as the mental image of a big, fat pig goring some Greek god crossed his mind. But Leo's grim demeanor served to keep Gibb from continuing to deny that yes, this truly was happening.

"Should we do that?" Leo had asked. "Prick our fingers and bleed onto this crystal for each other? For love? Even though it might be painful?"

Leo was leaving the next morning and he wouldn't be coming back. Still, Gibb tried to maintain at least a speck of humor in the proceedings.

"I'll do it if you will. But here on Earth tonight, which one of us is Adonis?" He chuckled. "And which one of us is Aphrodite?"

Leo had smiled when Gibb agreed to prick his finger, but Gibb's question, meant to be light-hearted, only made him frown again. He sighed softly.

"Each of us is both," Leo replied, patient but resolute. "Remember? Each equal parts the lover and the beloved. Separate, we're split into two halves. Together, we've joined up and now each of us has become whole. That's what that big Adonis/Aphrodite myth is about – love joining lovers together in spite of opposition and drama. Love can't ever exist without the equal energy of both: the masculine god and the feminine goddess."

Gibb looked confused. "Well somehow it sure exists between the two of us without a goddess," he muttered.

Leo laughed out loud for the first time all night. "I'm talking about our spirits, not our bodies, fool."

"You and me, we *are* that perfect combo of those energies. That's why this works, do you see? You need that perfect, natural balance of masculine and feminine and we both have that blend in certain measure within us. That's the balance of the entire universe. Yin/Yang, Boy/Girl, Love/Hate, Plus/Minus. Masculine/Feminine. Duality. Everywhere. It don't matter if you want to be any other way. You are who you are, I am who I am, and we are who we are. Naturally and perfectly."

"And…" Leo's eyes twinkled in the intermittent moonlight, "anybody who don't believe that can go fuck themselves."

Now it was Gibb's turn to laugh out loud. He didn't know if there was a single other person in the world as complicated as Leo Davion, but what did it matter? He loved Leo intensely, devotedly, lustily, even if he had a hard time keeping up with his intricate concepts about human existence. Leo sure knew a lot about a lot of things and Gibb was a zealous, if not always serious, student.

So yes, they did prick their fingers and bleed on that stone that gorgeous April night. And Leo did drive off in a cloud of spring mist the next morning to head back down south. And then, after all of that moon-stars-wind-Aphrodite-Adonis-briar-bush-blood-and-love blather, Gibb never heard from Leo again. Not a word. No call, no letter. Nothing.

Until this afternoon.

*Chapter 2*

# BLUES WALKIN'

Trying to walk the fifteen miles to the interstate was probably going to take more anxious time and energy than Gibb had tonight. But he was determined, even if he'd never walked even half that distance at one time.

As he walked, Gibb took deep breaths of the cool night air, doing his best to calm down and push himself forward, one long step at a time.

He was relieved that not one single car had yet passed by out here tonight. It meant that he wouldn't have to truly test his nerve just yet. Was he really going to do this? Stick out his thumb and then jump in a car to who-knows-where with a total stranger on some midnight whim? Or would he chicken out? As soon as he saw headlights, was he going to just dive into the woods and hide until they passed?

Suddenly, he didn't have another moment to think about it. A pair of long, stretching headlights came bending around a curve up ahead, heralding the appearance of a speeding sedan in the next split-second. Without thinking, Gibb dove right into the shelter of the tree line, lying flat and face-down until the car whooshed by.

Well, he had his answer. He closed his eyes. Rubbing his palms against the dead, dry leaves and damp dirt beneath him, he lay there for a moment cowering in the darkness, bitterly pitying himself. He silently cursed everyone and everything in his life for leading him to this pathetic point.

He could go back home right now – his mother wouldn't have even known he'd gone anywhere. She was asleep when he'd left. If he went home now, he could replace the two hundred dollars he'd stolen from her purse and tear up the nasty note he'd left for her. It was Sunday and the banks were closed, but she'd still refused to loan him the money for one lousy day. If he went home now, he could void the check he'd left to reimburse her for the theft, and then he could attend his high school graduation ceremony this evening. Life would return to whatever it was before. A loud and listless sigh escaped his lungs.

*Life would return to whatever it was before.*

That thought was enough to make Gibb finally open his eyes and sit up. He looked around feebly at the silhouettes of the silent trees and bushes surrounding him.

*Get up,* he finally told himself sternly. *You're not a criminal. For the first time in your life, you have somewhere important to be. You want change in your life? Come out of the woods and let those headlights hit you.*

But it still wasn't fair. Not even close. Because here he was, keeping his promise to Leo to be there for him no matter what. So, why was he keeping his promise when Leo hadn't kept his?

Gibb knew only half the answer, but what he knew had irked him from the moment he'd tramped out the door of his Eislertown home tonight. He hated to admit it, but it was because he *needed* Leo. But even worse, he needed Leo to need *him*. And now knowing that Leo needed him made him want to move Heaven and Earth to be there for him.

But that was the problem, Gibb thought, grinding his teeth in frustration. Who exactly was he doing all of this for, then? Sure, it was for Leo… to a degree. But this wasn't some huge sacrifice on Gibb's part. Look at how simple it was for him to just pick up and leave whatever life it was he'd had in Eislertown. Nobody truly cared enough about him to give Gibbon Mulcahy a reason to stay around. Hell, his own mother probably didn't even remember that he was supposed to graduate the next night.

But here was the tricky part. Now that he was on his way to see Leo, obstacles be damned, Gibb was beginning to realize that being needed was a lot more complex than having nobody really care about you. Because if nobody cares about you, you're free to do whatever you want without having to worry about what anyone else thinks about your choices. And if nobody cares, then nobody gets hurt. Simple.

But being needed…well, that was exactly one hundred percent the opposite. Being needed meant that somehow you mattered. Like it or not, that brought with it some real responsibility. And that responsibility could be, as Gibb was now finding out, a completely one-sided burden to bear. Leo needed him *right now*, so Gibb was the one hoofing it through the darkness in the middle of the night to try to hitch a ride to an open bus station instead of wasting time waiting around until tomorrow to find some other way. Would Leo ever do something like this for him? He strongly doubted it, rose quartz crystal and the god and goddess of love notwithstanding.

What did it really matter, though? Wasn't his impulse - to bolt Eislertown for Bache, Louisiana - the right answer when you love, when you're *in* love, with someone? Doesn't everyone else in the world just go ahead and do something like this when the person they love most in the world needs them?

Leo had been the one person, the *only* person, in the whole wide world, to ever call him amazing. Intelligent. Strong. Beyond that, Leo had been the only person he'd ever trusted. To share the hard secrets of his childhood.

More than that, Leo was the one person he'd ever had sex with, had ever been naked and intimate with. Sure, his was just another human body on a planet of billions of them, but showing it all to another person meant Gibb had to trust that Leo would be into what he was seeing. Gibb had been so unsure, but Leo had called him beautiful. Beautiful. And that was all it took.

It was the memory of those words that sent him running all the way down to Bache on little more than a whim. He needed to see Leo's face and hear him say those words again. And then, of course, he needed to be with him that way again.

Gibb shook his head, trying to clear his mind of the instant, futile erotic thoughts teasing him right now. *Everything will happen again once I get to Bache,* he thought resolutely.

But crouched down in the darkened woods, his spirits clouded again. Was he really doing this more for himself than for Leo? Was he really that self-centered?

A stern voice in his head interrupted his mental battle.

*Stop stalling...*

Gibb jumped to his feet, rubbing his hands together and brushing off the twigs and dirt that betrayed his cowardly plunge to the ground. He was no more confident than he'd been a minute ago, but he was going to go through with it now. He'd promised Leo and he was going to keep his word. Gibb strode back out to the road, heading south towards the interstate.

A half hour later, only three cars had gone by. He still hadn't been able to bring himself to turn around and stick out his thumb.

*OK, maybe this really was a bad idea,* he thought.

It had to be at least midnight. He was getting tired, yawning as he walked, occasionally glancing over to watch the moon glowing orange as it started setting in the western sky. Up ahead about a quarter mile, a lone bare bulb lit the darkened sign beneath it: *Seneca Gas and Go.*

He was now only about seven miles away from home, still less than half-way to where he needed to be to catch his first ride. Intervals of dejection rivaled his determination, but he kept walking, mumbling to himself.

"Why am I even doing this? This is madness."

A few minutes later, he reached the lighted sign. Maybe if he stood in the bright little pool of light underneath of it, it would be easier to flag someone down for a ride. He leaned his back against one of the sign's rickety wooden posts. It felt good to have something holding him up, even if it was gnarled wood. For a moment, he thought about sitting down on the ground to rest, but he knew he'd probably fall asleep right there.

Suddenly, without any warning, a man's deep voice boomed frighteningly out of the quiet darkness. The abrupt and unwelcome sound made Gibb jump and gasp as his heart reflexively started to pound in his chest.

"You there. Red-haired dude," the disembodied baritone called out. "Look, I'm over here!"

Aghast, Gibb whirled towards the voice coming from the gas station lot and saw a quick flash of headlights from a car parked right on the other side of the station.

What the hell? Someone in that car really expected him to just walk over there?

Suddenly, Gibb was really scared. He could make out the dark shape of what looked like a small station wagon. The headlights flashed again. Gibb took a deep breath through his nose. Was he really going to walk over there to that car? What if that guy grabbed him or hit him or worse? What if he wasn't even alone and there were a bunch of guys in the car, waiting to jump him?

Keeping his eye on the shadow car, Gibb reached into his backpack, fumbling around until his fingers felt the cold, hard quartz. He clutched the crystal and held it in his palm. It was going to have to be his amulet now, just in case there was any trouble.

"I ain't gonna hurt you, man. Just need you to give me some directions!" the voice called out.

Should he just take off running? The guy sounded normal enough, Gibb tried to convince himself. Warily, he took a few steps towards the station wagon. As he did, he heard the car door open. A tall, dark shadow rose slowly up from the driver's side. Intimidated, Gibb froze.

"Where do you need directions to?" he called out, trying not to sound as scared as he felt.

"Somewhere I can get some gas!" said the voice.

Confused, Gibb nervously scratched the back of his head, then loudly stated the obvious.

"Well, this place is closed! It's like midnight or something."

In reply, Gibb heard what sounded like a long sigh.

"Really, man?" the voice said sarcastically. "Thanks for pointin' that out."

Gibb didn't move any closer to the apparition, but the guy's sardonic tone was a little bit of a relief.

"Are you alone?" Gibb called out.

"Nope!" said the voice, its tone amused. "I got seven dudes in this car and we was all just waitin' on you to show up so we could make a human sacrifice out of you on this here gas station lot. You up for that?"

The shadow moved closer to him. Gibb backed up.

"Don't be scared," the voice said, trying to sound reassuring. "I really am alone. Just need your help."

"Then come over to this sign where I can see you in the light," Gibb called back, turning around to head back to the sign and stand under the bare bulb, relieved to feel a little more in control of the situation.

As the man moved to join him under the light, Gibb's jaw dropped and his blue eyes widened behind his glasses. The shadow guy was easily seven feet tall. He wore black from hat to boot. He was the tallest person Gibb had ever seen in person, for sure, and one of the thinnest. He looked like a strong wind could knock him right over. If it did, this guy was in for one long fall. Wait, was he famous?

Gibb squinted up at him. From where he stood, the guy's head looked too small for his tall body. But he marveled at the length of the man's mocha-colored fingers, each capped with a fastidiously manicured nail. The guy's odd physical proportions were fascinating, but his voice was even more intriguing. How could such a booming voice come out of such a skinny throat?

"How can I help you, sir?" Gibb said.

"Look at you, all polite," the man said, smirking. "A nice young man just out here in the middle of nowhere in the middle of the night."

Gibb gulped a little. This guy was weird. Sort of humorous, but weird.

"Relax, dude. My problem is I'm almost out of gas," the man said. "I been kinda stuck here waitin' for this place to open up 'cuz I don't wanna run out of gas on these butt-fuck Egypt roads y'all got around here, you know?"

Instantly, the man apologized. "Sorry for my language, kid."

Gibb laughed, reassured that the guy was being truthful. "It's OK! It's not like I've never heard those words before."

"Dude, what the hell do people even do around here?" the man asked, incredulous. "There ain't *nothin'* goin' on and it's barely past twelve. Are you from around here?"

Gibb nodded and chuckled.

"Born and raised."

"Well, all right then. Poor you," the guy said, a look of honest pity on his face. "Anyway, I don't want to wait no longer than I have to. If you could tell me if there's an all-night gas station real close by, then I might could jus' get this car there, fill 'er up, and get back on the road."

Gibb couldn't believe his luck. This guy could at least give him a ride out to the interstate once he got gas. If he got in that car with him, he would really be on his way!

"Sure, if you can make it another four or five miles, there's like an AM/ PM market that's open all night down in Watkins Glen. They have a gas station there."

Gibb offered to navigate the way down to Watkins Glen if the man promised to give him a ride out to the interstate.

"Boy, where you goin' in the middle of the night, talkin' 'bout hitchhikin' out on an interstate?" the man asked as they walked over to the car. He almost sounded concerned.

"Pretty far away," Gibb replied breezily, as if he were regularly out at night hitching rides. "It's a town call Bache and it's in Louisiana. Things are bad. It's a long story."

The tall man raised his eyebrows. "Bache, Louisiana? Maybe you ain't gonna believe this, but I swear it's true – I'm driving down to New Orleans. That's where I live. If you wanna help pay for the gas, I can get you that far, at least."

*What?*

Gibb's eyes widened. "No way. Did you really just say you're going to New Orleans?"

"That's right," the man replied. "New Orleans, Loozeanna, the center of the Universe. For cool people, that is."

"This is unbelievable!" Gibb exclaimed. "There's no way. How'd you end up here in the Finger Lakes of all places? In the middle of the night?"

"I just come from a reunion of buddies from 'Nam. We get together every couple years or so somewhere in the country. I bring my sax and play a little.

This year we was up in Rochester. And my dumb ass didn't get gas up there where civilized folks live. So then I got lost around here, and now I *swear* I can hear them banjos in the distance. You know what I'm talkin' 'bout." The man widened his eyes in exaggerated fear.

Gibb laughed again. "I don't think anybody around here plays a banjo. They just watch TV a lot. The only way they'd kill you is by boring you to death. There's pretty scenery, though, in the daylight."

"You don't say," the man said, "Too bad we ain't stickin' around for sunrise. You ready to roll?"

Gibb's own eyes widened. Could this really be happening? He nodded.

"What's your name, man?" the man asked as they got to the car.

"I'm Gibb," the young red-haired man replied, trying to give the older man's huge hand a firm handshake.

"Gibb?" the man asked, wrinkling his nose. "What kind of a name is that? Is it short for somethin'?"

Gibb was embarrassed for a second. "It's short for Gibbon," he replied dryly.

"Gibbon," the man repeated, like it was a word he'd never heard. Except it turned out that he *had* heard it, in a very different context.

"Gibbon, like the monkey Gibbon?" the man chuckled. "We had them li'l Gibbon monkeys over in 'Nam."

Gibb raised his eyebrows. He'd only met this man a minute ago and already this guy was making fun of him. At midnight. In a deserted gas station parking lot. Not a scenario Gibb could have imagined playing out only hours before, but...here he was. Well, this guy was weird but at least he didn't seem like a psycho.

"Yeah, like the monkey Gibbon," Gibb mumbled, resignation in his voice. "I can't believe I'm even telling you this, but yeah, that's how I got my name. My Dad thought I sorta looked like a monkey when I was born, so they named me that."

"Well, all right then," the man said with a deep chuckle. "Kind of a messed-up thing to do to a baby, namin' him after a monkey. But I guess parents do all kinda messed-up things, don't they?"

Gibb grunted. "Uhh, yeah," he said. "You could say that."

"Sorry to be doggin' you the first minute I meet you," the affable man said with a grin. "My name is SamWell. But you can call me Sam if you cool. Otherwise, it's SamWell, hear?"

Gibb opened the passenger side door with trepidation. How was it possible that he was thinking about putting his entire life in this stranger's hands the second he was in the man's car? Anything could happen. He truly could be some wild serial killer. He could be a mental patient or a prison escapee! He could be the worst human being on Earth.

"Do me a favor and stamp yo' feet to get rid of the dust on your shoes and just shake yourself off a little, OK?" the man requested in the darkness. "I seen some twigs and stuff on your shirt over and there might be one danglin' near yo' right ear. My ride ain't much but I like it clean and smellin' nice."

Sheepishly, Gibb complied with the request, a smirk on his own face. There was no way this guy was a serial killer. Before he got in the car, he carefully slipped the rose quartz amulet back into his backpack. It was almost like it had served its purpose.

*Chapter 3*

# WAKE UP CALL

F ive a.m. and southbound on Interstate 81, Gibb drowsily rode shotgun as SamWell Dreaux, a man he'd never met before last night, rolled wordlessly on through a state Gibb had never before visited. Shadowed for one last moment in ribbons of glowing pinks and purples out on the eastern Maryland horizon, the sun suddenly vaulted deftly into the early June morning sky, spearing its first rays right into Gibb's closed eyelids.

He'd slept only fitfully through the short and jouncy night and now, haplessly, he shifted his position again, trying to get comfortable in the dismal ergonomic confines of a tatty 1977 Volaré station wagon.

Suddenly, Sam laughed, raucous and feckless. The sound burst through the car like a wild punch, untroubled by who it hit or who it hurt. And, like a flying fist always does, it clocked someone who didn't deserve it: Gibb, sort of awake now and not even a little bit happy about it.

Grimacing, he sat up in his seat. Achy shoulders, unprepared for such a long car ride, voiced their complaints in the form of pins and needles stabbing along the length of arms unintentionally folded for too many sleepy hours. He glared over at Sam, the impossibly thin, ridiculously tall driver. With his seat pushed back as far as it could go, Sam's knees still pushed up against the dashboard. He kept his eyes on the road, but a smug smile crossed his lips as he saw his young passenger stirring himself awake.

"Where *y'AT*?" Sam hooted, entirely too loud for this time of the day. Gibb grumbled and fumbled around for his glasses.

"I don't know..." he muttered, irked and sleepy. "You got a loud laugh, you know that? Where are we? And what was so funny?"

"We jus' passed into Maryland. I think you musta dozed off right after we got into Pennsylvania," Sam replied, his deep voice much quieter now. "And then I looked over at you and you had yo' mouth hangin' open, lookin' like one of them fish you see layin' on top of the ice at the market. I wished I had a camera."

He chuckled again.

"Aren't you sleepy?" unamused Gibb yawned, glancing at the digital clock on the dashboard. "We've been on the road for more than five hours. Want me to start driving?"

"I'm a musician, man. This is my time of day...I'm hardly ever asleep at five in the morning. You can take over in about three hours."

"Do you know that I've never been out of New York State...well...until now? Never."

Gibb immediately felt silly at his admission to the almost total stranger, both for the truth of his words and for his blithe over-sharing but, nervous and still sleepy, he kept talking.

"Anyway, uh... I'm sorry about falling asleep. I really meant to stay awake to help keep you awake while you drove."

"Thanks fo' the help. It made all the difference," Sam said, grinning out of one corner of his mouth. "Seriously, though, I don't need no help stayin' awake in the wee hours. I'm jus' more surprised than anything that I got me a trav'lin' companion."

He looked over at Gibb, his eyes laughingly disapproving of the red-haired, disheveled sight in the passenger seat.

"'Specially one as ugly as you."

Gibb made a face, then yawned. "Not a pretty picture, is it?" he said flatly, scratching at his head.

Sam laughed again. "You ain't lyin'."

He fixed his eyes back on the road in front of him.

"Anyway, you awake enough now to tell me why you headed to New Orleans? Lookin' for adventure? You gonna find it there. Bet!" he said nodding, more to himself than to Gibb.

Gibb could feel himself tense up, not really sure how to respond to Sam's question. The lengthening pause in their brief conversation was quickly becoming awkward, adding to his dread of having to explain himself to Sam. Sure, he could lie, just make up a simple story that would seem plausible. He didn't know this guy so what would it matter? Sam was only giving him a ride from Point A to Point B, and even though Gibb was grateful for it, he didn't feel like he owed anybody an explanation about where he was really heading. Or why. Especially why.

Nervously, he cleared his throat and spoke up.

"So…well, look. If I tell you why I'm going to Louisiana," Gibb said, stammering, "I'll be honest with you. You might just pull over and tell me to get out of the car."

"Why?" Sam asked, suddenly sounding serious, his eyes only on the road. "You kill somebody or somethin'?"

"No!" Gibb laughed, then frowned. "I thought about killing my stepdad last night, but that's nothing unusual. That's not the story, though."

"Whew! That's a relief," Sam said, exaggerating his exhalation. "OK then, so are you pregnant with another man's baby?" he asked deadpan, still staring straight ahead.

"Uhhh…what?" Gibb asked, confused as he watched Sam snicker at his own question.

"Look man, only two things gonna make me put you out the car, OK?" Sam said matter-of-factly. "If'n you killed somebody would be the first reason. I don't want no murderers in my car bringin' no criminal bullshit to my passenger seat, OK? The second reason would be if you was my girlfriend and you was pregnant with another man's baby.

"So…" Sam held out his thumb to count, "number one…you ain't killed nobody, so you good there. Number two, we know you ain't no girl, and even if you was, with that ugly-ass face of yours, you fo' sure wouldn't be *my* girlfriend. So you good there, too. See? Now it don't matter what you tell me, I'll let you stay. Mainly 'cuz I'm-a need you to start drivin' in a couple hours."

"Well…it's kind of a long story," Gibb said, giving himself one more chance to back out.

"It's kind of a long ride," Sam replied.

"I guess," Gibb agreed, out of excuses now. At this moment, he was truly more interested in hearing himself admit the truth than he was worried about Sam's reaction.

"Umm…" he muttered, not sure how to begin. "Hmm…well…"

"Can't be much of a story," Sam said, feigning a yawn. "I'm already bored as hell."

"OK, here it goes." Gibb began. "Try not to get too wigged out. So, you already told me you've heard of the town of Bache…"

"Sure, I have," came Sam interrupted. "That's why you in this car…"

Now it was Gibb's turn to interrupt. "Well…"

He finally just let it fly, blurting out his reason and his desperation in one long, barely coherent, run-on sentence.

"I'm on my way to Bache because my boyfriend Leo's dad had cancer real bad and he just died and it's terrible because his family already had a lot of trouble but I promised him I'd be there for him because I love him more than anything even though we're not supposed to be in love 'cuz we're both guys but we're in love anyway and I don't care who knows it anymore."

As he rambled, Gibb could see Sam's eyebrows arch, a look of surprise and then a frown overtaking his almost gaunt countenance. His wide blue eyes searched Sam's face, not sure whether what he'd just confided had crossed a line that Sam hadn't even considered when he'd laid out the two conditions for leaving his hitchhiking passenger out on the interstate.

"Wow!" Sam finally said, his head nodding in a kind of appreciation as he turned towards Gibb. "I wasn't expectin' nothin' like that. Now *that's* a good story, see? OK!"

Now it was Gibb's turn to look surprised.

"I'm serious," Sam went on. "I'm sorry about what y'all are dealin' with, but at least it's not some lame-ass shit like, 'I knocked up my girlfriend and now I gotta leave town.' 'Cuz I'll be honest, that's what I thought you was gonna say. But *this*? Wow. Look at you! I got some new respec' for you, Gibbon-like-the-monkey-Gibbon. You got some heavy kind of grown-up shit goin' on, don't you?"

"I don't know what to call it," Gibb said, his nervousness still presenting itself in shaky hands and a galloping heartbeat. "I just know I need to get there. I already feel like I should've been there when everything happened. Now I feel like I'm getting there too late."

"Well, we gonna try to get you there as fast as we can. Heads up, though. I can't drive too fast. Police always thinkin' I'm up to no good if I'm drivin' over the limit. Trust me on this. Fastest way to get you there is for me to do the speed limit, OK? We can maybe go five or ten over, but that's it."

Gibb nodded, not sure what to say. Sam may have just awakened him with a too-loud laugh, but Gibb couldn't believe his good fortune. Not only was Sam heading to New Orleans, but he wasn't judgmental about Gibb's reasons for making this trip. And he seemed kind-hearted to boot.

"I...I really don't know how to thank you."

"No thanks necessary, dude. I mean, I was headin' this way anyway. There was room."

He paused and regarded his young passenger.

"But there's gotta be a good reason you didn't jus' find another way to get down to New Orleans. We do got buses and planes now, ya know."

Relieved by and a little astounded at the absence of any judgment from Sam, Gibb decided to trust him enough to tell him the entire story, up to and including the moment the two of them met in the darkness only hours before, just outside Eislertown, New York.

*Chapter 4*

# THE STRANGEST
# OF PLACES

E islertown was one of those places that everyone knew of but no one ever visited. Nestled secretly among the trees between Route 96A and a tiny stretch of northeastern Seneca Lake, locals could tell you the secluded village in the heart of the Finger Lakes was tucked away into the woods over there somewhere, but no one could come up with a reason to ever go there.

In most places, life's beauty and ugliness sit in stark opposition at either end of a long spectrum of perception as the countless shades of grey between them blend together to comprise most of life's experiences. But in Eislertown, to Gibb anyway, only the grey existed. The dark grey, the mostly ugly grey.

"What the hell is even *in* Eislertown? Aren't there only like five people who live there?" Gibb's favorite teacher, Ms. Mullan, asked him after freshman year English class one day a few years earlier. She was from Boston, and, well, she just talked like that. Direct. Gibb loved that about her. Despite her bluntness, she was only curious about what she was asking.

Gibb only replied that Eislertown was a weird place, but yeah, more than five people lived there, maybe two hundred, and that living there was kind of a "mixed bag of heck". What Ms. Mullan didn't know, as the bespectacled, nerdy adolescent snickered to himself, was that to Gibb the word "heck" was a perfectly innocuous combination of the words "hell" and "fuck".

His mixed bag of heck had actually begun the July before he'd turned four years old, the night his father was killed in a head-on drunk-driving accident. After finishing up a second- shift stint at a nearby salt-brining plant, Gibb's dad had been on a routine drive home on two-lane Route 414, a road he drove every day of his life.

As every earthly second passes, someone's world changes forever in that very instant. For Gibb and his mother, Lily, theirs changed the second it took a middle-aged inebriate to drift his two-ton 1969 Chevy Chevelle across the center line of a blind curve at sixty-five miles per hour. The aftermath of twisted metal and shards of glass strewn across that road became the perfect metaphor for their lives in the moments and years afterwards.

If someone had asked Gibb to reveal his clearest early memory of his life, he no doubt would have said it was the midnight knock on the door that awful night, the blue-grey uniform of a New York state trooper, and his mother's window-rattling screams carrying through the open screen door as his three-year-old self stood blinking against the glare of the living room light in footy pajamas, panicked and crying at the scene playing out in front of him.

Now, many years later, he couldn't picture his dad as well as he could remember the way he felt when he was around. Gibb's vague memories of his father and his early life had left him with a steady feeling of happiness and security. He called on those memories often to remind himself that something better could exist outside the sad confines of their broke-down Eislertown palace, wishing so hard sometimes that his dad could still be with them somehow.

But that was impossible, of course. Still, after marrying a great guy like his dad, how could his mother end up giving her hand to a bum like Jack Haydel? Was she that desperate for a husband? Beaten down by life? Shell-shocked because of what happened to his dad? Gibb knew that the questions and their answers were all pointless because there was nothing he could do about it. His mother did marry Jack, and life became what it became. But he imagined that his dad would have been appalled.

Jack was a weaselly little guy, just over five-and-a half feet tall. His furtive little brown eyes would dart back and forth during conversations and when he smiled, his slightly buck teeth were reminiscent of a certain cartoon rabbit. But Jack wasn't funny like Bugs Bunny. He just thought he was.

He loved calling Gibb any name that referenced his freckly, bespectacled red-headed looks:

"Archie", "Opie", "Carrot Top", "Four-Eyes", and when Gibb was a little kid, "Freckle-Face Strawberry." Old and stale, just like Jack's approach to life. And then there were his awful, malignant jokes.

"Hey, Opie, how many faggots can you fit on a bar stool?" Jack would crack, clearly picking up on Gibb's lack of enthusiasm at hearing this garbage for the millionth time.

"Jack...", Gibb would start to protest.

"Four!" Jack interrupted gleefully. "You just turn it upside down!"

And then he'd laugh out loud again, like it was the first time he'd ever told the lame joke. Gibb would just grimace and shake his head. Jack enjoyed his reaction immensely. He usually followed up with at least one more charming quip before shutting up for a while, satisfied that he'd gotten under Gibb's skin again.

A born loser, that was Jack. He knew it and he knew Gibb knew it. He lacked imagination and self-confidence, the two most important characteristics Gibb thought a person needed to make a better life for himself. Jack's vile jokes and comments came from the same universal source that all hate comes from, the perpetual feeling of anger towards anyone or anything he did not, could not, or even *want* to understand.

And he may have been mistaken, but Gibb suspected he knew why Jack enjoyed repeating those awful jokes to him over and over. Because if Jack was doing it for the reasons Gibb thought he was, then they were both right.

Gibb had never once spoken about it to Lily or Jack, but he was gay. And in spite of Jack's never-ending spew of derogatory bullshit, Gibb wasn't ashamed of it. Confused what to do about it, sure, but not ashamed, no matter how many times sawed-off little Jack needled him about not having a girlfriend. Jack loved to open up to the *Playboy* centerfold and ogle the picture, laughing lewdly as he tried to get Gibb to expound upon his favorite physical assets of the photo. Gibb would just get embarrassed and tell Jack to leave him alone. The last thing he wanted to do was give Jack any insight into what, or who, he found attractive.

One thing remained true, though. Gibb lived in Jack's house. And regardless of the jerk's antics, he knew he needed to keep his cool or risk Jack taking his frustration out on his mother Lily. To Gibb's knowledge, Jack had never been physically abusive to her, but he yelled at his mother a lot. He was controlling and manipulative, keeping her guessing at all the ways to satisfy him. It seemed that just when she thought she'd figured it out, Jack would change the game again.

Gibb couldn't remember one dinner where Jack didn't have something to say about whatever Lily made them. Everything was too dry, too undercooked, too salty. Jack would complain about it to Lily with a superior look on his rat-face. Her face would register another defeat, and Gibb would wonder how it was possible for him to despise Jack even more than he did the day before.

It was after one of those boringly predictable dinner episodes that Gibb, deciding he'd had enough of seeing his mother kowtow to her rotten husband, excused himself to go for a long walk. He had a lot to think about.

Senior year was starting in a little over a week and he was on edge about it for a few reasons. As much as he hated living in Jack's rundown house, he was still nervous about experiencing what came next: applying to colleges, maybe not getting accepted, *paying* for college if he got accepted, dealing with his sexuality in secret in this town, this whole area, for another whole year. Knowing he wouldn't be asking anyone to the prom in spring. Relieved about that. Anxious about that. Tired of thinking about that. Just ready to leave and start something new. But it was still scary to think about it.

He'd write his feelings down in pedantic, self-conscious poetry, then revel in ripping the pages out of the notebook so he could light them on fire whenever he was the only one home. The first time he burned up his journal pages, he told himself that destroying his words by fire made the most sense because talent-wise, well, he was pretty much the exact opposite of Robert Frost.

He could never explain the feeling of freedom those flaming acts of desecration brought him, and he got pretty good at pretending that his feelings were disintegrating right there in front of him along with the ink and paper. But reality was a persistent pest, and soon he'd be back in his room, writing more of the same old tortured crap.

Tonight's sky would have been worthy of a new attempt at poetry, though. It was only late August, but it had already begun to feel like autumn in the Finger Lakes, especially in the evenings. Gibb put on his lightweight jacket and slipped his beat-up, taped-shut four-year-old cassette Walkman into the front pocket. He crossed through Jack's junk-car littered front yard, adjusted his headphones and pushed "Play."

Heading onto a path beaten long ago through the darkening woods, the orange and purple twilight draped itself over the tops of the trees and Gibb, struck by both the beauty of the scene and the music in his ears, stopped to take in the tranquil power of the moment.

The beautiful voice in his headphones was actually singing about summer turning into fall, magically freezing the moment into his memory. The sky, the trees, the feel of the air, the crescent moon just over the tree line. Minus the music, he'd dreamt this exact scene in his sleep many times. Now that he was experiencing it awake and alert, it felt like a sort of *déjà vu* moment, something he couldn't quite explain, like the sign of a huge promise about to be fulfilled.

He quickened his pace along the path in anticipation of… of what? Nothing? Something? Maybe everything.

# Chapter 5

# INCONVENIENCE STORE

G ibb stared ahead blankly as he approached the bright fluorescent lights of the little Kountry Korner convenience store. The walk through the dark woods under that breathtaking sunset sky had inspired some big thoughts in him, thoughts like what a perfect future life would look like. Happy in some sort of medical career. Having a couple of dogs. Finding an awesome guy to share that perfect life with, far away from here. Glad to have the dogs, at least, if he never found the guy.

And then he walked out of the woods and saw it, the silly spelling of the name of the only store close enough to walk to. Kountry Korner. The purposeful misspelling of "country" and "corner" with a "K" instead of a "C" seemed to be the peak of artistic creativity around these parts, and it brought him joylessly back to the boring reality of Eislertown.

As he walked in, he was greeted by the familiar cigarette gravel voice of Nicotina. That's what Gibb called her, anyway. Not to her face, just to himself. Her real name was actually Lois, she of the perpetually lit-cigarette hanging out of her mouth, in her hand, or in an ashtray. Nicotina was one of the store's owners and the likely mastermind behind the Kountry Korner name.

"Hi, Gibb!" she croaked.

Turning to return the greeting, Gibb managed to get out the words, "Hey, Ni…err…Lois," before his heart stopped for a second.

*Holy shit, who is that guy?*

No warning sirens sounded; no bells rung in Gibb's ears. Just a shocking, but somehow familiar jolt right through his skin, skeleton, and spirit as the customer at the counter casually turned to regard him.

The guy was tall, at least 6'1", a lanky boy about Gibb's age with flawlessly unkempt longish sandy-blond hair. His sizable right hand clutched a Coke and Gibb noticed that two of the rangy fingers sported rings, rings that seemed to gleam in the glaring fluorescent light above the cash register.

Both of the guy's ears were pierced and to Gibb's immediate approval, he was wearing a black Grateful Dead T-shirt emblazoned dead-center with the iconic "Steal Your Face" red-white-and- blue skull-and-lightning logo. Gibb's breath actually got a little short as he wondered if the guy loved the Dead, Gibb's favorite band, or if he was lame and just liked the design on the T-shirt. Actually, he didn't care.

*That dude is freakin' hot.*

To Gibb's slight alarm, his eyes locked with the guy for just a split-second too long, but the friendly, spontaneous smile he returned relieved any sudden anxiety Gibb felt about possibly being caught staring. He nodded a brusque hello and shuffled away towards the candy bars, pretending to be stumped by which one to choose, glancing back at the counter to check out the hot dude.

*No chance, none whatsoever, not now, not ever,* he thought forlornly to himself as he stole one last look at the concluding transaction between Nicotina and the stud. It wasn't the first time he'd seen a guy and wished for himself better looks, a better physique, a better everything. *Anything* to stand a chance at getting a guy like that.

For a moment, again, he wished he wasn't gay so he wouldn't be attracted to someone so out of reach, out of his league. The most appalling part was that the guy probably wasn't even close to being gay, rendering Gibb's instant, mighty attraction a worthless waste of energy.

He caught Gibb's eye as he moved towards the door and gave him a quick nod as he headed out. Nothing to get excited about, just a nod. Didn't mean anything.

*Hi,* Gibb thought to himself sarcastically, *I'm Gibb, the local nerd-boy. Sorry for my slack jaw and the drool, but I thought you were hot. I'll just go ahead and fuck right off now. Have a great night!*

He shook his head and sighed, still peering over the top of his glasses, watching his latest stranger-crush stride confidently through the glass door and around the corner of the building.

Nicotina called over to him from behind the counter.

"I see you shaking your head over there, Gibb. Having trouble finding what you want?"

"Nope, I'm pretty sure I found it," he called back, glancing in vain towards the door for maybe one last glimpse.

⌘

The woods were pitch black on the way home, but Gibb barely noticed, focused instead on the jumble of random thoughts careening around in his brain. Usually, he kind of liked walking around in the dark. In fact, he preferred it to daylight if for no other reason than it allowed him the illusion that he was totally, completely invisible. It made it easier to hide from the world's judgment of his flaws and hopes and dreams. And if he was being honest, his own judgments, too.

But even darkness couldn't help him tonight because, at this moment, nothing was making sense. He just could not shake the memory of that guy's handsome smile back there at the stupid Kountry Korner. It bugged him. The guy was just some random dude buying a Coke. A random guy whose ridiculously handsome smile had rattled every bone in Gibb's body.

He stopped walking. For one long second in those dark woods, shrouded there in the darkness, he wished that he was straight and that that good-looking guy had been a beautiful girl. It would have made life so much easier. Because if that guy had been a girl, and if Gibb had been into her, he probably wouldn't have been as embarrassed by the power of the attraction. A girl would have picked up on his reaction right away and either a) flirted or b) sent the silent message that she wasn't interested. Next.

But some random gorgeous guy at the Kountry Korner grabbing a Coke? He'd have absolutely no idea that Gibb felt or even *could* feel that way. Worse, that same guy would never even *think* about Gibb again, not even for a second. Meanwhile here Gibb was, traipsing back home, back to a silly, rundown little house and a silly, rundown little life. Invisible in this darkness. In a confused and discontented daze over some random, hot stranger.

He sighed, shaking his head hard in a vain attempt to just forget the whole thing – the guy, his same-sex attractions, his life at home, high school.

The possibility of ever even seeing the dude again, let alone having some kind of relationship with him, was exactly zero.

*Why am I even thinking about this?!* Gibb thought, his inside voice exasperated.

He continued to shake his head, kicking at unseen rocks and twigs along the darkened path back into Eislertown, every one of his exhalations a sigh of frustration.

⚏

*I hate my life*, Gibb thought to himself, sighing as he moved his hands up to cradle the back of his head to stare up into the dark void of his bedroom ceiling. *Everything about it is so stupid. Everyone else is smarter, better-looking, happier or funnier than me. I just get to lie here in this bed feeling ashamed of myself. Because I'm weird. A friggin' dorky weirdo.*

Then, from the back of his mind, a stronger, familiar and irritatingly cheerful voice spoke up, a voice he often heard when he was pathetic and full of self-pity.

*If you couldn't deal with this life, you wouldn't have this life,* it said. *You'd be somebody else and then you'd have to deal with **their** shit. You have it hard, others have it harder. Don't go comparing your life to anyone else's. You're all right.*

There was a short pause before the voice left him with one last directive.

*And stop being a pussy.*

Gibb just shook his head. The voice usually ended its sermon by saying something profane like that. It was almost funny, but he didn't laugh. The voice was right, and he knew it.

*Chapter 6*

# STATE OF THE STATE

A week later it happened, just like in a romantic movie. No, not really. Unless you can get past one of the most unromantic settings in humankind: a dull, fluorescent-lit American high school history classroom. And if you can pretend really hard that whatever happened that morning was romantic. Because it wasn't.

But that's *where* it happened, at least, on the first day of senior year. *He* walked in. The handsome dude. The Kountry Korner guy. And Gibb would soon learn that this...this... *phantasm* had a name: Leopold Davion.

*No freakin' way!* Gibb yelled in his mind, feeling his face flush with excitement, as the guy entered the classroom. Quietly, he took a deep breath and held it, looking away as he closed his mouth and unconsciously bulged his cheeks before exhaling an airy, unintentionally lip-buzzing sigh.

*Look at that. (But not too hard).*

There was that perfect blondish hair, but as the guy moved closer to Gibb's seat, Gibb could now see the color of his eyes. Blue-green, the color of tropical ocean water Gibb had only ever seen in pictures.

*Oh my God. It's even worse than I thought,* he lamented to himself.

A wicked skull ring grinned grimly from the guy's left middle finger and, yep, Gibb hadn't been wrong. Both of the guy's ears were pierced with small gold hoops.

Gibb slouched down in his chair, glumly wondering to himself how in the world someone could just show up looking that cool. Effortlessly. It was disgusting. No one person should be able to just…to just…*look* like that. Breaking peoples' hearts without even knowing or caring. What a jerk.

There had to be a word for what Gibb was seeing, but his intellect was failing him. For the first time in his life, he was being confronted by the severe limitations of the English language in real time. What in the world was the word he was looking for? He needed something better, but he had to settle on one paltry description: *Beauty.* Actually, make that two words. *Intimidating* beauty. That was it. Was there a word that combined those two things?

He hadn't been mistaken when, from a safe distance, the guy's looks had unintentionally knocked him out at the stupid Kountry Korner last week. But now? Being up close to this much beauty was like being out under a brutal summer sun. Blinding. Too Hot. For a second, he mulled crawling under his desk to hide from it. He could feel himself begin to sweat.

There was an open seat next to Gibb and he really hoped the guy wouldn't take it. Lies. Yes, he did.

*Sit here! No…go sit somewhere else! OK, please sit here. No…go away!*

"Is it cool if I sit here?" the guy asked, because of course he would, gesturing towards the empty seat next to flustered Gibb. His voice was gentle and quiet and Gibb wasn't sure, but the guy's question may have been slowed down by a bit of a drawl.

Snapped out of his mental wrestling match, Gibb could only mumble.

"Sure, go ahead," he said, nodding and gesturing to the chair, trying hard not to look the guy in the eye again and working even harder to sound casual. Unpredictably, impulsively, almost as if he was listening to someone else's voice asking the question, Gibb addressed the handsome stranger and… immediately wished he hadn't.

"Are you new?" Gibb asked, his face reddening as he realized how stupid his question sounded.

*I am easily the lamest person in the Universe. "Are you new?" Really?*

To Gibb's relief, the good-looking stranger didn't seem put off by the question at all.

"Yep. My family got here early last week," he replied, his gentle drawl much more noticeable now. "My Dad's job took us up here from Loozeanna."

*Loozeanna.* Gibb liked the sound of that. He suddenly realized he'd never met a real person who spoke with a Southern accent. Anything he knew about the South came from history books, or movies where hapless travelers ran into southern hillbillies commanding them to "squeal like a pig," and TV shows where waitresses said things like "kiss my gree-its." But he'd never met anyone who really talked like that. He was charmed and for some reason, he felt a quick shiver run right down the front of his body, all the way to his feet.

"Cool," Gibb said. "I really dig that skull ring. My name's Gibb, by the way."

He was surprised and kind of proud that he actually introduced himself, almost believing that the beautiful guy would actually care to know his name.

"Hi, Gibb. I'm…"

Just as the stranger was about to introduce himself, the bell rang and their teacher, Mr. Mellon, walked in, quietly closing the door behind him. As Mr. Mellon took roll, Gibb found himself setting his jaw in anticipation of finding out the new guy's name.

"Davion, Leopold."

The good-looking guy shyly raised up his hand as Mr. Mellon scanned the room. Gibb noticed three girls across the classroom all stare over at Leopold, then turn and look at each other, all wide-eyed. One of them mouthed the words, "*Oh. My. God.*" to the others as they both nodded their eager assent.

Gibb frowned. In his mind's eye he could see ol' Leopold over here holding hands with one of them by the end of the week as they walked down the stupid school hallway between classes.

"Aha – there's a hand. You're Leopold?" Mr. Mellon confirmed.

The new guy nodded.

"OK, good. Welcome, Leopold. You're a new face around here."

*Yes, yes he is a new face around here,* Gibb thought wryly. *And there's never been a better-looking one to brighten up this lame place.*

"Where are you from, Leopold?" Mr. Mellon asked, his question sounding nosier than he probably intended.

Either way, judging by the way the guy slouched down in his seat and mumbled, Gibb could tell that Leopold wasn't too excited about being the center of the class's attention, even for a brief moment.

"Umm…" Leopold stammered, his posture slightly worsening. "I'm from southwestern Louisiana, like about a hundred miles from New Orleans," he said, this time with almost no trace of an accent. Gibb wondered if the guy had practiced those pronunciations so he wouldn't stand out too much among all the Yankee natives in the room.

"Kind of a big adventure," Mr. Mellon prattled on, oblivious to his new student's discomfort, "starting your senior year in a new place and in a whole different area of the country."

"Yes, sir, I do believe it will take some time gettin' used to. I go by Leo, though," the gorgeous guy stated quietly, his accent slipping through this time.

*Yep, in about one week, this guy is gonna be the most popular dude in school,* Gibb thought, *at least with the girls. Every guy is gonna hate him. Except me. I won't have a girlfriend he can steal.*

Leo turned to Gibb and gave him a friendly nod, which Gibb tried not to return too eagerly, as Mr. Mellon began his lesson. Gibb didn't listen to a word of it. He was too preoccupied trying to figure out a way to ask the handsome guy…er…Leo…if he wanted to hang out.

Under ordinary circumstances, which was every other single day of Gibb's life up to today, he wouldn't have ever once considered doing any such thing. But the guy was new and probably didn't know anybody yet. That would probably change within in a week, but damn. This guy's presence shook him up hard. Gibb really wanted to get to know him better, even if it meant certain rejection today, tomorrow, or next week. What did he have to lose?

When the merciful bell rang at the end of the period, Gibb let his reluctance lose its battle with his courage. Turning to Leo, he faked a breezy tone.

"Hey, what time is your lunch period?"

Leo consulted a printed class schedule.

"I think it's this period now, sixth period."

"Hey! Me too. If you're cool with it, maybe we could hang out at lunch," Gibb said, surprised at the steadiness of his own voice. He mentally crossed his fingers in hope of a "yes" from Leo.

"Sure, bud. Sounds good."

Gibb was in.

⚍⚌

They didn't say much on their walk through the humdrum maze of hallways, but once they got to the cafeteria door, with the clamor on the other side of the open door threatening to drown out Leo's gentle voice, Leo had a question. He asked it with a self-conscious laugh.

"Man, I know this is gonna sound weird, but it's almost like I've met you somewhere before. Sounds crazy, I know but, way off-chance, bud – you ever been to Loozeeanna, maybe New Orleans or over by St. Mary Parish?"

Gibb stopped, surprised. "I've never been to New Orleans, but yeah, I've been to St. Mary's Parish."

Leo stared at him intently. "Really? When were you at St. Mary Parish?"

"Well, my dad is buried in the cemetery there."

"What's that now?" Leo said, amazed. "Your dad is buried in St. Mary Parish?"

Gibb didn't understand why Leo would think anything was strange about that.

"Yeah. You're looking at me like you think that's weird. Why?"

"So, you're telling me that your father is buried in St. Mary Parish cemetery in Bache, Louisiana?" Leo said, still looking confused.

"Uhh...no," Gibb said, more confused than Leo, wondering where the disconnect was coming from. "He's buried in St. Mary's Parish Cemetery, like twenty miles from here."

They stared at each other quizzically for a split-second until Leo suddenly understood. He let out a big laugh, a laugh Gibb loved the second he heard it.

"Daaamn, man. OK, now I getcha," Leo said, with a grin. "For some reason...never mind. I getcha now. This is kind of funny. See, down in

Louisiana, we have parishes. Like y'all have counties up here - like Seneca County - we have parishes, like St. Mary Parish, where I'm from. So that's why I mentioned it. Coincidence is all. And I'm sorry, bud, I didn't really mean to make you think about your dad's grave and whatnot."

"Oh, no, it's OK." Gibb said, restraining himself from patting Leo on the back. "I was really little when it happened and…yeah. No sweat, dude."

"So, just to make sure. You've never been to St. Mary Parish, Louisiana, then."

"Nope, I've never even been out of New York state. Seriously."

Intrigued that Leo maybe remembered him from the Kountry Korner, Gibb felt comfortable enough to tell him he'd seen him there.

"So, yeah, don't you take this weird, either, but when you walked into History today I could've sworn the same thing, like I'd seen you around before but couldn't place where, y'know? Then I thought, wait, wasn't that dude wearing the Dead shirt at the Kountry Korner last week?"

Leo's eye lit up.

"That's it!" he exclaimed. "I knew I'd seen you around somewhere. I was beginnin' to believe in déjà vu and all that mess," he drawled. "Never had that happen before. I do apologize if you thought I asked a weird question."

"No, no. I really didn't think it was weird at all. Like I said, I was thinking the same thing," Gibb reassured him. "I can't really explain it but…" he held up his hand to high-five Leo, trying to think of something not weird to say. He said it anyway.

"Welcome to the Finger Lakes. I'm glad you made it up here."

A second of uncomfortable silence, a couple of quick, dismissive laughs, and into the lunchroom cacophony they went, Gibb's face reddening as he silently kicked himself.

Mentioning Leo's Grateful Dead shirt over lunch made for an easy transition into a musical conversation where both guys discovered they had a mutual love for not only the Dead, but for other bands as well. Pink Floyd, Rush, Allman Brothers, the Beatles, Led Zeppelin. But the Dead was easily each one's favorite for similar reasons, although Leo's love for the band was far more nuanced. Gibb didn't know it when they sat down, but he was about to get Leo's starry-eyed and well-reasoned opinions on why the Dead were bigger and more important than just their music.

Leo spoke quietly, but his animated voice and twinkling eyes colored his side of the conversation with fervor. Gibb reveled in Leo's knowledge of the band's history, the best tapes of their stand-out shows, his favorite versions of their songs. But where Gibb's appreciation of the Dead was relegated to his collection of a couple of worn-out live albums, Leo took it a step further. He truly believed that the Dead changed the world through their music, and he used a quote from Plato, the philosopher, to illustrate his point.

"Plato said something like, 'Any musical innovation is full of danger to the whole State and should be outlawed. Because when modes of music change, the State always changes with them.' You see what he meant by that? Plato was one hundred percent right. Rock and roll – Elvis, Chuck Berry, Little Richard, Buddy Holly – they all shook up 'the State' pretty good. Then the Stones and the Beatles fine-tuned that chaos," Leo went on. "And the entire culture changed. Overnight, once they were on Ed Sullivan, ever'body wanted to be the Beatles".

He slapped his hands down softly on top of the lunch table, the skull on his ring smiling, almost like it was enjoying the conversation.

"But when the Dead came along, they *really* shook it up. Blew the lid off and that shit just splashed *everywhere*. There is no denyin' their major impact on musical and societal culture changes all over the world. Nobody played like them. Nobody."

Gibb raised his eyebrows, impressed, as Leo's sermon continued. Without thinking he leaned in closer to Leo across the lunch table to look and listen more intently.

"Y'know, the whole hippie movement was a tit-for-tat response to the crazy American political scene at the time. And the Dead was that underground band providing the soundtrack and the whole mind-expansion thing, the acid trips, the 'live your life, be free' trip.

"I might be wrong, but I always think of them as like these innocent, sorta dorky guys smokin' dope and laughin' as they sent electric musical smoke signals out into the sky. But they couldn't have known anything about the energy they were messin' with, because they had *no idea* on God's green Earth how many aliens, includin' you and me, were gonna pick up on those signals and home in on where they were comin' from, y'know?"

Aliens. Gibb was all for that label. If this smart, hot guy considered himself an alien, then he'd be a proud alien right next to him. He had never had a conversation like this with anyone. Fascinated and more than a little dumbfounded, he let Leo continue to speak his mind uninterrupted.

"Because look at what happened first in San Francisco, then all across the country, into Europe and Asia too. Hippies, yippies, the Black Panthers, the SLA, the whole feminist movement, gay rights, all of it. People who were involved in those causes, a lot of them heard the Dead and said, 'Ahaaa, this is the musical sound of what it is we're doing.'

"Because what those movements were doin' was takin' the *traditional* way of doin' and thinkin' about things and then twistin' it into a narrative that fits our time and place in American history. That is exactly what the Dead was doin' with their music. Symbiosis!

"So," Leo concluded, holding up his hands and entwining his fingers together for emphasis, "they were a perfect fit for the times…and all they were doin' was playin' music," Leo said with a laugh. "Here in the 80's, some of those movements are stronger than ever – gay rights, women's rights, civil rights – and maybe the band has now evolved out of being the soundtrack to the causes. But at the beginning? Look out lightnin', they just caught you in a bottle."

*Who talks like that?* Gibb thought to himself. This guy seemed pretty shy at first but look at him now. As far as Gibb was concerned, Leo could go on all the talk shows and make his case for the Dead's place in musical history. He was that passionate, that knowledgeable, and that charismatic. If he'd been on TV, he would've gotten Gibb's attention for sure. But Gibb was suddenly grateful, and he smiled to himself for the pun, that Leo was actually sitting right in front of him in the here and now. He wasn't sure that he agreed with everything Leo said, but he'd still made a pretty good case.

"I never really thought about it that way," Gibb finally broke in. "I've always just been blown away by the music. I can't describe it like you. But it's just…real. There's nothing 'show biz' about them. Right now, when you listen to stuff on the radio, there's so much bullshit going on. Electronics, doctored voices, songs obviously written just to be lame Top 40 hits. So boring. There's some cool stuff, but it's gonna sound so dated in ten years.

"I think the Dead's music will still be relevant because it's real – it's genius and it's flawed and it's great and sometimes it's not – all at the same time. But at least it's real, everyone playing their instruments, singing live even when they're not always in great voice or the sound system is jacked up or whatever. It's *real*. It's the humanity of it that makes it cool, the very *American* humanity of it. I think they're a *great* American band, singing about real American life. And there's no put-on. They're just playing. But I have to agree with a lot of what you said, even though I don't know near as much about it as you."

Leo shook his head and demurred.

"I don't know that much, bud. I think you just described it all way better than I did. I just know that here it is 1983 and all these years later that band still has a whole world of people following them around – hangin' on every word, every note. Still relevant, just like you said. They didn't just turn the musical world on its ear, they helped turned *society* on its ear. There ain't no way they could've known that what they were doin' was gonna lead to all that.

"So, this is all just my long way of sayin' that their innovation changed 'the State', and I do believe Plato was talking directly about future bands like the Dead and the Beatles when he said that a couple thousand years ago."

Leo's voice faltered as he finished his summary, an uneasy half-smile on his face, suddenly aware that he'd probably said way too much way too soon in his brand-new friendship with Gibb.

"I do get to babblin' on when I'm into somethin'. Sorry 'bout that."

Gibb didn't think Leo had said too much. He was just trying to wrap his mind around all of it. And yet, to Gibb, Leo didn't sound the slightest bit pretentious when he spoke. Plato's quote was merely a reference, a good one, to support his viewpoint. It sure gave Gibb something more to think about. Before he graduated high school, he knew he needed to learn a lot more about a lot more just to hold up his end of a collegiate conversation.

While he was talking, Gibb realized that Leo sounded older than his years, more mature and centered somehow. Maybe he was a little further along in his emotional development than the rest of the kids Gibb knew from around Eislertown. Maybe he was just a natural charmer who got by on his good looks and endearing drawl. Was he real, or was his whole persona just a careful creation, like someone in show business? Gibb didn't know what to think – the guy looked, talked, and acted like no one he'd ever met before. He really was like a character in a movie, with all the potential to be a hero at the end…or just an incredibly good-looking villain who would ruin many lives by the time the credits rolled.

The weird thing was, Gibb hoped Leo truly *was* a villain. That way Gibb couldn't continue holding him in such vaunted and wholly unearned esteem, awesome lunchtime conversation notwithstanding. Sure, they'd just met in person, but Gibb was smitten in a way he had never been about anyone before. Ever. Yet, as excited as he was, he really didn't like the way it felt, the way he didn't like walking barefoot over a driveway full of sharp rocks.

Still, he couldn't explain to himself the instant connection, the confounding familiarity or the unwanted and excruciating instant attraction, but there it was in all of its vain and unwieldy eminence. Leo Davion had walked into History class and, with one innocent, aquamarine grin, ripped Gibbon Mulcahy's heart right out of his chest. And that wasn't even the worst part. The worst part was that Leo didn't have a glimmer of an idea that he was even guilty of such a crime. He probably wanted possession of Gibb's heart even less than Gibb wanted him to have it.

That was what made it tough. It wouldn't have mattered if Gibb was the most attractive, desirable guy on Earth. He was a *guy*. He didn't have a chance with Leo. At that moment, he'd never been so truly tormented and totally enamored at the same time. Hating the feeling. Exhilarated by it, too.

The bell rang, announcing the end of their lunch period and, without his even knowing, the beginning of Gibb's new life. Forty minutes after sitting down to lunch with Leo, the entire world was different.

# Chapter 7

## AIN'T NO PLACE I'D RATHER BE

"So that's nice how y'all met," Sam yawned from the passenger seat, his eyes closed in a subtle message to Gibb that he'd be more interested in the story after a little more sleep. Gibb was oblivious. Wide awake and fired up now, his life story tumbled from his mouth in a rattling assault on poor Sam's tired ears.

Poor Sam for sure. There was just no way for a seven-foot guy to stretch out those long, long legs in a car this small, even with his seat reclined and pushed back as far as it could go. Talk about pins and needles when he woke up. But Gibb kept talking.

He couldn't help it, though. Once he'd gotten behind the wheel, he exhilarated in the new-found feeling of open-road freedom, stoked from the moment he'd started driving up there in northern Virginia. He gripped the steering wheel, working hard to restrain himself from flooring the accelerator.

Many hours after his impulses had convinced him that hitchhiking to New Orleans would be the most expedient way to get there, Gibb's emotions were bordering on frantic. His earlier elation had now given way to a straight up urgency just to get to Leo, a goal that felt somehow more, not less, pressing with each passing mile. Sam had earlier admonished him to only go five over the speed limit, but whenever Gibb looked over and saw Sam had his eyes closed, he couldn't help but push it further.

The noontime sun, annoyingly cheery as it waved them happily southward, was way too bright without the sunglasses Gibb wished he was wearing right now. Squinting hard, he yanked down his windshield blind and checked the gas gauge. They'd need to stop soon.

He still couldn't believe that he was really all the way down here in Tennessee, especially on the one day it would have been sort of important for him to be back home up in Eislertown – his high school graduation day. The one event that pretty much everything in his life had been leading up to. The only thing that was supposed to matter.

It didn't matter. As far as he was concerned, no one except Ms. Mullan was going to miss him anyway. He doubted again that his own mother even remembered he was supposed to graduate today. He shook his head, a sardonic smile on his face, imagining her oblivious and chainsmoking in front of the TV, not even slightly worried about where he was right now.

Really, though, graduation was only one thought fighting for his attention. He loved the idea that he'd had the nerve to just jump into some stranger's car and disappear. At the same time, he was thinking of Leo and how sad he was for him and the whole Davion family. Why did Mr. Davion have to get cancer so young? Why did Leo's family have to go through this?

Then he was sad for himself. Why had his own father died so young? How would Gibb's life have been different if he'd lived? If his dad had lived, would his mother have turned out different? There was no way she couldn't have. She'd married two men: one awesome guy, Gibb's dad. The other: Jack. Enough said. Jack had ruined her life, really, and she'd let him. It was a pretty sad story.

But who was he to judge anybody else's life, driving through the unfamiliar, hilly terrain of eastern Tennessee, miserably believing he was probably nothing more than Leo's last resort? A back-up plan. But here he was anyway, practically standing on the accelerator, to get to Leo as soon as he possibly could. Maybe he should have his own head examined.

He wished he'd packed his cassettes of the Dead's *Europe '72* album. That would've cheered him up a bit, if only for the knowledge that he got to crank up *Tennessee Jed* while he was traveling through the actual state of Tennessee. That would've been much better music than the cavalcade of assorted baritone snorts and wheezy snores coming from the passenger seat. Wow.

"Whatchu sighin' so heavy fo'? You tired of drivin'?" Sam asked sleepily, his eyes still closed as he reached for his own blind. Gibb whipped his head around, startled to hear Sam's voice.

"Sorry," Gibb said sheepishly. "I didn't even know I was doing it. We gotta stop for gas."

"Do whatchu gotta do. You gotta pay for it this time anyway. I got it back up there in Virginia or Maryland or wherever we was. I'll be sleepin'."

"No problem, man. But aren't you gonna want to get out and stretch? You look like a pile of laundry all mooshed into that seat," Gibb muttered.

"You just watch yo' speed there, Casey Jones, and we'll be a'ight. You got it?" Sam said, turning towards the window again.

"Casey Jones?" Gibb asked, incredulous. "Wait a minute - you know the Dead?"

"Dude…" Sam sighed. He started mumble-singing the song in a sleepy stupor, "Drivin' that train, high on cocaine…"

"You DO know the Dead!" Gibb exclaimed. "That's so cool."

"Only a little," Sam murmured in half-agreement. "Plus they got the idea for dat one from an ol' Mississippi folk song. They didn't jus' come up wit' the idea out of nowhere."

"What?" Gibb replied, bewildered, staring quickly over at Sam whose eyes were still closed. "I didn't know that."

"Everything come from something, right?" Sam mumbled. "Nothing start all by itself. Now shut up for another hour or so and then wake me up."

Gibb did half of what he was told. He finally shut up, but still kept moving at seventy-five mph for the entire next hour, keeping a wary eye out both for state troopers and a stirring Sam. Yawning now as he pulled off the interstate for a quick fill-up, he knew what he really needed most was sleep. For now, he'd have to settle for coffee, something he'd hardly ever drank in his life up to this point.

The gas station was a step back into an earlier time, probably the 1930's. Judging by the old Esso and new Exxon signs fighting for top billing outside, and the overalls-clad Grandpa-Walton-lookalike coming out to fill the tank, the place was in no hurry to catch up to the 1980's.

Grandpa told Gibb there was free coffee inside.

"Go on in there and gitchu some!" he said cheerily.

Gibb moseyed inside first to find the bathroom and then to find his quarry: a single Bunn hot plate warming a half-full glass pot of black sludge, the slightly burnt aroma mixing with fifty years of gasoline, oil, and rubber. North or South, it didn't matter. All old-time gas stations smelled like this. And all of them seemed to have a wall calendar with a picture of a topless girl gracing the top half of the page.

As he walked back to the car, Gibb took a sip of the coffee. Suddenly, his eyes flew wide open. He almost gagged on the scorched muck in the cup. Terrible! Not only was it too hot outside to be drinking something hot like this, it was a crime against humanity to ever serve coffee like this to another person, even if it was free.

Sam was up and towering high above the roof of the small station wagon nearby, his black sunglasses reflecting the rumpled appearance of his passenger, that red-headed remora carrying the coffee cup. Sam watched, intrigued, as Gibb placed his cup on the ground, then struggled to pull off his sweatshirt under the glaring sun beating down on the gas-station blacktop. The sweatshirt seemed unwilling to come off, fighting Gibb, making him twist and pull harder than he should've had to. Gibb won, but as he re-emerged from under the pullover, his cockeyed glasses and tortured, unkempt hair made it clear the shirt had gotten the better of him.

Sam just shook his head as Gibb, clueless, made his approach.

"Dear God, you are ate up."

"What?" Gibb said, not sure what he'd just heard.

"I said, you are ate the hell up, that's what you are," Sam reiterated with a throaty laugh.

"Are you speaking a foreign language?" Gibb asked, wrinkling his nose in confusion, "'Cuz I don't have a clue what you're saying to me. No, I didn't eat anything – I just have this coffee."

Sam laughed out loud and shook his head.

"What?! No, dude, when I say you 'ate up', I mean that *You. Are.* All. Ate. Up. You a mess! Have you checked yo'self out? No wait, don't," Sam said as Gibb moved to look at his reflection in the car window. "I don't want you shatterin' my windows with that reflection."

Gibb laughed in response. "What do you expect me to look like, Richard Gere? Should I go ask the gas station dude if I can go make myself look pretty in their classy bathroom? It doesn't even have a mirror anyway, by the way."

Sam grinned.

"My first thought is to say yes, take yo' ass back inside and do something with yourself. But I'll jus' do myself a favor and try not to look over at you the rest of the way to New Orleans. Damn," he muttered, "that hair is bringin' my morale down."

Gibb could only shake his head and chuckle. *Where does this guy come up with this stuff?*

"Whatever," he said. "You want some of this coffee? It's terrible."

"Nope, get in. I'm-a drive awhile. We makin' good time, lead-foot, but we still got about seven hours or so. How you holdin' up? You doin' OK?"

Gibb, surprised by the hint of concern in Sam's question, didn't answer right away.

## Chapter 8

# AN INVITATION

Two weeks into the school year, Gibb couldn't help but be surprised by two things: the growing intensity of his feelings for Leo and the fact that Leo hadn't become as popular as Gibb thought he would.

It turned out that Leo really wasn't an outgoing guy. As good-looking as he was, he just seemed shy when he got around people. Sometimes people mistook shyness for snootiness, but that wasn't Leo's personality. He was just quiet. He loved to read, he loved music and, without ever really saying anything about it, he seemed to prefer his own company to almost anyone else's, Gibb being an exception. In other words, he was a lot like Gibb.

That didn't keep Leo from escaping the notice of some of the more popular girls in school, though. Suddenly Gibb, who would have rather been stretched on the rack, was fielding their questions about him. One particularly good-looking girl, Bramble Andersson, was more than a little smitten.

Bramble, whose parents must have hated her or at least been high when they named her, surprised Gibb at his locker this morning just as the day was getting underway.

"Hi Gibb," Bramble said with a pretty smile. "My friends and I were wondering, do you know if your friend has a girlfriend?"

Gibb was taken aback – he had no idea this girl would have even known his name. She'd never once talked to him before, nor him to her, even though he'd known who she was since they were in middle school. She was beautiful, though. Gorgeous face, perfect blonde hair, no makeup and she didn't need it. This close up to Bramble, Gibb noticed for the first time that she had light freckles across the bridge of her nose. Even *he* thought about what it would be like to kiss her. Bramble was gorgeous.

His mind raced as he thought about how to answer her question.

*If Bramble and Leo got together, they would be one of those awful couples that dressed exactly the same, in gleaming white tennis outfits with their blond hair tousled just right. Or they'd be on some page in a lame store catalog wearing matching robes and gorgeous smiles, peering at each other mischievously over cups of coffee. Ugh.*

Perfection was so seriously gross.

"Umm…I…" Gibb stammered as usual, debating with himself whether he should lie to this girl or not.

Bramble stared at him patiently.

"I…hmm. You're talking about Leo, right?"

"Yes!" Bramble replied, the mild exasperation in her answer making it clear she knew Gibb didn't have any other friends.

"Well, I know he's planning on going right back to Louisiana after graduation," Gibb replied.

That part was true. Leo had said as much. But as Gibb contemplated telling Bramble anything more, it jealously dawned on him that whatever he told Bramble wouldn't really matter, truth or not. Because if Bramble wanted Leo, as gorgeous and popular as she was, there wouldn't be a reason in the world for Leo to turn her away.

So, after being truthful with her at first, he figured he might as well make up the rest of the story. Just for the heck of it.

"He basically said that he promised his girlfriend he'd be up here for the school year and then he'd go to college down there and be with her."

"What's her name, do you know?" Bramble persisted. Now Gibb could understand how the girl got her name. So irritating.

"I don't know, really. I mean, we don't talk about too much stuff," Gibb replied vaguely.

"Oh, I don't know about that," Bramble replied, suddenly all officious. "You guys seem to be doing a lot of talking at lunch all the time."

"Yeah…" Gibb said, starting to become uneasy imagining that people were actually watching him interact with Leo in the cafeteria. "I don't know. I mean, we talk about music a lot, I guess. Bands we like…just stuff like that. School stuff. Nothing like…I don't know…too personal," he said haltingly.

"OK, I was just wondering," Bramble said, satisfied enough with Gibb's answer. "I think he's super-cute but he seems so shy and quiet. I don't know if he'd ever, like, just come up and talk to me."

"Well…" Gibb said with a shrug, "if you wanna talk to him, why not just go up to him like you came up to me just now?"

"Mmm…I don't know," she half-whispered. "I don't really approach guys."

"Well, you approached me," Gibb said with a laugh.

"Yeah, well, you're different," Bramble deadpanned. "Look, just do me a favor, will you? Just tell him I was asking about him and let him know I told you I think he's super-cute. That might help break the ice."

*Yeah, I'm different, all right,* Gibb thought sarcastically. *Welll, Miss Hot-To-Trot, guess who's now not gonna be breathing a word about this little conversation to Mr. Super-Cute? I'm so different, I don't even know how to relay a message. How 'bout that, Bramble? You can literally go scratch.*

"OK," Gibb told her, trying hard not to show his annoyance. "I'll let him know."

Later that day in the cafeteria, Gibb saw Bramble but avoided her. If she and Leo were going to get together, that was between the two of them. He wasn't going to play Cupid on her behalf, that was for sure.

In truth, Gibb and Leo had been talking about a lot of things over the past couple of weeks. Things Gibb had never talked about before with another person. Why certain music mattered, how badly he wanted a dog and would get one right after college, why he thought the Finger Lakes region was the most beautiful place on Earth, even though he'd never once been out of New York state to be able to make a true comparison. Leo listened to him intently, like what he said mattered. And that's why Gibb didn't feel weird talking to

Leo about anything, really, except the fact that his feelings towards Leo were getting more intense every time they met up. Leo began to be the constant occupant of Gibb's thoughts and the reality of that was making it more difficult for Gibb to keep his feelings to himself.

An hour's bike ride away there was a beautiful spot called Kimberly Hill. At the top of the hill, there was a little glider plane runway. It was always cool just to sit up there and watch the planes take off, especially this time of year. The trees changing color all around the valley below and sunlight gleaming off the lakes was a pretty magnificent view.

Gibb finally got the nerve up to ask Leo if he wanted to ride up there with him the next time he went. He took a swig from the half-warm carton of milk on his lunch tray and put the idea out there.

"Definitely!" Leo said without hesitation. "I need to get out there and check out as much of this place as I can while I'm here. I've heard people mention the gliders and the views and stuff from up there on Kimberly Hill. I'm up for it. You wanna ride up there this weekend?"

"Sounds like a plan," Gibb replied casually, trying not to sound too enthusiastic even though he couldn't have been more stoked.

"Now it's my turn, I guess. I got kind of a crazy question for you." Leo spoke quietly as his long fingers picked through a ketchup-red pile of soggy fries.

"Shoot."

Gibb sat marveling at how anyone would ever want to eat whatever those fries had become under the weight of at least 10 of those little ketchup packets.

"Well…it's my birthday next week and…"

"Oh, wow. Happy early birthday, man."

"Oh…thanks," Leo said, not expecting the interruption. "Anyway, let me tell you why I mentioned it. And, hey, if this sounds stupid or weird, just feel free to say no, OK? It'll be cool either way."

Gibb nodded. "OK…"

"OK, so, when my birthday rolls around," Leo stammered, "Mama makes dinner and they always offer to let me invite a friend. I don't really know anybody else around here yet, so…"

"So I'm your best, worst, and only choice," Gibb said with a laugh.

"Well…" Leo replied with a sheepish smile, "kind of."

*Unless I tell you about Bramble. Which I'm not going to do, especially now that I'm the one who is getting this invitation.*

"Sure," Gibb laughed, "as your only Finger Lakes friend right now, I'll be there. Just tell me what day."

"Very cool! It's next Thursday, the 29th. I'm really glad you're gonna be there. You can meet my sister!"

*Sister?* Gibb tried not to frown. *Oh, no. Is he trying to fix me up?*

"Sure, that'd be great," Gibb replied with a grin, ashamed of the sound of his own voice feigning interest.

*Well, whatever*, he thought. He'd just be happy to be hanging out with Leo two times in the week ahead, no matter the circumstances. They were going to be riding bikes up on Kimberly Hill this weekend. And then next week he was going to meet Leo's family! All he hoped was that his growing crush on Leo wouldn't be too obvious to them.

## *Chapter 9*

# TO THE POWER
# OF TRUTH

Gibb barely slept that night. For the first time in his life, he'd met another person he believed in, someone who seemed to know a whole lot more about the world than he did, someone who actually seemed to want to hang out with him. It was weird, actually.

His emotions were now controlling him, not the other way around as was usually the case, and he hated it. For the first time in his life, he really cared about what would or wouldn't happen next, and that did a fine job of keeping him from getting much sleep not just tonight, not just last night, but this whole past week.

Gibb knew he needed to talk to someone. He didn't have any close friends and, no, family wasn't even a consideration. The only person he could talk to was Ms. Mullan, his freshman year English teacher. He could tell her things he couldn't tell his own mother, and Ms. Mullan never judged him or made him feel weird or ashamed. She was, at this point, his best - and only - confidante.

Ms. Mullan was a sort of larger-than-life, mythical figure in Gibb's life. The woman easily stood over six feet tall. She wore big, owlish glasses and didn't give a damn that they awarded her exactly zero style points. Her hair was cut short in a practical, frosted-blonde bob that required almost no maintenance. A little eye make-up, but not always. No lipstick. Ever. And it was hardly her goal to dress to impress in her grey slacks, plain white blouse and black flats.

Gibb had never had another teacher like her. The way she spoke, the way she carried herself – Gibb would always say that what Ms. Mullan had was *presence*. She spoke with authority and command, with complete confidence in her knowledge of the subject - sort of like a man, for lack of a better comparison - but not as an *authoritarian*, which was very *un*like Jack and most of the male teachers Gibb had had in the past. She was just…herself. Confidently herself. Smart. Probably smarter than you. Tough shit if you didn't like it. No apologies.

Gibb was drawn to her "stick-it-up-your-ass-if-you-don't-like-it" attitude and she seemed to take an early liking to him. She looked students in the eye when she stood in front of the class to teach, willing their participation in the proceedings, quietly gauging their interest and understanding. Maybe Ms. Mullan liked him because he always seemed to be looking right back at her, undistracted by side conversations with friends he didn't have, or daydreaming or passing notes.

Whatever it was, one day after class, he'd waited at his desk until the other kids hustled out of the classroom. Gibb asked Ms. Mullan if he could talk to her about an assignment, but he really just wanted to hang out with her a little bit.

That afternoon was the beginning of what became the most important mentorship relationship of his adolescent life. Not that he knew what mentorship was. Gibb just respected and liked Ms. Mullan enough to be open with her about what he was up against at home and in school. In turn, she was open to listening and giving examples of similar things that had happened in her own life.

She'd been married twice. She had a young son from her first marriage. Her current marriage was interracial and she'd gotten a load of shit about it from some old friends and members of her family back in New England. She'd said that their reactions sort of hurt, but because she wasn't in any relationship to please her friends and family, they could keep their feelings about her life to themselves.

She'd also gotten suspended from her first teaching job for not complying with the school's dress code. It was less than ten years earlier, but female teachers were required to dress in skirts at school in those days. When Ms. Mullan and a couple of other female teachers showed up wearing pants one day, they were all suspended for a week. When the women returned from their suspensions, again wearing pants, the situation got noisy enough to reach the school board.

During a raucous board meeting, the pants-wearing women were called "rabble rousers" and "showboaters" by members of the all-male school board. Not quite out of earshot, they were called "effing bitches" (she didn't say the real word as she related the story to Gibb) and worse by some male members of the public. Some of the female members nodded their agreement with that assessment, casting cold stares at the offensive pants-wearing teachers. But other women in the community, actually more women than Ms. Mullan had ever seen at a board meeting, stepped up to have their say. This group included, to their chagrin, the wives of a few of the male Board members.

The policy got changed.

It wasn't happy-ever-after, though, because nothing ever is, Ms. Mullan told Gibb. She called it a *pyrrhic* victory, a term Gibb would have to look up in the dictionary. The cost of winning that fight included strained relationships with other school faculty and staff, having to engage with angry parents of students, and less-than-stellar teacher evaluations.

"All over a stupid pair of pants," Ms. Mullan shrugged with a frown. "But who cares now, right? When's the last time you saw one of your female teachers in a skirt?"

She was right – Gibb couldn't remember the last time. Maybe early elementary school, but what did it matter? Ms. Mullan's point was that you had to push back against stupidity. If something seems stupid, say something, do something about it. But don't let your opponent use a tired old argument to keep the status quo because you're threatening the "way things have always been done." You have to fight for real change, she'd said, but you have to know there will be a price to pay. Be prepared.

It was with that story in mind that Gibb had mustered up the courage a year ago to trust Ms. Mullan enough to come out to her. He'd figured she'd be supportive, but he hadn't expected her to high-five him and tell him she thought it was awesome. That meant everything to him. Ms. Mullan hadn't just been kind to him, she'd *celebrated* a huge part of him that many others would have outright rejected on the spot.

Ms. Mullan's affirmation probably played a huge part in the way Gibb had been able to accept his queer sexuality. He didn't feel so alone in his own life, he wasn't ashamed of it, and he had her to thank for that, at least partially. Because even though he had to live with a jerk like Jack at home, Ms. Mullan was a reminder that there were a lot of people in the world who weren't like Jack. She was a great example of a person who let other people be who they were naturally, with no pretense, no fake smiles, no playing games. She was real and allowed you to be real, too.

So now, in his senior year, Ms. Mullan remained Gibb's closest confidante. But now he had to go to her all lovesick and pathetic and he knew, as cool as she was, she was going to call him out for being lame.

The next afternoon, Gibb skipped lunch to see if he could catch her. He knew Ms. Mullan preferred to spend most of her free periods in her classroom after she slipped down to the faculty room for a quick smoke. Lucky for Gibb, she was in the classroom when he popped his head in the door to check.

After she waved him in, Gibb hemmed and hawed but eventually got to the point. In hushed tones, he told her everything, from first seeing Leo at the Kountry Korner to their upcoming hangouts up at Kimberly Hill and his birthday dinner.

"I'm not seeing the problem here," she said, almost sarcastically.

Ms. Mullan's words weren't as casually dismissive as her words suggested. She was a practical person. Get to the point, her Bostonian tone implied. Gibb grimaced as she shrugged her shoulders and stared back at him through those big, round glasses.

"The problem is that I think I'm in real trouble," he griped. "I can't seem to get my head on straight because of all of these stupid feelings. And yes, feelings are stupid, even if *anthropomorphizing* them is even stupider. Check it out, I got to use that word." He chuckled.

Ms. Mullan rolled her eyes indifferently.

"Look, I know what it's like to really like someone and not really know how to tell them," she said with brusque understanding. "And I know you don't wanna scare this guy off by seemin' like some kind of creep, comin' on too strong or whatever. I get that."

*Yeah, if she only knew.*

"But what bothers me here is that I think you actually really *feel* like a creep just for having those feelings. You're actually beating yourself up because of who you really are. That's what's bad. You gotta learn that your feelings about him are as normal as the way a straight guy feels for a girl when he first meets her or vice-versa."

Gibb's voice wavered as it faltered.

"Hmm…I don't know about that. It's pretty powerful."

"You don't know about that…" Ms. Mullan gently mocked him, then lowered her voice, too. "Emotions are powerful regardless of your gender or sexuality. Makes it tough to be human sometimes. So, this is about more than being physically attracted to some guy. You *feel* something for him and that's a good thing, not a bad thing. Caring about somebody isn't a bad thing, no matter what anybody says. And it's definitely not a criminal thing when it's between two consenting adults. Which you're gonna officially be soon, right, Mr. Senior?"

Ms. Mullan's words were kind and encouraging, but Gibb was still frowning.

"Yeah, yeah. Soon. November," he said, indulging her own aside. "All of what you just said there is great, but it doesn't change anything. I don't *want* to feel this way, about anyone or anything. *That's* the problem. I'm not in control of my own emotions."

"So, go ahead and try to stop it," Ms. Mullan said, her mouth slanted in her own half-frown. "Ignore it, do whatever you can to avoid it. That can work for a while. Just be prepared, though. No matter how much energy you put into doing that, it's not gonna go away, even if you pretend it's not there. Because your feelings are *true*, see? Whether you want them to be or not."

She pursed her lips.

"Gibb, look around you. There's not a lot in this life that's really true. A lot of life is just a big put-on, like the way all the girls in this school have to get the same haircut to fit in. Same with the boys. Haircuts, clothes, sneakers. Whatever. No original ideas of their own. They call it fashion so they can feel OK about it, but it's just another box they put themselves in. Everybody following everybody else because everybody else is doing it. To me, that's weird.

"Y'know, I've seen tacky trends come and go every year I've taught school. But there are some kids, like you, who just don't care to follow 'em. Put it this way, it would be *really* weird if you walked into school wearing an O.P. jacket, OK? I think it's because you know trends are garbage, whether you're aware of it or not. So, you just blow them off and do your thing. Great!

"But turn that around for a minute. The stuff that's *not* garbage, the stuff that *is* true, both good and bad, is never gonna leave you alone until you deal with it, till you face it somehow. See what I mean?"

Gibb scratched absent-mindedly at the back of his neck.

"Maybe. But it's scary as hell to face some stuff…like this whole thing with Leo."

"Don't I know it?" Ms. Mullan muttered, the resignation in her expression highlighting the faint lines around her eyes. "But you should know, even if it doesn't work out with this guy, you're gonna run into this again. And again. And probably again. And you're gonna have to figure out a way to deal with *those* situations until you figure 'em out.

"It sucks," Ms. Mullan said humorlessly, "but sometimes life's a shitsicle."

Gibb just stared at her. He didn't know what he'd expected to hear from her but…well…maybe what she'd said was exactly what he'd expected after all. It wasn't like he thought she was going to wrap her arms around him, smooth his hair, and call him "poor baby."

"Thanks, I guess. I feel a lot better now," Gibb said grimly.

"Really?" Ms. Mullan asked.

"Nope," came the reply, simple and dour.

They stayed there in silence for a long minute, Gibb staring off into space, Ms. Mullan looking down at a pile of unmarked quizzes from an earlier class. Standing up from her desk, she turned towards the blackboard and picked up a piece of chalk.

"I don't have the answers," she said, her back to Gibb. "If I did I'd write 'em on the board like we do in class."

She turned around.

"But this particular lesson, this lesson about loving yourself for who you are and not hating yourself for what you aren't, doesn't ever have an easy answer for you, for me, for anybody. Maybe it takes a whole lifetime to learn. Who knows? Maybe it'll take a lotta lifetimes. I don't know if I believe in any of that, but anything's possible, I guess."

Ms. Mullan patted Gibb on the shoulder, then shrugged.

"I know it all sounds trite and cliché. But I don't really have the words to clearly explain this stuff. Because the truth is, if words, if language, were enough to teach people the importance of loving themselves without any conditions, we would have all learned that by now. Think about that. The world would be a hell of a better place with a lot less anxiety, wouldn't it? But that's not the way it works. Because understanding truth takes a lot of work, a lot of time, and a lot of new experience, y'know? It's not just words on the board."

"Maybe...I don't know," Gibb said, but guessing she was probably right about that.

"Look," Ms. Mullan said matter-of-factly, "all you can do is be honest with yourself. Then do your best to make peace with the way you feel. Then maybe, if you have the courage or the will, tell this Leo guy how you feel. Or not. But whatever you do or don't do about Leo, you still gotta accept your feelings. Because they're true."

As she always did when she wanted to make a strong point, Ms. Mullan looked Gibb straight in the eye.

"If I've learned anything in life, it's this. You can't get away from your truth, Gibb. It's with you wherever you go."

⊰⊱

He was glad he'd talked to Ms. Mullan, but Gibb wasn't sure she understood the perilousness of his situation. Yes, he had deep feelings about Leo, but he didn't want that to drive Leo to drop his friendship. Being Leo's friend was more important to Gibb than anything else. And so, after all of the midnight mental wrangling and incessant obsessing, he decided the best thing to do was to give himself some more time before he spent any time around Leo one-on-one outside of school. It was lame, but it was the right choice. He couldn't trust himself not to say or do something stupid, something that would make him look like the infatuated fool he was.

The next day, Gibb told Leo he couldn't ride up to Kimberly Hill with him on Saturday. Gibb wasn't good at making fake excuses, but the one he made was good enough to obscure the real reason for why he pulled out. He just told Leo that he'd forgotten about a stupid home project his mom and stepdad were doing that weekend. They expected his help and he had to be there, he said, lying through his teeth. In the twelve years since the unholy day they were married, his mom and Jack hadn't lifted a finger to even paint, let alone do any sort of "project" in Jack's hovel.

Leo was surprised, disappointed even, but he understood.

"I know how that goes, bud. We can go another time. But still hopin' you can come by for dinner next Thursday."

Feeling especially guilty now, Gibb knew he had no choice but to go. He had to commit.

"For sure!" he said, over-enthusiastically. "Count on it."

## Chapter 10

# BIRTHDAY BOY

It would have been encouraging to say that Leo's birthday dinner had been a fun family affair, with lots of laughs and camaraderie and food and cake, where Gibb had been welcomed to their home as Leo's new friend. That would have been a heartening description for sure, but it wouldn't have been even a tiny bit true.

To be fair, there had been a cake. A yellow cake with festive blue and white frosting, decorated on top with two candles in the shape of the numbers "1" and "8". The cake would have been easier to eat, though, if it hadn't been smashed and smeared up and down the steps leading to Leo's family's front door, the candles strewn backwards in a sad, wide "81" on the brick walkway approaching the house.

As Gibb rode his bike into Leo's front yard, it appeared that the only ones celebrating Leo's birthday were a couple of large crows gorging themselves on the sloppy remains of a literal broken promise. Whipping their heads around at the sound of Gibb's bike wheels, the big black birds squawked their white-frosted beaks at him in antipathy and reluctantly flew off, leaving their sweet spoils behind.

The birds' noisy exit left the yard completely silent now. Gibb regarded the multi-colored mess on the walkway warily. He knew something wasn't quite right here, but what had happened?

Maybe it was something as simple as somebody tripping up the steps as they carried the now- doomed confection up to the house. Hoping that was the case, Gibb knocked timidly on the Davions' front door.

The birthday boy answered, the smile on his face a mix of relief and the look of someone who'd just finished laughing at something.

"Hey," he greeted Gibb. "Watch out for flyin' cakes."

Leo shook his head as he surveyed the mess on the steps.

"You didn't step in that, did you?"

"I think I got around it OK," Gibb said, his own face confused, not sure whether this was funny or not.

"Ah, don't worry none about this," Leo said, waving his hand towards the steps. "Come on in."

Smiling nervously, Gibb stepped across the threshold into a comfortably decorated living room. Two long, beige sofas faced each other, their broad-cloth backs set to wall and window. A love seat, beige and comfortable brown, sat perpendicular between them to create a large, perfectly U-Shaped conversation area. Throw pillows decorated in a crimson and plum-purple flower pattern decorated both ends of each piece of furniture while a handsome wood-framed and glass-topped coffee table sat in the middle of it all, ready to graciously accommodate the visitors sitting around it.

There were black and white photographs of what looked to Gibb to be some recent and also some distant ancestors of the Davion family, some faded braided rugs and a couple of paintings, too. The place was unpretentious and homey, much better kept than his own living room over in Eislertown.

Gibb suddenly realized he hadn't heard any other voices in the house.

"It's pretty quiet for a birthday party," he said. "Where is everybody?"

"They're gone," Leo said, chuckling and shaking his head.

"Gone?" Gibb asked, not sure what was going on. "Like gone, gone? Gone where?"

"Well…" Leo said, his mouth in a crooked smile. "I was hopin' to spare you a little of this, but if we're gonna be friends you might as well know the truth."

He stopped smiling, his blue-green eyes solemn now.

"My Mama deals with some real mental problems. They truly don't have a name for what ails her, but they treat it like bipolar disorder. They used to call it manic depression, but it really don't matter what they call it. No one's been able to get a good handle on it.

"Mama's havin' some of her troubles today and I gotta say, it's not rightly unexpected. We've all kinda been waitin' for the big blow-up…it's been buildin' these last couple days…and it just so happens that today's the day it all come tumblin' down."

"Is it because it's your birthday?" Gibb asked, not sure what else to say.

"Maybe. Part of it is her bein' stressed out over makin' dinner and all, but I believe my birthday is just a small part of it. The woman just won't take her medication on a consistent basis. She tells Daddy it makes her feel like shit all the time, so she goes off it for a while. That's the first warnin'.

"For a little while ever'thing's fine and she's happy, 'cuz she's proud of showin' us how competent she is without the pills. She's smilin' and laughin' and cookin' and showin' interest in what we got goin' at school and stuff. It's really kinda nice.

"But then things start to slip a little. She starts talkin' a little faster or she starts talkin' more - a lot more - like she's some kinda expert on things she's never done or places she's never been. That's the second warnin'. But we know from experience that's when you gotta really nod and pay attention, and you best look her in the eye while she's talkin' and give her some affirmation. When you do that, she stays right high and happy. Otherwise, the trouble comes sooner than later. But it always comes."

"What happens?" Gibb wasn't sure he wanted to know, but he asked anyway.

"Well, the first real clue is when she can't sleep. She just…I don't know…I think it just keeps gettin' noisier in Mama's mind. Then nothing she does can help her turn the noise down. She stays up all night doin' stuff – cleanin', cookin', writin' stuff down, makin' lists of instructions how to do stuff she's never gonna do. I guess the only way she knows how to try to finally make it stop is by makin' a lot of noise herself, hollerin' and yellin' and throwin' shit. Can't tell you the number of full jars or bottles I've seen her smash when she gets worked up."

"Really?! She smashes stuff?" Gibb was incredulous. His own mother was the exact opposite. She had her problems, but she kept them in her own head, smoking her cigarettes and watching TV, barely saying a word. He'd never once heard her raise her voice.

"She does smash stuff," Leo replied wryly, shaking his head. "I don't know why, but I believe it's because her mind has gotten to racin' so fast that her actual *comprehension* of what's happenin' around her just gets real distorted. I imagine it's sorta like takin' a tape of someone talkin' and speedin' it up a little. But let the tape keep speedin' up and up and up, now there's no words any more. It's just super-fast squeaks and squawks and gibberish and it's confusin' as hell. And that's when she pretty much loses it.

"She'll throw stuff and smash stuff. Or she'll grab her car keys and stomp out the door, screamin' stuff at us like 'Y'all made me do this again! Y'all ain't fit to live! I'm never comin' back to this blankety-blank house!' Meanwhile, we're all shakin' our heads like, 'Oh no…here we go again…'

"If Daddy's home, he'll try and stop her but she'll jump in the car and fly off in a rage and that's when it truly gets scary, 'cuz we're always afraid she's gonna hurt herself or, God forbid, someone else in a wreck. It's pretty terrifying sometimes."

"Holy shit, Leo. That's a…" Gibb blushed as he struggled to find the right words. "That's…a lot to deal with."

"Yeahhh, buddy," Leo drawled. "But what's worse is afterwards. Afterwards, she can get so low, sometimes she don't come out of her room for days. And then when she does, she might be cryin' and all messed up, needin' a bath, lookin' like a damn haint. She's a sight, bless her heart. And there's nothin' anyone can say or do to help her. Except Daddy. He does his best, but it's a tough go. She hates to make him miserable, but she can't help herself. He gets her to go back to the doctor and the doc works on a new treatment plan or tells her she just needs to stay on her doggone medication.

"The doctors need to get it right, though, so she doesn't feel like shit and keeps takin' it as it's prescribed. So far, nothing has really helped for a long period of time."

Gibb just stood there, forlorn and full of dread, as he listened to Leo.

"She gets real controlling, too," Leo added. "I do have a car, you know. It's a 1974 Ford Maverick – it's kind of a badass little ride. I had it lowered three inches and tricked it out with dual pipes, painted it an orangey-red. Mama was in a mood and pitched a fit when I told her I was gonna drive the car up here."

"Why?!" Gibb wanted to know. He wished he had a car, but he'd put all his savings from his summer landscaping jobs into planning for college. It was better than nothing, but not enough to buy a car *and* afford tuition.

"No reason for it, really. Just a way for her to hold on to some illusion of control she has. Daddy took me aside and told me he understood why I was pissed off but asked me not to fuss about it. He's just tryin' to keep the peace. I promised him I wouldn't say another word about it. I'm going back home after graduation anyway. I'll be drivin' her again," Leo said emphatically.

"That's...umm...pretty big of you. You know, to handle it that way," Gibb said.

"Nah, it's really not," Leo replied, shaking his sandy head. "We love her and we worry about her. When Mama lost her shit and tossed that cake today, she flew out right behind it. Daddy wasn't home and we couldn't stop her.

"She took off at high speed like she always does and we don't know where she went. When he got home, he took Sissie with him to try to find her. He told me they'd try to bring back dinner. It doesn't matter - only thing that matters now is that they get Mama home safe tonight."

He grimaced. Gibb tried to think of something to say.

"Well, I'm glad I got to see you on your birthday, anyway," he stammered self-consciously. "Even under these circumstances. You sure you're doing OK?"

"Yeah, I'm good," Leo said, reflexively rubbing at his eyelids, like he was tired of talking about it. "This stuff happens in our family. Last thing Daddy said before he went out the door was that he was sellin' Mama's car, he didn't care how big a fit she pitched. I believe he'll do it, too. It's a way to finally help keep her safe and himself sane.

"Anyway, I just wanted to stay behind 'cuz you were due to arrive soon and I wanted to let you know that my birthday dinner got sort of...cancelled."

"Anything I can do?"

"Nah, it's all good. No wait, there is one thing. You could stop wussin' out on that bike ride over yonder up to Kimberly Hill. You're makin' me think you're afraid of a little exercise," Leo said with a playful shove to Gibb's shoulder. "Wanna just plan to ride up there this weekend since you chickened out last time?"

Gibb couldn't say no now, not after what Leo was dealing with today.

"Yeah, sorry about cancelling last weekend. Definitely not afraid of a little exercise!" he said, more cheerfully than he felt. "For sure, let's do it this Saturday!"

More than anything in the world Gibb wanted to stay here at Leo's house and hang out with him, but he was feeling uneasy again. He didn't have a clue what to say or do in this situation. Plus, he'd come over here all churned up about Leo, as he had been for weeks now, for entirely different reasons. Now there would be a whole raft of raw emotions that Leo's family would surely be grappling with, if and when they got his mother home. Probably not the best time to meet everyone.

Fifteen minutes after he'd arrived, he was pedaling home, feeling truly sorry for Leo and hoping that their ride this Saturday would be a good escape for him. He also hoped that he wouldn't do or say something stupid to make Leo regret hanging out with him.

# Chapter 11

# ON KIMBERLY HILL

Gibb didn't want it to, but Saturday came anyway. Too many conflicting feelings – hope/despair, worthiness/unworthiness, lust/shame – were dampening his enthusiasm for meeting up with Leo for their ride up to Kimberly Hill. But the sun was shining, the Indian summer air was warm, and he'd promised Leo he'd meet him at nine-thirty a.m. He wasn't going to back out again.

Gibb was already waiting at Rogers Park, their planned rendezvous point, when Leo rode up without a word. They nodded a silent hello to each other and then they were off, Gibb leading the way on the fifteen-mile ride down to Kimberly Hill and then the steep half-ride, half-walk up the half-mile high hill.

Every so often, Gibb would turn around to make sure Leo was keeping up. Leo would nod or give him a thumbs-up. From the moment they'd met up this morning to the moment they'd finished their slog to the top of the hill neither of them had uttered a word.

Gibb appreciated that Leo was staying quiet. Somehow, as soon as the reverie was broken, their time together this morning would begin to take a definite shape. For now, in silence, every possibility still existed for what this day could hold. Gibb liked thinking about it that way, anyway.

They reached the top of Kimberly Hill, passing by chair swings and lookout points where they could have stopped to take a break and look at the view.

They didn't, though. Gibb wanted Leo to see all of it at once, to feel like he himself did whenever he got up here, in the middle of more than just a breathtaking 360-degree view of these amazing hills and valleys. Up here, as far as Gibb was concerned, if you were alone and it was quiet, you could feel like you were at the center of forever itself, a single point equidistant from every other thing in the Universe.

Leo followed Gibb's lead as he walked his bike all the way to the lip of the western slope of the hill. To Gibb, the best view of everything was from this very spot. Years ago, someone had thoughtfully constructed a sturdy, chesthigh retaining wall here. It was a good, solid something to lean against after the long walk-and-ride, and one last barrier to keep a person from falling right off what felt like the edge of the world.

They stood, both quietly astounded by how far they could see across the valley from this spot. Gibb had been here many times before, but he couldn't seem to remember a day when he could see this much so clearly. In his mind he imagined he was seeing the Pacific Ocean out there on the horizon line, almost three thousand miles away.

Leo finally broke their morning-long silence with one whispered word. "Wow."

"Unreal, right?" Gibb whispered back.

The squeaky whine of a winch tow somewhere up on the field behind them brought them both back to earth. A moment later a glider plane sailed right over their heads, banking northward off the hill to soar high above a ribbon of blue river cutting through the green and gold valley below.

"I wanna do that someday," Leo said, following the little plane with his eyes until it finally disappeared into the sun.

"Me too. Maybe after college. Man, I love it up here," Gibb said serenely. "High up above everyone and everything. High up and *away* from everyone and everything."

Leo kept looking at the sky. "I'm pretty sure this is as high up as I've ever been," he said, his awed voice barely audible above the noise from another departing sailplane. "I believe I'm right when I say the highest point in the whole state of Louisiana is only like 500 feet. Never been to it, though."

They took a few more minutes to stare in wonder at the amazing scenery before Gibb jumped on his bike.

"C'mon, there's a lot more awesome stuff to see up here."

At the very top of the hill, smooth and winding bike and walking paths split a couple hundred acres of grass into well-manicured swaths of perfect green incongruence. The glider runway, the ideal launch pad up and out to the blue skies above them, sat right in the middle of it all.

As taken as he was with the beauty of it all Leo was more astonished that, aside from the occasional glider rider and one middle-aged couple on bikes, no one was up here on a day as remarkable as this. Gibb just shrugged. This was one of the places he came to escape. The fewer people who came up here, the better.

After an hour of riding around - with Gibb taking great satisfaction in Leo's slack-jawed reaction to the scenery up, around, and below them - they took a break. Gibb chose a grassy area just beneath the northern crest of the hill. The view was great but, even better, it was probably the most shaded and private spot up there.

With the mid-afternoon sun riding high behind them, they were now lying in the grass, staring up at a few interesting cloud formations in the almost-empty blue sky. Heads cradled in their clasped hands, the long and quiet gaps in their conversation were as weighty as their few words.

Leo eventually spoke up.

"Let me ask you a question."

He paused, waiting for Gibb to consent. When no response came, Leo resumed, his question thoughtful and deliberate.

"What if everyone you've known is everyone you've ever known?"

Gibb pondered the question for a minute, not sure what Leo was getting at.

"Hmm...not sure I know what you mean," came Gibb's laconic response. He sat up and looked over at Leo. "I mean, everyone I know *is* everyone I've ever known. Isn't that, like, true?"

He laughed, more out of confusion than humor. Still staring at the sky, Leo clarified his question.

"Sure enough. But what I mean is, what if everyone you've ever met is someone you've met before, maybe in other lifetimes, other dimensions, somehow, some way? Wouldn't that be kinda wild?"

"What's making you think about that kind of stuff?" Gibb asked.

"Oh, I dunno. I just think there might be something to the whole idea," Leo replied. "Like take your mama, for instance. You ever get the feeling you've known her before somehow? Or other people in your family? Or friends?"

*Oh, that's definitely happened,* Gibb thought, turning his head to look over at Leo. *Just this month.*

"Sure, I've experienced that. I never thought about it in terms of like, my mom or whatever. I'm pretty sure I never met her in another lifetime," he said with a laugh. "If I had, maybe I'd understand her better. She's kind of weird. But yeah, I know what you're talking about."

He hesitated, then let go of the idea of telling Leo he was one of those people. Their conversation gave way to another long holding silence as the clouds morphed shapes again, each young man completely alone in his own perception, a single foot and a million quiet miles apart.

Swallowing hard, Gibb summoned up his courage. He sat up, still facing away from Leo.

"Leo, can I ask you something, man?"

"Yep, sure."

"Has anybody ever, like, really confided in you? Like some dark secret or some kind of weird drama in their life?"

He gauged Leo's response to measure how much farther to take any kind of revelatory conversation. Leo looked over at Gibb.

"Well, sure they have," he said self-assuredly. "Mostly the women in my family. For some reason, my sister, my grandma, female cousins – they all just tell me stuff. Some stuff I have absolutely no business knowing, stuff they don't even know about each other. They always feel like they can talk to me about whatever's on their minds," he said, shaking his head in resignation and rolling his eyes a little.

Gibb smirked. "So, you're like the family counselor or something?"

"Mmm…no, not really," Leo answered. "More like…well, look, this is gonna sound real sexist and I don't mean it ugly, I really don't. But the women in my family? They just like to talk, buddy. They like to talk a *lot*. And *I*," he said, pointing to himself, "I don't talk much at all.

'Cept when I'm nervous. So it's good for them, I guess. They talk about what's botherin' them and I end up doing a lot of listenin'. Afterwards they're happy and I'm usually just bored stiff or completely blown away and tryin' to act cool about it. So, umm, I guess I'd call myself the family listener, but not any kind of counselor," he concluded with a laugh.

"Well, when they're telling you stuff, do they ask you for advice?"

Leo shook his head. "Nah. Cause I'm gonna tell you what's the God's-honest truth: women, *especially* southern women…well, at least the women in my family…they don't need advice. Before they even start talkin', they already know the answer to the question they're askin', whatever it is. So, if they ask you what *you* think about somethin' *they're* thinkin' of doin', trust me, it's just a set-up. They already got the whole thing planned out, even if they act like they don't know.

"And if they're *not* gonna do somethin', they know that too. So, if they ask me how *I* feel about somethin' they're thinkin' about doin', I just shake my head and say 'I don't rightly know.' Because they're gonna do whatever they want anyway, and they already have a plan.' Rule Number One: never give your opinion. About anything. Stay neutral."

Gibb grinned.

Leo adjusted his hands under his head, his left hand inadvertently grazing Gibb's right wrist before settling into their new position. Pure electricity pulsed through Gibb's entire hand from Leo's fleeting touch. He wished Leo hadn't moved his hand away so quickly, but it wasn't like Leo would be into holding hands. Especially after all this talk about women.

"So anyway, why did you wanna know about people confiding in me?" Leo asked.

Gibb took a deep breath and, stretching his arms above his head he turned to Leo. *Let's see how he deals with this. Here goes…*

"I don't know. It's kind of hard to explain and I'm like you, I don't talk a lot. But I write a lot of stuff down, try to turn it into poetry, stuff like that. I'd like to be good someday, like Robert Frost or Dylan or Robert Hunter or John Barlow, ya know? I really don't think what I write is any good, but sometimes it helps to write stuff down. Until I light it on fire and just sit there and watch it burn. That helps make it kinda fun."

He chuckled. Leo sat up and looked at him.

"Now why would you go and do that? It's prob'ly a lot better than you think. I'd like to check it out some time," he said.

"Mmm…maybe some time. But not any time soon. It's not always, like, terrible, but it's too…I don't know. Self-conscious or something. Too me, me, me. One of my teachers told me once, and it made a lot of sense, that people only choose to read stuff to learn about themselves, not about you, the writer.

"So right now," Gibb explained, "they wouldn't, *you* wouldn't, get a whole lot out of it. It's too self-centered and my life is pretty boring. Gimme some time, though. Maybe at some point I'll come up with something that means something to somebody somewhere, once something interesting happens in my life."

"Oh, I don't know. You're an interesting enough cat. Maybe you're too humble," Leo said, his eyes following the flight path of a couple of crows squawking overhead.

"You think so? I don't," Gibb muttered, blushing as he stared off in the opposite direction, feeling itchy from a thin sheen of sweat beginning to silently creep from every pore on his body.

*Well, this was awkward.*

Leo glanced over at Gibb. "You're looking kinda perplexed there, bud."

*Am I? Weird.*

Gibb twisted his mouth diffidently. "I'm always perplexed," he said with an uneasy laugh. "When I'm walking around, does my mouth droop open, like," he slackened his jaw and starting talking in the voice of a cartoon dunce, "'Duhhh…my name's Gibb. I live in Eislertown with a bunch of other losers.'"

He went back to his normal voice. "That's what I feel like I look like, anyway."

"Come on now, buddy," Leo said, laughing. "Not at all. Good impression, though."

He grinned, almost affectionately, his eyes shining as they caught the sun. Gibb had to look away for a moment. He shivered, less from the cold sweat trickling between his shoulder blades than the lewdness of his thoughts about Leo at that moment. He cleared his throat and his mind with a strong cough, then sat up and turned towards Leo.

"I guess I'm perplexed because I want to tell you something true and something heavy, but I don't know why, since I've almost never felt the need to talk to anyone about anything heavy."

Leo raised his eyebrows, surprised at Gibb's sudden intensity.

"Uh-oh. You some kind of serial killer or something?" Leo kidded.

"Why yes, yes I am," Gibb said. "All the serial killers are from the Finger Lakes, in case you didn't know."

Leo smiled.

"Seriously, though…if you wanna talk about something…"

Gibb, nervous, cut him off.

"Well…I do have one true friend I can talk to. She's like, way older than me, though. She's like thirty-two. But other than her, I've never told anyone anything like this before. So, if I start to stammer and stuff, just bear with me, OK? I can't promise that any of it is gonna make any sense."

"OK…" Leo said, a wary expression on his face.

Gibb did start stammering, but then he took a deep breath and calmed himself.

"All right, here we go."

## Chapter 12

# RIPPLES, PART I

"Nah, nah. There ain't no way. I know you didn't just blurt out 'I love you and can't keep my mind off you!' or some shit like that," Sam said from behind the wheel, lifting up his sunglasses so Gibb could see his eyes.

Gibb hesitated, staring blankly at him for a second.

"Well, what if I did?"

"I'd put you out the car right here in nowhere Tennessee, that's what," Sam said, maybe half-seriously. "Even though I said I wouldn't. I had not previously considered you being lame as hell as a condition for dumpin' yo' ass on the side of the road. But I'll do it, hear? I will do it."

"You won't have to worry about that," Gibb said with a grimace. "Even though that's exactly what I wanted to tell him, that's not what happened."

"Well, what happened then?" Sam demanded.

※

In retrospect, Gibb hadn't really been sure what it was that he was going to tell Leo that afternoon on Kimberly Hill. It didn't matter anyway because he didn't get the chance. Not that afternoon, anyway.

Literally, the second Gibb was about to lay bare his emotions, to tell Leo all the anguished secrets of his burning heart, they'd heard a sudden commotion behind them. From the direction of the glider runway up the hill behind them, the distant sound of men's voices had quickly turned into urgent, ominous shouting.

Instinctively, both Gibb and Leo jumped up to look back towards the runway over the crest of the hill. For a split-second Gibb thought that an angry, hateful mob might be descending on the two young men lying just-a-little-too-close-together on that grassy slope.

That wasn't it, not even close.

"WHOA!", each of them hollered, bolting in opposite directions faster than they'd ever run, then diving out of the way of a rapidly descending glider plane that, unbelievably to both guys staring wide-eyed from their prone positions on the grassy hillside, crashed nose-down right on the wide expanse of lawn where they'd just been sitting.

"Ohhh, SHIT!" they both hollered, jumping to their feet at the same time and running towards the crumpled plane.

Leo got to the plane first, chagrined to realize that a Plexiglass canopy, not a door, was the only way to get to the motionless pilot slumped over in the cockpit. The canopy's latches were bent, but with some desperate effort, Gibb and Leo each got their respective sides to open. Then, to Gibb's astonishment, Leo reached into the glider's little cabin and, without another word, hooked his arms under the pilot's armpits, pulled him out of the cockpit, laid him prone on his back in the grass and began performing CPR on him! Three men, presumably the ones who'd been shouting from way back there, came running over the hill's crest towards the glider.

"He's alive," Leo called to them urgently, "but he's unconscious."

As his own adrenaline and shock began to subside, Gibb could only stand back and marvel at Leo's knowledge and experience as he worked on the pilot. Gibb's mind could barely process everything that had just happened in the last two minutes, but there was Leo right out in front of him, cool and calm and actually helping, not getting in the way like he himself would have. Gibb sighed.

*So, in addition to everything else, he knows CPR, too. How...where... do people like this even come from?*

But his feelings of inadequacy were overmatched by his admiration and... now he had to admit it...love... for the handsome young guy trying to do his best to assist in the face of someone else's misfortune. Leo was every bit as amazing as Gibb had imagined he was. Every bit.

Considering the relative distance of Kimberly Hill from any nearby town, an ambulance arrived much quicker than Gibb had imagined it would. First responders whisked the injured glider pilot away, and a few short minutes later Gibb and Leo were readying themselves for the bike ride back home.

"You were unbelievable up there," Gibb said as they glided down Kimberly Hill.

"Nah," Leo demurred. "I just took a CPR class before we moved up here. It wasn't a big deal. Everybody should prob'ly take that class. Then they could do it, too."

"A class isn't even close to the same thing as jumping into a little plane and actually *doing* CPR on a real person," Gibb insisted. "That guy's whole life was in your hands right then."

"Aww...come on now," Leo said dismissively.

"Come on, nothin'!" Gibb exclaimed. "If you hadn't been there, he might have died! I wouldn't have known what to do, and I'll bet those other three guys didn't either. None of them offered to step in and help.

"You were all cool, calm, and collected, too," Gibb laughed. "Like you'd been doing it your whole life."

"Well..." Leo said haltingly, "thanks. Maybe my dad's calm is rubbing off on me after all. Hasn't always been that way, sure as shootin'."

"Maybe..." Gibb replied.

"Now that you've been by my house, you kinda have an idea of how things can go there. Y'know, with Mama and all her stuff. It's not easy to be cool when shit starts flyin', but we make it work."

"You sure made it work today," Gibb said, wanting to tell him even more. "Pretty impressive."

And that was the last of their conversation that day, riding silently until they got back to Rogers Park and parted ways with a simple goodbye.

⊰⊱

"Whoa! Did the pilot live? Or did he die later?" Sam asked, his interest in Gibb's story clear.

"Oh no, the pilot lived," Gibb said eagerly. "He was messed up, but he lived!"

"OK, then!" Sam said, playfully mocking Gibb's enthusiastic tone, before his voice dropped back to a matter-of-fact tone. "So, when the hell did you ever get around to tellin' ol' Leo about your feelin's and stuff?"

"Christmas Eve," Gibb said bluntly. "Three whole months later. And I'm glad I waited."

"Aww…Christmas Eve," Sam repeated. "Ain't that romantic?"

"Stop," Gibb laughed. "It's not as corny as all that. It just happened that Christmas Eve was another day of big trouble at Leo's house. So, he came by and picked me up and we went riding around. It started out sad and then got kind of…I don't know…beautiful."

⊰⊱

Mid-afternoon on Christmas Eve, Gibb heard a polite knock on the front door. Looking out his bedroom window onto the fast-fading day he saw something that made his heart stop: Leo's family car, their white sedan, parked right in front of his house. Without another thought he hustled downstairs, the smile on his face as big as the dog-eared wreath adorning the front door he couldn't open fast enough.

"Hey, Merry Christmas!" he exclaimed to his drop-in visitor.

Leo, much more sedate, dressed in a long, grey woolen coat that looked more like it was his dad's than his own, smiled wearily.

"Merry Christmas yourself. You up for riding around a while?"

A minute later, the amount of time it took for Gibb to grab his coat and shoes, they were out the door and on their way to nowhere.

"Mama lost her shit again today," Leo said somberly as he drove. "Daddy's home looking after her. Sissie pissed her off by telling her she was going to the mall to do last minute shopping and Mama expected her to be home helping to get stuff ready for Christmas. Anybody could've seen it comin'. She's been off her meds for at least a week."

"Yikes," Gibb said.

"Yeah, yikes. It almost got physical. Daddy had to step in to separate 'em and then Sissie run out of the house...who knows where she went? Hopefully to her friend's house. Daddy give me the keys and said, 'Just go on out for a while. I'll deal with Mama.' He didn't want her tryin' to jump in the car and take off. She's still pissed Daddy sold her car after the last time. But he had to keep her from bein' a threat to herself and everybody else out there.

"So, first I drove around lookin' for Sissie but I didn't see her walkin' on the side of the road anywhere. And I kept lookin' for her, but somehow I ended up here."

Even after almost four months of hanging out, Leo had never once been to Gibb's house, so it was pretty unlikely he'd just "somehow ended up" there.

"Glad you came," was all Gibb could muster to say. "Wanna go anywhere in particular?"

"Nah, let's just drive around the lake to where all those little Amish farm stands are on the other side. Prob'ly nothin' open but maybe we can get some pie or somethin'."

They drove in silence for a few minutes until Leo spoke up.

"You wanna know what I think about somethin'?"

Gibb shrugged. "I guess."

"Kindness. This world needs more kindness."

"Yeah, well...I kind of already knew that," Gibb said before suddenly catching himself with a laugh. "Sorry, I didn't mean to add to the unkindness of the world with a smart-ass comment."

Leo ignored him.

"The world needs more people to stop expecting *other* people to be kind and to just start being kind themselves. Or continue being kind, even if they're tired of other people not being kind. You get what I'm sayin' here? *Everybody* needs to be kind. You can't just sit around and wait for other people. We're all in the same bowl of soup. Why is that so hard to understand?"

Gibb was puzzled. "What's got you thinking about this stuff? The whole deal with your mom?"

"That, yeah," Leo said, quietly exasperated. "But it's Christmastime and you see people stealin' Christmas gifts out of other people's cars, or people goin' hungry 'cuz no one's helpin' 'em out. And Sissie runnin' her big mouth even when she knows Mama don't mean to be crazy, makin' everything worse. Shit, everybody in the world needs to be more like *you*."

"Me?!" Gibb was floored. He'd never thought of himself as any paragon of kindness.

"Yes, you. Folks need to just shut the hell up and follow the example of Mr. Gibbon Mulcahy. Kind. Humble. Nice all the time."

Gibb stared at Leo stone-faced as he pulled into the empty parking lot of one of the farm stands he'd mentioned. It was definitely closed and, by the looks of it, wouldn't open its doors again until springtime.

"What are we doing here?" Gibb asked, looking around the deserted parking lot. Darkness was falling. He could see Seneca Lake in the distance and a small parade of three boats, festively lit up for Christmas, chugging south towards the Watkins Glen boat launch.

"I don't rightly know. Just sittin' here for a few minutes, I guess," Leo mumbled gruffly. "I'm gonna leave the car runnin', though. I don't know how y'all deal with this cold all the time. Glad I'm goin' home in June."

And there it was, just like that. The perfect opening, and this warm idling car overlooking Seneca Lake, was the perfect setting for Gibb to finally tell Leo everything he'd wanted to say that afternoon up on Kimberly Hill. This polite and gentle Louisiana boy was about to get shelled by the soft pitch he'd just lobbed.

"Looking forward to goin' home?" Gibb asked, mimicking his accent as he looked Leo straight in the eye. "Well, that makes one of us."

"One of us what?" Leo replied cluelessly.

"One of us glad you're going back to Louisiana, that's what. And that one of us isn't me."

"See, there you go again, bein' all kind and nice," Leo interjected. "You don't gotta say stuff like that, Gibb."

"It has nothing to do with being kind or nice. It has to do with something a lot bigger than that."

Gibb's reply was sharper than he'd intended, and it surprised both of them.

"Meaning what?" Leo asked, still oblivious.

Gibb took a deep breath through his nose and nervously rubbed the side of his face. Now was the time, but now how was he going to say it? A minute ago, he was so confident. Now he was starting to wuss out again. He turned his gaze back towards the lake, the sky dark enough now that one remaining Christmas boat blazed bright in light and color, sitting quiet and still in the middle of the now-black water.

"I'm taking a big chance here with what I'm about to tell you, but at this point I don't have another option. I've gotta be honest with you."

"OK..." Leo said, drawing out the word.

"You see that boat out there?" Gibb asked, turning to him.

He saw Leo nod.

"That boat is you."

"Me?" Leo replied bewilderedly.

"Yep, you. Did you notice that when we first got here, that boat was sitting there with two others? Maybe not. Its lights didn't look as powerful because it was still too light outside. But when it began to get kind of dark, the other boats just sort of drifted away, leaving it all alone there in the middle of the lake. Who knows where those other boats went?

"It always seems like when it gets dark, some things and people just kind of drift away, and some just get left there in it. Like that boat we're seeing, all alone out there. But look, it's blazing brighter and brighter the darker it gets. See that?"

"Yes, I see that," Leo replied.

"Well, th-that's you," Gibb stammered. "Maybe you don't know it, but you blaze brighter when it gets dark around you."

"That's a pretty nice thing to say…" Leo began. Gibb cut him off.

"I'm not done. If I don't say this now, I may never will. Back in late August it was getting dark out, just like this, when I headed to the stupid Kountry Korner for a snack or whatever. That was the night I first met…no, that's the night I first *saw* you.

"It was getting dark outside and," he tapped himself on the chest, "it was starting to get dark in here, too. I was getting pretty tired of a lot of stuff and having to deal with every freakin' thing on my own. My family was, still is, no help and…well, you know that whole story. No real friends, either. No one. But then I saw you and, like it or not, it was like seeing that boat out there. Even though you were a total stranger, you lit things up for me in this weird, big way."

Leo, as still as a Rogers Park statue, stared silently at Gibb.

"That evening, there was the same kind of distance between me and you as there is between us and that little boat out there tonight. See how we can see the little Christmas lights all lighting up the water and the darkness all around them? If those lights weren't on right now, we'd barely notice that boat. Only its silhouette. And once it gets totally dark, we won't be able to see it at all."

"What are you trying to say here, Gibb?" Leo asked, almost, but not quite, impatiently.

"I'm saying that the evening I saw you at the Kountry Korner, I walked home through the dark woods amazed at how a *complete and total stranger* lit up that night for me. Just like that boat out there is doing right now! I've never been on that boat, I've never even seen that boat, and I probably never will again. But I'll remember it for sure. Why? Because its light defies the darkness, *simply by being there.* Do you understand? That's what you did at the Kountry Korner that night in August, and you had no freakin' idea."

Leo leaned further towards Gibb, more intrigued now at what Gibb was telling him.

"Just like, right now, all the way out here where we are, that boat and the people on it have no clue about the effect those lights are having on us,"

Gibb said, pointing. "That's because they're too close to it to see it. They're just going about their business on board right now, clueless that they're even being talked about.

He took a deep breath, then exhaled, giving himself a second to collect himself before really going for it.

"Anyway, same goes for you. You had no idea on that night that you were a light like that, and there I was in the distance, mesmerized by it. I walked home in a daze, figuring I'd never see you again 'cuz I thought you were just passing through. But then you walked into History class and the rest is… well…"

"History," Leo said, almost somberly.

"Yep, history," Gibb acknowledged quietly.

"I still don't know…" Leo began.

Gibb interrupted him again with a wave of his hand and a command.

"Turn off the car," Gibb said stoically reaching over and turning the keys in the ignition himself.

"What? Wait, what are you doing?"

"Turning off the car."

Save for the rush of blood in Gibb's ears, the car was now completely quiet in the farm stand parking lot. The scent of old cigarettes hung thick in the front seat without the warm air hissing through the vents. Now it was just Gibb and Leo, quietly breathing. The shivery December air took quick advantage of the idle car and slipped quickly inside, frosting their breath now, as Christmas Eve fell into complete darkness outside. Gibb slid further away from Leo on the bench seat and leaned back against the passenger side door.

"What are we doing?" Leo half-whispered.

"I need to finish what I'm telling you and I want to make sure you hear every word," Gibb said, matching Leo's low volume as the inside of the windows began to fog up.

"OK," Leo half-whispered again, comically this time. Gibb didn't smile.

"Leo, I need you to know something. In the last four months you've shown me more about how to make my way in this world than anybody I've ever met over the course of all eighteen years of my life. In the face of some really tough shit you've got going on at home – you know, with your mom and stuff - you've never been anything but kind and understanding and cool to me. You know a lot of things about a lot of things and you've shown me, without really meaning to, how much I have to learn and how far I have to go. You've been the best friend I could have ever dreamed up and…"

"You've been the best friend I could have made up north here, too," Leo broke in. Gibb held up his hand, a playfully impatient half-smile on his face.

"Still not done here," he laughed. "I know I'm taking forever to get to the point but I've never had to say this before so *please*, just kinda bear with me for one more minute. I think under any other circumstances I would be pretty embarrassed right now. But ya know something? I'm not!"

"EMBARRASSED ABOUT WHAT?" Leo whisper-shouted.

*Here goes…*Gibb thought as he took a deep breath.

"About the fact that I am head over freakin' heels in love with you. *In love.* **With *you*, LEO DAVION.** There it is, in bold-type and capital letters. And even though that might freak you out or upset you or make you hate me or not wanna be my friend anymore, that is the stone-cold, hard-ass fact. I. *Love.* YOU. I'll put it on a billboard, scream it from the treetops, hire a sky writer. I don't even care anymore."

Gibb could see Leo's silhouette stiffen behind the steering wheel. He said nothing in this silent, interminable one-second void. Gibb, more nervous now than before he began, took that as a cue to keep talking.

"Just like that stupid boat out there I kept trying to compare you to a minute ago," Gibb continued softly, gesturing awkwardly again towards the lake. "You lit everything up. Your handsome, beautiful face. That's right, I said it. Your handsome, beautiful face. And then I heard your handsome, beautiful voice. And things got more intense, like, immediately.

Gibb's voice was stronger now, confident. Whatever the consequences of this emotional admission would be, he'd deal with them. He kept going.

"So now this has gone…well, shit, for me this has *always* gone…*wayyy* beyond friendship. The truth is I was into you from the moment I saw you. And then we became friends, and I knew it was much more than a feeling of friendship, for me anyway.

"And then we went up to the top of Kimberly Hill. And what happened there? Geez, dude. A glider almost crashes into us and *you* jump right into the cabin to perform CPR on that pilot. You saved his life until the ambulance got there," Gibb said, suddenly getting choked up.

"And that was it. That's when I knew for sure. Well, I already knew I loved you, but then seeing you in action I had to finally admit it. Own it. I had to say it to myself and now I'm saying it to you: It was *love*. It *is* love. I don't ever want you to leave here and go back to Louisiana.

"So now you know. Now you know and I don't have to pretend anymore. I'm not gonna try to hold your hand in the hallway at school or anything, OK? But at least now you have the whole picture."

Gibb's voice cracked, exposing his feelings even more.

"I want you to know, even if you drop me as a friend, and I won't blame you if you did, you've given me the chance to see who you really are and it's amazing. Earlier you called *me* kind. No way. No way ever. That's like me stealing a picture you painted and claiming I'm the artist. I'm following *your* lead. I swear to God, no matter what happens, I'll be inspired by you for the rest of my life, whether you're in it or not. I love you, Leo. I know that like I've never known anything else."

In the cold silence and stale tobacco air, Gibb ran the knuckle of his forefinger quickly in and out of the corner of his eye, trying to blot a tear. Half-elated, half-miserable, he sat still, his back now pressed hard up against the inside of the car door. It was done.

And now, maybe, so was their friendship. Suddenly, every negative feeling Gibb had ever had, came rushing in. Shame, self-loathing, self-doubt, anger, fear, pain, sorrow, regret. Maybe it was only twenty seconds of *real* heck, that perfect combination of the words "hell" and "fuck", but in that short space he felt like he was being whipped, hard, lashed by wind and rain, alone and afraid.

He could barely see Leo's face now in the dark, only a silent, breathing shadow, betraying no evidence of any of the color or light Gibb had ascribed to him. For a moment, he rocked slowly back and forth on the driver's side, arms wrapped around his drawn-up knees, his head bowed.

Finally, Gibb saw movement. Leo lifted his head, but in this dark space there was no face, no expression to read, no way of knowing what he might say. If he even said anything at all.

Gibb could only look away and shake his head, his humiliation complete. What a blunder. *This* was why he never told anyone how he was feeling about anything. He had beclowned himself at the exact moment he was hoping to be met with…well…if not the same amount of ardor, at least some empathy.

Suddenly, Leo spoke, enunciating clearly into the frigid air in the car.

"I feel the same way."

And that was it. Two seconds. Two seconds to say five words. Five little words. The sky didn't rain fire, the ground didn't shake, and Gibb didn't explode into a million pieces upon hearing them. But those five little words were all it took to change the world, in ways neither of them could have predicted or understood on that cold, dark, amazing Christmas Eve.

*Chapter 13*

# RIPPLES, PART II

A chilly breeze skittered eastward across Seneca Lake, lightly slapping Gibb's face before disappearing with a sigh. After the universe exploded in Leo's car up there at the farm stand, he needed to calm down alone. Here, rooted in place on this log, the only intrusion on his solitude was the watery whisper of the chilly lake lapping at the shore.

Despite the fact that their entire world had changed just two hours earlier, Leo still had to get home to be with his family, and he'd probably stayed out later than his dad had expected. There was nothing going on at Gibb's house tonight anyway, so after one last incredulous kiss, he'd asked Leo to drop him here on this side of the lake. Just like the first night he saw Leo, he'd walk the last couple miles home through the dark. Only this time, everything in his mind would be true.

The sky above Gibb blazed with stars, the multi-colored lights on houses and Christmas trees all around the lake doing their best to twinkle in imitation. On a day when everything got turned completely upside down, the lights from these lake houses provided stability, some proof that life was still going on as usual, regardless of the new disorder in his own world. He was grateful for every lit-up house he saw, even though he'd never met, and probably never would meet, a single person who decorated them.

He'd grown up today. And even though his voice had cracked and he'd teared up, he'd followed through. He was actually brave enough to tell the truth to Leo. Ms. Mullan would be proud when she found out.

His emotions were all over the place: inchoate, rambling, completely disconnected from each other. The usual way they were when it came to Leo. He was all at once and then one at a time elated, sad, proud, confident, embarrassed, happy, and then bummed out again. It was unbelievable to Gibb that Leo felt the same way about him. Leo had told him tonight that he loved him, too. On Christmas Eve! It was too mawkishly awesome to be true.

But the whole thing made him sad too because, no matter what, Leo was going back to Louisiana after graduation. What was going to happen then? There was no doubt he would have missed Leo when he left, but the stakes were way higher now.

This was the first time anything like this even mattered. And as he continued to replay over and over in his mind the outrageous emotional and physical highs of tonight, he could understand why. Up until today, except for the ten-years-ago death of his young cousin Billy, or Little Bill as the adults called him, he had lived within the safe pattern of not getting caught up in anyone else's emotional conflict or baggage.

He was engaged enough in his classes, but not enough to stand out. Teachers seemed to like him OK, but apart from Ms. Mullan, they didn't give him any extra attention. He was more emotionally detached from the world around him than he'd ever acknowledged before.

He guessed he was destined to be one of those kids who would never be remembered for anything when classmates pulled out their high school yearbooks twenty-five years from now.

"Who's that guy?" they'd ask, then shrug. It was an odd thing to admit, that in his detachment he was more like his mother than he'd ever realized. But, the truth was, that's exactly how he wanted it. Not to be like her, but just to be left alone.

Naively, he hadn't expected that falling for Leo would ever get complicated. Mainly because he'd never expected that Leo would *really* have any feelings for him. Up until tonight, Leo had just been a fantasy. Beyond that, he'd never once given any thought to relationships beyond the fun part of them – the companionship, the laughs, the sexual exploration.

Like pretty much anyone else his age, all Gibb really knew of love was the good and bad stuff he'd hear about in songs or see in movies. He didn't have any experience with any of it so, up to now, anything he saw or heard of love was just somebody else's story. Besides, in those stories and songs, the love was always between a man and a woman. There really was no obvious road map in popular culture for two young gay guys in the early 1980's. They'd have to figure it out their own way.

Yet even as he thought about how awesome tonight was, sitting there alone at the edge of the dark lake he let his mind begin to wander a bit. This was his big mistake whenever he was elated about something. Because it was when he was at his most excited and upbeat that here it came again, to haunt him and hurt him, the grim face of his most difficult memory. It was Billy's awful death, bobbing right up to the surface of his attention span, torturing Gibb again with its brazen invasion of his thoughts and its agonizing clarity.

Gibb hated the memory. Mainly because, here on this almost-silent Seneca Lake shore a whole decade after it happened, Gibb had to grapple again with the fact that he'd never really let go of the fear, the raw anger, or the deep grief connected with the death of his beloved cousin. Somehow, he could never let himself be too happy again after that terrible day without having to remember all the terrible details of what happened.

Billy had been Gibb's best friend and, even though they weren't siblings, they liked to tell people they were twins. It was a close enough resemblance: Billy was only two months older than Gibb and had his own red hair, freckles, and challenges with nearsightedness. That's about where the similarities ended, though.

It didn't matter to them when they stood next to each other that it was easy to tell them apart – Gibb noticeably taller and lankier with blue eyes, Billy built more like a little pug-nosed tank with dark brown eyes. But they'd considered themselves brothers and they were so inseparable in those early years of life that many people mistook them for the real thing. Billy was the best, and remembering him tonight, Gibb's eyes welled up with tears as usual.

Billy's father was Gibb's mother's brother. Gibb only knew him as Big Bill or Big Uncle Bill. Big Bill was a physically imposing man - loud, unsmiling, and one mean drunk.

Billy, even though he had only just turned eight years old and often had no part in it, seemed to get the blame for a lot of stuff that went wrong around their house. If the dog pooped on the carpet, Billy got yelled at or, if Big Bill was drunk, Billy usually got hit and hit hard. If the trash wasn't taken out by the time Big Bill came home from work, it was the same scene. Billy lived in fear of his father and he really worked hard not to mess stuff up. It never seemed to work.

One time, for reasons Gibb still couldn't remember because there was no excuse for it anyway, he witnessed Big Bill angrily, drunkenly pick Billy up off the ground by his ears, oblivious to how much the boy, and Gibb, were crying and begging him to stop. Gibb could still see Billy's feet kicking the air above the ground as his father reminded him again "who was boss."

Gibb hated Big Bill even more than he despised Jack. Jack was a real jerk most of the time, but he never did anything like that. That memory made Gibb's eyes overflow as he sat there on the log tonight, his tears both angry and sad, still incredulous at how anyone could do anything like that to another person, especially their own kid.

This was exactly why he would try so hard not to let those memories come back to him. All they brought was pain. Tonight, Gibb cursed Big Bill in whispers as he wiped away the tears.

Still, Gibb did have a lot of great memories of those days. In fact, in the oddest of twists, one that made him do a double take the second he heard Leo mention it at lunch, Billy and Leo shared the exact same birthday. September 29th. Same date, same year.

*How the hell does a coincidence like that happen?* Gibb thought to himself.

And it was ten years ago on that date, on a sunny Saturday afternoon, that Gibb attended Billy's eighth birthday party. Big Bill and Jack both had to work that day and, without their dark presence, the party was fun and light-hearted. No anger, no drinking, no stupid, unfunny racist jokes. Just a bunch of boys riding bikes around, playing kickball in the backyard, and a couple of moms cutting and serving a bakery-bought cake and Kool-Aid.

But later that night, something happened at Billy's house, something that made the boy sneak out and zoom away on his Huffy bike under cover of darkness. Gibb wasn't there, so he couldn't say for sure, but he never once doubted that Big Bill had hurt Billy again. Billy actually told Gibb only days before that if Big Bill ever hit him again, he was going to sneak out of his first-floor bedroom window in the middle of the night and run away forever.

The driver who hit Billy on that moonless night admitted to the cops that he'd been speeding, but "the kid came out of nowhere," riding his bike straight through the unlit two-way stop at Ovid Street and Canoga Road in the eleven o'clock darkness. The driver, never imagining he'd have to avoid hitting a kid in that intersection at that time of night, barely blunted the impact as he sent Billy flying up and away from ever having to deal with Big Bill's abuse again.

It was as terrible a scenario as Gibb could have ever imagined. In fact, up until that night he'd never dreamed something so terrible could ever happen to a kid. It was bad enough that his own dad had been killed in a drunk-driving wreck, but this was different. At least Gibb's dad was a grown-up when it happened. Billy was still a little boy, for God's sake.

For the first few years after the accident, Gibb couldn't shake from his imagination the vision of the impact between that car and Billy on his bike. He blamed Big Bill and wished something terrible, something worse than Billy's fate, would happen to him, too. Tonight's recollections made Gibb realize those feelings hadn't changed.

After Billy's death, Big Bill and his wife, Kate, got divorced and the guy had moved away. Michigan or somewhere like that. Gibb's mother never tried to contact him, and he couldn't remember the last time she mentioned her brother's name. Good. Gibb hated him and wished him nothing but the worst.

He hated that awful intersection where the accident happened and every stupid two-way stop he observed on the country roads around them. How hard was it to put up two more stop signs?

And even now, whenever he thought about all of this, he was still angry and resentful toward his mother and Jack for not understanding how deeply affected he'd been by the loss of not only his cousin, but his best and only real friend, too. It was like he'd lost two people that day. Lily and Jack didn't seem to understand or care about his sadness, how alone he felt, or how scary and tragic the whole pitiful thing was, especially for a little kid. A week after the accident, Billy was buried and those two were back to normal, going about their lives as if the world hadn't just come to a complete and total end.

Gibb hadn't even been allowed to go to Billy's funeral, but he gave Lily a pass there. It was probably the best choice she could have made – he knew he'd still be having nightmares about it all these years later if he'd had to witness that. He'd often imagined shoving Big Bill into Billy's open grave in front of horrified onlookers, kicking as much dirt on that bastard as he could before they hauled him away, kicking and screaming and blaming Big Bill at the top of his lungs. He awoke screaming from that nightmare many times over the last ten years.

But Gibb did learn something from watching how his mother and Jack dealt with the emotions around Billy's death, from not allowing Gibb to go to the funeral or to even talk to them about how pissed off and freaked out he was. He learned avoidance. Avoidance of all things emotional. The strange thing was, he never really tried to learn how to avoid emotional interaction. It just sort of happened.

As time passed, the trauma of young Billy's death had naturally scabbed over but, like many unresolved traumas, Gibb's grief and rage still roiled underneath. That emotional scar, though, had allowed him to become exactly what he was now: an observer outside the front windows of life, safely guarded from engaging in the higher stakes of true participation in it.

That's probably why Gibb had never had another close friend. He'd never had a boyfriend or a girlfriend. He'd had his crushes like everyone else does, but he never once mentioned them or acted on them. He'd say his goodnights from the bottom of the steps rather than walk over to the couch to kiss his mother and, all things being equal, she never made the effort to kiss or hug him, either. He'd never even had a pet. As much as he wanted a dog, he was glad he didn't have one. He knew he wouldn't be ready to deal with the pain of losing it.

But then a few months ago, Leo came along like a damn Siren. Sirens were female in Greek mythology, but gender was irrelevant in this case. Siren was the perfect word for Leo because not only was Gibb ridiculously physically attracted to the guy, he'd even become captivated by the sound of his voice.

One minute Leo would be describing himself in a goofy way: "I'm happy as a possum eatin' a sweet tater." And the very next moment he'd be articulating the deeper meanings set forth in music and art and poetry, their connection to and reflection of the human condition throughout the ages, the arts' overlooked associations with math and science and, most incredibly, their inexorable weave into the braid of something Gibb had rarely, if ever, considered: the Sacred. The All. The Universe. God.

Leo had come along with his Southern manners and his quiet charm and his beautiful face with those otherworldly eyes and that smile, that mouth, instantly driving Gibb to involuntary sexual distraction every time he couldn't force himself to look away.

And after all that, today Leo *really* came along, responding to Gibb's unwieldy overtures of love and desire by sincerely telling him, with quiet confidence, that he felt the exact same way. Telling Gibb things he'd never once heard before from anyone – how awesome he was, how good-looking he was, how amazing he was, how smart and funny he was, leaving Gibb's mind to swirl like the barely visible little eddy near the shoreline in front of him.

The shoreline. Yes, there it was in all its revelatory glory. Revelatory not because Gibb had never seen a beach before – he'd been down here at the lake a million times – but at one of their lunch discussions last week Leo had, as usual, taken a simple concept – in this case, the beach – and framed it in a way Gibb had never before thought about.

Shorelines and beaches, Leo told Gibb, were more than just places to wade or swim. They were actually sacred spaces, holy places where two connected but decidedly separate worlds blended together. At those first shallow, distinct points, where two different worlds meet, a living being can make a choice to enter one or the other.

These holy places crackle with the clashing energy of colliding worlds, Leo had said, but you can't see it. You can only feel it. That's why people are drawn to be near the water, because more than just being beautiful, water is an archetype of their own unconscious, its depths daring us to explore them in order to foster our own growth and change.

Leo went on to explain that at these sacred places, living beings either stay safely where they are or they enter the other, unfamiliar world based on their own curiosity, desires, and capabilities. These sacred places were hubs for physical, spiritual, and emotional risk. Without self-awareness and a true understanding of these things, any creature could lose its entire self, *physically die*, if it makes the wrong choice.

"How many people have drowned after going in too deep?" Leo had asked. "And from another perspective, how many whales have been doomed after beaching themselves?"

Standing on the sacred line that straddles these two worlds, Leo said, a person is at his most vulnerable. If your curiosity outweighs your capability, trouble and anxiety will surely follow once you become aware of your limitations.

But what if you switch it? If you have the *capability* to safely enter and thrive within a new world, but you don't have the *desire* because you're afraid to face potential challenges that come from leaving the safety of your own shore, you're still stuck with Trouble and Anxiety. Leo had written both words on a napkin with a capital "T" and a capital "A". They'd both snickered at the unintended double entendre, but Leo still had a point to make.

"Both of those problems, Trouble and Anxiety, arrive prim and proper," he said, underlining each letter, "dressed in threads woven from a million 'what if's', should have's,' 'could have's' and 'would have's', and both born from a terrible mother: Fear. Do you see what I mean? Trouble and Anxiety exert a powerful and constant control over their creators if they're not slapped and then forbidden by them."

Remembering that conversation as he sat on the lake shore of where two different worlds connected, Gibb shivered in the cold Christmas Eve air. He took a deep breath and closed his eyes, running his hands over his face and the top of his head, exhaling hard as he recalled word for word what Leo had said. What eighteen-year-old talks like that? How did he ever get so…deep or whatever?

"Straddling two worlds is risky," Leo had said just before the bell rang, "because you have to decide which is worse. Dying as you reach for something you want? Or dying as you sit on your hands and watch what you want slip back beneath the surface? Everybody has to answer that question for themselves, y'know?"

Leo gave Gibb a lot to think about that day, but at that time Gibb truly had no idea that Leo could have been referring to the two of them. He thought he'd been alone in this, struggling with the choice to enter an uncharted world of honest, demonstrated feelings, regardless of how they were received or perceived.

Now, late this afternoon, Gibb had been brave enough to not "sit on his hands" as he took the risk to reach for the something he wanted. Funny enough, this afternoon he'd thought *that* would be the hard part.

What he hadn't considered, though, was that reaching out would draw him much farther out into the metaphorical water. Right now, he felt like his feet were still able to touch the bottom. But if he went any further with this, he was afraid he'd be entering a world where his curiosity outweighed his capability.

He couldn't help but be a little afraid. This was a risk, making himself vulnerable to another person. This could end really badly. Was Leo really who Gibb thought he was, who Gibb wanted him to be, *needed* him to be, to make this risk worth it? And what about himself? Did a potentially awesome or possibly crazy relationship with Leo matter more than just finishing high school, laying low, and prepping for college?

Now, alone and concealed within the remnants of this mind-blowing day, with every winter star above and every house light below painting dots and streaks of color and gold on the cold, still lake, Gibb realized how invisible he was here - a literal bump on a log. He smiled humorlessly at the familiarity of that feeling. At the comfort of that familiarity. Yet somehow, the realization that he was invisible here didn't bring him the same reassurance it usually did.

Maybe it was because he didn't want to always be invisible anymore. Maybe treading water in this new wide-open sea wasn't going to be such a bad thing, if he could keep it up. But what if he went so far out into the depths of this new unfamiliar world that he drowned? What if he didn't have the strength to make it back to safety? That's what all those songs and stories seemed to be about. Tonight, he understood those concepts just a little bit better.

In the end, though, he knew that this whole internal conversation was nothing more than a lot of stalling. He already had his answer, had it pretty much the moment he lay eyes on Leo. Unaware at first that he'd been caught in some sort of emotional riptide, Gibb now realized that he was already way far out there, and had been for some time. It was pointless to try to make it back to shore.

No matter how hard he tried to imagine another possibility, there wasn't one. He'd be there for Leo no matter what – emotionally, physically, in love and friendship - and he'd hope that Leo would keep his promise to do the same.

On the shore of Seneca Lake this Christmas Eve night, everything was completely different from the way it was just the night before. High above him, Orion's belt twinkled bright and clear. Maybe it was a sign that everything was going to be as smooth and clear as the sound of Leo's voice after all. Wouldn't that be awesome?

# *Chapter 14*

# YIELD

"Thanks for inviting me to your New Year's Eve party. The food is exquisite," Gibb laughed as he offered a half-eaten can of cold cocktail weenies to Leo, the tip of his glitter-strewn paper party hat scraping the wall of the cheap motel room as he sat on the queen-sized bed. After an inauspicious start to the evening, Leo had surprised him by driving to this tiny roadside joint far enough away from Eislertown that no one would know their names or faces.

Gibb sat in the car as Leo went into the office to check on a room. No way was he going to walk into that office with Leo and risk raising suspicion from the motel staff. Who knows, they may have even kicked them out without renting them a room. Nope. Best to know your place, stay in the car, then sneak into the room once Leo had the key. Funny how no one ever tells you these things, he thought. You just kind of know.

"The decorations and hats are pretty awesome, too."

"So glad you made it, Mr. Mulcahy," Leo replied with a smile, pulling down a couple of now-annoying crepe-paper streamers he'd haphazardly taped to ceiling above the bed. "Can't have a party without the guest of honor."

They'd each told their families they were going to some kid's New Year's Eve party tonight down in Watkins Glen but that wasn't even close to the truth. A few hours earlier, Gibb could barely contain his excitement as he said goodbye to his mother, slipped out of the house, and ran full speed through the dark woods out to the Kountry Korner where Leo was waiting in his dad's car to whisk them both off to Rochester to go to a movie.

As they walked up to the theater, Gibb had no idea what they'd choose to see. There were a few new movies out and one, "A Christmas Story", looked pretty funny. For some reason, though, Leo wanted to see the only one Gibb hadn't heard of, a flick called "Terms of Endearment." Gibb shrugged and agreed.

After it was over, he'd wished he hadn't.

At first, the whole set-up had been cool and Gibb couldn't have been more stoked. As the lights in the three-quarters empty theater darkened, Leo had reached down to hold Gibb's hand. Instinctively, Gibb looked around to see if anybody in the theater was paying any extra attention to the two young men sitting together without proper female company. No one was. Gibb's breathing quickened as he gripped Leo's hand hard, every part of his body now on fire, completely distracted now from whatever was happening on the screen.

He'd barely been able to follow the plot, but he was eventually able to calm down enough to see that the young woman character on the screen, played by Debra Winger, was sick with cancer. *Ugh.* He'd had no clue what this movie was about before it began, but now he was trapped. It only got worse from there. Gibb sat stone-faced while the young woman's mother, played by Shirley MacLaine, went through all five stages of grief in the next half hour or so. By the time the daughter died in the film, Gibb was long past wanting to walk out of the theater and get to celebrating New Year's Eve. What had Leo been thinking when he chose this movie, tonight of all nights?!

Gibb glanced over at Leo, hoping to get his attention so they could ditch this tripe and make an early exit. The bright light of the movie screen was just enough to allow Gibb to see silent tears streaming down Leo's handsome face. Uh-oh.

*Dear God. We're not going anywhere,* Gibb pouted to himself. Half-appalled, half-charmed by Leo's sensitivity, Gibb sighed and settled back in his seat, re-tightening his grip on Leo's hand. Mercifully, the movie finally came to an end five hours later. Well, it was more like twenty minutes, but it felt like five hours.

They walked out of the movie in silence, Gibb not knowing what to say and Leo not giving him any signal that he wanted him to say anything. By the time they got back out to the mostly empty parking lot, Leo's mood had brightened a bit. Slipping the key into the driver's side door, he grinned embarrassedly as looked over the car roof at Gibb and said, "Sorry to be such a crybaby in there. I guess you're ready to head home?"

Gibb just shook his head, a smile of resignation on his face as he climbed back into the car. He couldn't believe how damn cute Leo was with that look on his face. No, he didn't want to go home. Not now, not ever.

They drove instead to a nearby supermarket where they grabbed snacks and drinks, including the goddawful cocktail weenies. Leo saw New Year's Eve party hats and streamers and grabbed those, too.

"Why are you buying all that stuff?" Gibb asked with a laugh. "To hang up in the car?"

Maybe Leo hadn't heard him because he didn't answer as he headed to the checkout line with his cache. Gibb followed but, rather than stand in the line with Leo and draw unwanted attention to the two of them, he cut through an empty register stand and stood waiting for Leo on the other side of the checkout line. Silently, he kicked himself. If he really wasn't ashamed of his true feelings for Leo, why was he standing here waiting instead of standing *with* Leo in the checkout line?

There weren't many customers in the store at 10 p.m. on New Year's Eve, but there was one other line open and it was moving a lot faster than Leo's. Leo probably should have gone over there because right now he was standing behind two other people and the first one, an old woman with a change purse, was counting out the exact change she needed to make her purchase. Her shaky arthritic fingers were in no hurry to find the last four pennies she needed to make good on her two-dollar-and-ninety-nine-cent grocery tab.

More bored with the scene than impatient, Gibb's eyes wandered over to the other checkout line again. Two new customers had joined the line and, well, weren't *they* just perfect? Two college age kids, a very handsome, tall athletic-looking blond guy and an extremely good-looking brunette girl, also tall and athletic-looking. Gibb could see them openly holding hands. At one point, the guy drew her closer to him and quietly kissed the top of her perfectly-coiffed head. All she could do was smile and make goo-goo eyes back at Mr. Wonderful. The hefty middle-aged lady running the register had noticed the sweet kiss, giving the perfect couple a big smile as they approached her. Gibb's contempt for her was almost as strong as it was for young Mr. and Miss America over there.

He could only imagine the look the old bat would have given them if he'd kissed Leo on the top of his head in the checkout line. And not only do those two people over there get to be beautiful, but they also get to hold hands and hug and kiss in public and then have that public display of affection be *celebrated* or, at the very least, *tolerated* by everyone else around them.

So, here he was over here, trying not to be obvious, not even standing in the line with his own hot date, irritably remembering the way he'd looked around the theater to make sure no one was looking when Leo had reached down to hold his hand during the movie a little while ago. He scratched his stubbly chin and looked back towards Leo's line. The cashier was finally handing him his change. A merciful moment later they were heading back to his car.

Gibb turned around and glanced at the good-looking couple now coming right out the door behind them. He envied them as much as he despised them. And they had no idea. No idea of the contempt he was feeling. No idea how privileged they were. No idea how much of a struggle it had been for him to even admit his own feelings to Leo for fear of being totally rejected, beaten up, or worse. All Barbie and Ken had to do was just be themselves, their wonderfully blissfully, perfectly *normal* selves.

*God bless those two amazing, naturally heterosexual specimens of perfection,* he thought bitterly. *The rest of us can only dream about being as superior as they are.*

"What's going on with you?" Leo's voice broke through the cacophony of voices in Gibb's head as they got in the car. "You OK?"

Gibb hesitated but finally told him what had been on his mind in the store, pointing out the couple to Leo as they now both watched them get in their car.

Leo shook his head. "Who gives a shit?" he muttered. Then, right there in the parking lot, with the bright lights of the supermarket illuminating the car's front seat, Leo leaned over and kissed him, not caring who might be seeing them from inside or as they passed by. Gibb, scandalized for a fleeting second, kissed Leo back just as intensely.

"Can't change it, so let it be what it is," Leo said with a mischievous smirk. "Besides, we got somewhere we need to be. Let's go."

Leo's dad had made him promise he wouldn't drink and drive and told him he'd prefer it if Leo didn't drive home at all. He wasn't only thinking of Leo's safety. With a wry grin on his face, Leo confessed that his dad was probably hoping he might meet up with a special girl tonight and, well, whatever happened might just keep Leo off the road until the morning.

"You still have time," Gibb remarked sourly.

"What's up with you tonight?" Leo asked, legitimately surprised after the way Gibb had just kissed him. "I've never seen you like this."

"I don't know," Gibb responded. "I hated that movie, by the way. Not just because I thought it sucked, because it did, but I kept feeling like we were running out of time while we were in that theater and now it's after ten and we're gonna have to head home soon. Those two that just left in the car, they're gonna get to be together all night somewhere. Not us. We've gotta pretend to our families we went to some stupid party just so we could hang out together. It's lame that we have to sneak around."

Leo started the car and, with a matter-of-fact look on his face, simply dead-panned, "Well…it's sneak around or nothing. You choose."

His words were cold water and they woke Gibb up. Leo was right. There was no use getting pissed off that their new relationship would never be considered equal in anyone's eyes. Well, Ms. Mullan was cool with it, but in her own way she was as much of a square peg as they were. He remembered her telling him there would always be a price to pay for rocking society's boat.

Tonight, Gibb was better able to understand what that meant. He set his jaw and looked over at Leo.

"Let's sneak around."

⊰⊱

The "somewhere they needed to be" that night was Tranquilla, that quaint little roadside motel. Leo paid for the little room in cash while Gibb waited in the car. The grandfatherly, Italian- accented motel owner had shaken his fist as he warned his young customer not to have any loud parties and people parading in and out all night.

*This is a nice-a place, you understand?* Leo promised him that they'd respect the rules, backing out of the little office as quickly as he could.

They ate their snacks, laughingly mimicked the motel owner's accent, hung their streamers, wore their party hats, never turning on the TV. And there in that nice-a place, on the nowhere side of a two-lane road somewhere between Rochester and Eislertown, with only the muted glare of neon lights and passing headlights coming through the closed curtains, Gibb and Leo discovered the explosive power that results when two people, in love and uninhibited, can truly connect.

They did their best to kept their explorations and discoveries as quiet as they could, but that phenomenal New Year's Eve was anything but "tranquilla."

Gibb and Leo didn't know it at the time, but that astounding first night together was going to be the last night they would be in the same bed for months. After New Year's, Leo's dad would let him borrow his car sometimes, but fooling around in a car was awkward and it was winter and Leo couldn't help but feel a little guilty about what they got up to in the backseat whenever he was driving them home.

Despite the gyrations they always had to go through to make it happen, though, their relationship was about way more than sex. Leo wasn't just Gibb's boyfriend. He was also Gibb's best friend, confidant, and mentor. Leo seemed to know so much more about life and the world and really, Gibb was in awe of him.

Leo was perfectly content in his own skin, somehow visible and invisible at the same time. It was hard for Gibb to describe. When they were at school, Leo didn't go out of his way to talk to anyone. Not even Gibb. Somehow, as good-looking as he was, as much as he would stand out in any crowd or photo, Leo kept his head down and his mouth quiet. He had no problem going through a school day saying almost nothing, deliberately portraying himself as exceedingly shy and quiet.

But he wasn't really shy or quiet. In school, they were just two under-the-radar nobodies – one by choice, one with no other option – but one-on-one, everything was different. Gibb woke up every morning amazed that Leo was in his life, in freakin' nowhere Eislertown of all places, another social misfit who just happened to be into other guys. For a couple of months, everything was perfect.

Perfection, though, is that lone, sparkling minute in a humdrum string of a million other moments in time. Incredible to experience, but it passes just as quickly as it arrives.

*Chapter 15*

# THE BECKONING SHORELINE

April budded out in glorious spite of a lengthening lull in Gibb and Leo's relationship. As he always did when he needed to think, Gibb found his way down to the driftwood log there on the Seneca Lake shore again, thinking back on what winter with Leo had really been. Life-changing. It had only been a few months, but it seemed longer, maybe because Gibb lived every moment of them twice – once in real-time, and then again soon afterwards, usually in the middle of the night, totally recalling every detail. Almost all of it had been awesome. Well, except for the last few weeks. Something was going on with Leo and Gibb suspected it had to do with the unpredictable state of Leo's mother's mental health.

By now, they'd gotten used to sneaking around and keeping their secret relationship to themselves, but the situation had real limitations. They'd still never met each other's parents – Gibb hadn't been invited back to Leo's house since the birthday cake incident. Mrs. Davion would just hang up the phone whenever she heard Gibb's voice ask for Leo on the other end, so Gibb just stopped calling.

Right after the New Year started, just as their relationship had kicked into high gear, they'd both agreed it was best not to sit together at lunch anymore or hang out at school. They didn't need any additional stress thrown into their lives by being the targets of would-be tough guys. Gibb ended up spending a lot of sixth periods in the library or hoping to catch Ms. Mullan if she was around at that time.

One bright spot in Leo's family situation, though, was that Gibb had sort of become friends with Leo's sister. Sissie was just one year younger than Leo. Before he met her in person, he'd somehow never once seen her in school. Now, for whatever reason, he saw her in the hallway all the time. And she wasn't easy to miss.

Sissie's real name was Tara, a southern girl seemingly named after a plantation mansion, but she hated the whole "Gone with the Wind" inspiration for her name and that was, in her own words, only because she looked nothing at all like Vivien Leigh's Scarlett O'Hara. Everything about Sissie was big: her blonde hair, her blue eyes, her height, her bones. But Sissie was easygoing and full of fun with a loud and infectious laugh. Where Leo was quiet and mysterious, Sissie was, in Leo's words, a "wide-open heathen."

"Let's just face some facts, OK?" she'd said to Gibb early on, exaggerating her drawl for maximum humor. "I'll just go ahead and say it: I got some weight on me. Other folks wanna call me fat. Whatever. I'm almost 6 feet tall and I got size 10 feet, OK? Ain't an eating disorder in the world gonna change any of this, so they can all kiss where I cain't, OK? God knows it's the truth!"

Sissie was a character but she'd taken a liking to Gibb right away. The feeling was definitely mutual. Gibb couldn't be sure, but it seemed to him that Sissie was onto the nature of his relationship with her brother. And she didn't seem to mind at all.

Gibb was glad Leo had Sissie. They were close and they needed to be for the difficulties they were facing at home. But her love and support of her brother wasn't enough to keep Leo's moods from shifting and, eventually, Leo began to sort of pull away from Gibb. Without much explanation or fanfare.

They'd gone a whole week without meeting up or talking when Leo casually asked Gibb to meet him at Rogers Park after school to "just ride around". What he really wanted, though, was to tell Gibb that they really needed to take a break, "just to reflect on what was happening here." They still hadn't figured out anything about their future beyond high school and graduation was fast approaching. Leo said it was probably best to put the brakes on this thing now in an attempt to avoid deeper complications later.

Gibb was as hurt as he was surprised – he'd never once doubted their bond and he hadn't been wrestling any worry about the future. He was completely on board with Leo's fears, but why wouldn't they want to make the most of the time they had left together? They'd figure out the rest later, wouldn't they? It didn't make a whole lot of sense to Gibb, especially because Leo had straight up told him that their relationship was the best thing he'd ever experienced in life.

Both had their challenging home lives: Gibb's an empty, loveless monotony, Leo's a constant and unpredictable assault on anything resembling a normal routine. Being honest with himself, though, Gibb had to admit that given the choice between their two lives, he'd choose the boring, annoying life in the tumbledown Eislertown hovel over the up-and-down madness of the Davion household.

Leo didn't need to make this, their almost perfect distraction from each of those wounded worlds, so difficult. All Gibb wanted to do was laugh and have fun and there was no one better than Leo, when he wasn't bogged down by torment. But at times like these, when they hadn't hung out or talked since Leo pulled away, Gibb couldn't help but think that maybe his own easygoing nature was starting to bore Leo. Maybe Leo just didn't want to tell him that, in order to spare his feelings.

It wasn't like they had every single thing in common. Leo was fascinated by the dark depths of painters like Goya and mystical poets like Rilke and he could talk about their work for hours, unintentionally intimidating Gibb who'd never once been introduced to the seemingly secret world of artists of their renown. It wasn't like they covered those kinds of guys at his high school.

At least Gibb could talk about the Grateful Dead with Leo in painstaking detail, and the band and their music was an integral, effortless link between them. But when it came to a deeper awareness of the arts beyond rock music, Gibb had a lot to learn. He couldn't help but think that maybe Leo wasn't up for waiting around for him to catch up.

Four months ago, being with Leo was the best possibility life could have ever offered, and when they connected it was magic. But just like anything else, magic has its flip side, and Leo's new disappearing act hurt.

Still, Gibb had wanted to do something special for both Leo and himself and he'd finally managed to do it. Just by coincidence or luck or *something*, the Dead's Spring tour was taking the band up to Rochester in mid-April, just two weeks and an hour's drive away. As far as Gibb was concerned, going to that event together would be the experience of a lifetime, something that neither of them would ever forget. All their talking about and listening to this band, and neither one of them had ever been able to get themselves to a show. Until now. Gibb had scored two tickets and couldn't wait to spring the news on Leo.

A whole week later, those damn tickets still sat in their little Ticketron envelope, untouched since Gibb brought them to Rogers Park, hoping to surprise Leo with them on the day he dropped his stupid bombshell.

Afterwards, Gibb was too bummed to even mention the show to Leo, but he was still hopeful Leo would be up for going with him. But maybe he wasn't. He didn't even want to consider that possibility.

All Gibb felt right now was defeat and betrayal. He was back to feeling embarrassed again that any of it even mattered to him.

Moping about all this crap only made it worse. But there was no one else to talk to about it – he wasn't about to whine to Ms. Mullan – so here he was, again, in his well-worn driftwood seat on the shore of Seneca Lake, feeling like the loser in one of life's little games. Again.

For a moment he wished he had the nerve to just grab some meager belongings, skip school, and thumb it to Virginia for the start of the Dead's spring tour. Most of the shows, like Rochester, were going to be there in the northeast anyway. It really wasn't that far to go when he thought about it.

Who cares if he'd be gone for weeks? His mother? Come on. Isn't that what being a fan of this band was all about? Breaking ties with convention and just *going*, wherever it was? Letting the music be the soundtrack to a whole carnival of people like Gibb who needed to experience a community, a whole world of color and sound and freedom that had only existed in their dreams before they found it for real?

But then, of course, the reality of his life settled in heavily, right on top of his dreams. Spring break ended the day tour started. How could he miss a few weeks of his senior year in high school and still graduate? Would he really just stick out his thumb and hitch rides all over the place, promising people gas money if they'd take him as close as they could get him to Philly or New Haven?

*No, no you would not.* He frowned as the rational voice in his head squashed his fantasies.

"I'm not even a good Deadhead," he mumbled to himself. *And that's just about the worst thing I can say about myself, because it kind of sums up EVERYTHING!*

Suddenly, Gibb was pissed off. Still staring at the rippling blue water, he stood up. Without warning and astonishing even himself, he suddenly, angrily kicked the log as hard as he could.

*Uh-oh, that's gonna hurt.*

The log was a lot harder than he'd realized. Pain flared from his throbbing toe all the way up to his ankle as he jumped around, trying to shake it off.

Furious and humiliated, Gibb reached down, picked that heavy log up off the beach and, raising it high above his head, hurled it into the lake along with a long, snarling string of four- letter epithets.

The offending log bobbed merrily around on the lake, undisturbed by this sudden turn of events. Gibb could only stare at it floating out there. In his misery, he kind of felt bad for it. Nah, he was actually only feeling bad for himself.

"Sorry," he called out to the unhearing log, his voice rueful. He'd just taken all his frustration out on a stupid piece of wood. Because it was there. He felt even more ridiculous now.

"Yeah, I'm sorry all right."

*Chapter 16*

# TOUCH OF GREEN
# WITH GREY

G ibb scratched at his stubbly face, suddenly realizing as he looked around the wet, leaf- sheltered alcove, that he had absolutely no recollection of riding into Rogers Park or these woods just now.

He remembered the phone call, easily recalling the thick catch in Leo's voice. But he couldn't remember the ride. So pre-occupied with the mystery of what Leo was planning to tell him this time, Gibb's mind raced as fast as the wheels beneath him for the entire five-mile ride to the park. And before he was even aware of it, he was there.

He looked around. *Still alone. Good.* There would be time enough to catch his breath and calm down a little before Leo got there. The damp earth smelled like springtime, familiar, but new and comforting at the same time.

Rain drizzled down, little arrythmic slaloms gathering in fat drops, dripping leisurely off the new green-gold canopy of leaves sheltering Gibb from the worst of it. His right foot still smarted from that embarrassing incident with the driftwood log over on the shore of Lake Seneca yesterday and, for the third time in less than minute, he had to dry his glasses on the raggedy hem of his well-worn T-shirt. An irritated glance upward rewarded him with another big, sloppy drop, this time right in his wide-open eye.

Cursing quietly, he stuck his finger in his eye to get rid of the intruding water. Whatever Leo had to tell him better have been worth this aggravation. Just for the hell of it, he gave his moppish red head a good, frustrated shake, rain drops flying everywhere like a dog after its bath.

"What are you doing?"

Gibb whipped his head around. There he was. King Leo, only six-foot-one but towering above any and everyone else in Gibb's world, standing silently, regarding the wet and bedraggled vision in front of him with a mixture of affection and impatience. Mainly impatience.

"Getting soaked waiting for some stud to show up," Gibb deadpanned, ignoring Leo's chagrin. "And I think he just arrived."

Leo rolled up slowly, his young face somber and, Gibb could have been imagining it, creased with worry. Somehow from this distance, he looked older than his eighteen years, like he'd been weighted down with woe for more than a little while. As he got closer, Gibb saw that Leo's perpetual air of cool and calm had been replaced by a quiet but wild-eyed look of anxiety.

Saying nothing, Gibb just furrowed his brow as Leo pulled up next to him and looked Gibb in the eye. He didn't want to rush Leo into speaking, but just grimly staring at each other was getting awkward. Gibb finally had to break the reverie with a whisper.

"OK, what's going on?" he asked.

Leo took a deep breath, looked down at the ground and shook his head. When he looked back up at Gibb, he had tears in his eyes.

Gibb put his hands on Leo's shoulders. "Tell me," he whispered. "What's up?"

Leo rubbed his hands over his reddened eyes. "It's terrible news. Daddy got cancer. Real bad, they think."

He dropped his head down again, looking at the ground as he continued speaking.

"He's gotta get treatment. But he can't get it 'round here, so..." His voice trailed off before he set his jaw and looked backed up at Gibb. "We gotta go home. Back to Bache. Like, right away."

Stunned, his eyes wide with disbelief, Gibb stayed silent for a few long seconds before slowly moving his hands down to hold onto Leo's handlebars.

"I'm blown away right now," he said, pulling Leo's bike closer towards him. "Oh man, I am so sorry. I'm speechless. Why can't your dad just get treatment right around here? People get cancer all the time around here and they don't have to move away. Why would you have to go back to Bache, Louisiana…?"

Leo held up his hand to shush Gibb, his response suggesting he knew these questions were coming.

"Listen now. Just listen. There's a couple reasons. First, they figure Daddy can get just as good treatment in New Orleans or Houston or even Atlanta as he can up here. He ain't gettin' treatment, like, in Bache proper."

He paused before speaking again, his voice now emotionally intermittently in high-pitched squeaks.

"We come up here 'cuz of Daddy's job, but all the people Mama and Daddy got are down in Loozeanna. Me and Sissie can do our damnedest here, but Mama…well, you know it's complicated with her bein' the way she is. We gotta go home, be around people who can help us help Daddy and help us with Mama, too, when we need 'em to."

Gibb was looking down at the ground now, too, trying not to show the tears welling up in his own eyes as the reality of what Leo was saying set in.

Running a quick finger under his slightly drippy nose and shaking his head a bit to ward off the tears, Leo looked around to make sure he and Gibb really were alone there. They were.

He put his hand under Gibb's chin, raising his face to look him in the eye as he whispered, "Problem is, the person I love most in this whole damn world is right here."

Gibb didn't want to cry. Still, as soon as he heard Leo say those words a steady stream of silent tears spilled up over the brim of his eyes, streaking the lenses of his glasses before sliding off to help further dampen the ground beneath his feet. He looked up at Leo.

"The person I love most in the world is right here, too," he whispered hoarsely, the words catching on his tongue.

He took a moment to compose himself before bursting out, "Oh Leo, holy shit! This is terrible! Terrible for your Dad, awful for you. Your whole family! Just…everybody," Gibb lamented, quietly adding himself into the mix. "I don't know what to say or do. *Is* there anything I can say or do?"

Leo shook his head and looked away for a moment without speaking, his pain showing dark and clear and powerful. In the silvery light around them, his somber features looked taut and grey, like a tombstone. A tombstone set with a handsome, human face.

Gibb took two steps towards Leo, and then he was holding him, silently telling himself he would do his best to protect him from whatever was coming. Leo buried his head between Gibb's neck and shoulder and, finally giving in, began to sob quietly. They held on tight as their dark new reality engulfed them both, but Gibb would still not allow himself to break down. He was going to be a rock for Leo today and he wasn't giving in.

"I'm here, Leo," Gibb whispered. "I promise, I'll be there for you no matter what happens. Even if I have to come to Louisiana to be with you, I will make it happen. Anything you need, I'll do it."

He paused, trying to compose himself as Leo held him tighter, sobbing even harder. Gibb kissed Leo's ear and whispered one more word.

"Somehow."

Leo lifted his head from Gibb's shoulder.

"I love you too, Gibb," he whispered. "I really need you to know that. Everything was going so great for a while there. And I know I've been screwing everything up with you, too. But this is how things always seem to go in my life and my family."

He shook his head and looked Gibb in the eye.

"I don't think I'll ever understand why everything that's beautiful in this world always has to turn into something ugly."

## Chapter 17

# PACK IT UP

Their worlds had changed entirely just a few months ago when Gibb and Leo had begun their relationship. Now everything would be changing again. Immediately.

The urgency of Leo's father's illness set into motion a whirlwind of activity at the Davion house as the family prepared to move back down south. At Leo's surprising request, Gibb was on hand to help.

It seemed odd to meet Leo's parents for the first time just as they were packing up to move, but in the context of his complicated relationship with Leo, somehow it made perfect sense to Gibb. And even though he knew Mrs. Davion probably didn't want him there, it wasn't going to hurt to have another young body on hand to help do the heavy lifting.

"Mama's gonna be like a drill sergeant," Leo told Gibb. "Very loud and very, very bossy. Don't let it bother you any. That's just how she is when she gets focused in on something."

Yep. The second Sissie sat down after packing and carrying a room full of boxes out to the garage, Mrs. Davion would be hollering for her to "get her lazy ass" to the store for white bread, berating Leo for not instantly being there to move something heavy the second she bellowed for him, shouting for "someone" – meaning Gibb – to come to the kitchen and take out the garbage, and all the while yelling at Mr. Davion to sit quietly and take it easy.

She was built like Sissie, tall and big boned, only with dark hair and dark eyes. It was impossible for Gibb to tell how old she was. Mrs. Davion had no wrinkles or creases on her face, but her perpetually serious expression gave her the look of someone easily ten years older than her husband.

Her loud voice made Gibb's ears ring, but Gibb could tell Mrs. Davion wasn't being unkind. In fact, Gibb really wanted to like her. She didn't seem to want to be liked, though, and kept her guard up the entire afternoon and evening. Gibb kept a respectful distance.

As sick as Leo had said he was, Mr. Davion didn't look it. Gibb was glad of that – he hadn't known what to expect when he walked into their house today. Mr. Davion was an older, not quite as handsome version of Leo. He had significantly bigger ears, too, Gibb noted.

Mr. Davion was quiet and calm as he talked through the tricky logistics of packing up the entire house in time to load out a moving truck tomorrow, and then get the family back to Louisiana.

Leo would be driving the family to Syracuse early the next morning to allow his parents and Sissie to catch an early morning flight to New Orleans. Leo would stay behind to oversee the loading of the moving truck, return the house keys to the landlord, and tie up whatever little loose ends were left before jumping in the car and driving the family's sedan back down to Bache.

"So, Daddy, let me just make sure I got this straight. Sissie is *definitely* flying with y'all back to New Orleans?" Leo asked, suppressing a grin as he looked straight at his sister.

Mr. Davion turned to look at her, too, and then both father and son inexplicably burst out laughing at her. Gibb was confused. Sissie rolled her eyes and shook her head.

"Y'all need to stop," she said.

Mr. Davion let Gibb in on the joke. When the Davion family moved up to the Finger Lakes last August, Sissie had turned so green from car sickness on the ride from Louisiana that they swore they had some kind of alien in the car.

"She looked like Frankenstein," Leo laughed. "By the time we got to Pennsylvania, this poor thing," he laughed, gesturing towards Sissie, "had thrown up ever'thing she had ever ate from the beginning of time."

"Well, it's a damn sorry thing, spendin' all that money to fly her turkey tail home," Mrs. Davion harrumphed from the kitchen. "That girl's lucky she got such a good daddy. She knows I'd-a told her sorry ass to hang her head out the car window again and just deal with it on the way back home!"

Sissie rolled her eyes again, then looked over at her dad who winked at her in solidarity. Mrs. Davion was a challenge, but at least she hadn't thrown anything, or anyone, out the door today.

For the moment, at least, Leo's family appeared to be unified and strong. Without words, they all seemed to want to put on their best face for their dad and husband, and maybe just a little for Gibb, too. Who knew? But by letting down their guard a little around Mrs. Davion, she seemed to be working harder not to come unglued at the slightest provocation. Right now they were almost normal, Gibb thought.

Still, who was he to judge what "normal" even was? Gibb couldn't imagine anything, not even a potentially terminal illness, bringing his own family together. Gibb and Jack tolerated each other, but really couldn't care less if the other lived or died. That was a cold truth, but if he was being honest, Gibb would have to say it was a fair assessment. It was only part animosity, the rest just boring, immutable indifference.

And then there was his relationship, or whatever you wanted to call it, with his own mother. She was a nice enough person and he felt bad for the way Jack browbeat her all the time, but Gibb thought of her as sort of cigarette-smoking ice sculpture. Maybe somewhat interesting at first, but an ice sculpture is all surface. Nothing underneath it but more ice, no matter how close you get to its center.

Gibb could only surmise that his mother was just one of those women that didn't get much fulfillment from being a mother. She didn't revel in Gibb's academic achievements or support his collegiate endeavors. But she didn't discourage them, either. She simply didn't show any interest one way or the other. She never asked to look at his report card, or about the classes he was taking, what he wanted to do with this life.

Once, when he was a sophomore, he'd asked her, frustrated, why she was so blasé about his education. All she told him was that she "just knew" he was a lot smarter than she was, and she knew he'd always get good grades. She seemed to mean it as a compliment, but Gibb saw it as nothing more than a lazy cop-out.

Her lack of interest in who Gibb was becoming as a young adult came to completely define their interactions, so Gibb just stopped trying. Gibb, his mother, and Jack lived blandly in the shabby old house like unrelated roommates: one a high school kid getting ready to graduate, the second a racist jerk who loved making fun of gay people, and to finish off the odd trio, a nice enough woman who smoked too much and may as well have been some random lady from the bank or the grocery store sitting there in front of the TV.

Gibb knew it was twisted, but in the face of that sorry assessment of his own family life, he was sort of envious of the fragile camaraderie the Davions were enjoying at that moment. *Pretty sad*, he thought. *Pretty freakin' sad.*

He was also envious that Leo would be allowed to drive the family car on his own all the way from the Finger Lakes back to coastal Louisiana. He wished so badly that he could ride along with Leo and leave silly, broke down Eislertown behind.

He didn't want to ask the question in front of Leo's family, but Gibb really wanted to know how long Leo would be staying around after everyone else flew back to Louisiana. It sounded like Leo would be alone at the house all day tomorrow after dropping everyone at the airport to see the moving truck off, then beginning the drive home on Saturday. It *really* sucked that he had to leave only two days before that Dead show in Rochester.

Under the circumstances, there was no way he'd burden Leo with his disappointment over having to miss that show, but there was no way Gibb was going without him. He'd be out twenty-five bucks for the tickets, but he'd be miserable the whole time thinking about Leo and how much he'd be loving it if he were there.

*So close*, Gibb thought. *If only he could stay here for just a couple more days.*

But there was no way, and he wasn't even going to suggest it. There might be a silver lining in all of this, though. If Leo were able to stay all day and night tomorrow, would the two of them be able to have a whole night to be alone together after the family and the movers were on their way?

By early evening the Davions, with Gibb's help, were packed up and ready to move. Gibb got ready to leave, throwing on his sweatshirt to stave off the spring evening chill. Before he said his goodbyes, he promised to come back in the morning to help Leo break down their beds and have them ready for the movers.

Gibb didn't know what to say to Leo's parents. Mrs. Davion basically pretended he didn't exist and Mr. Davion was, well, very sick and possibly dying. He wished for the right words.

"Goodbye, Mr. and Mrs. Davion. And you too, Tara Lynn," he said, grinning at Sissie, knowing how much she hated when people used her real name. "I hope you all have safe travels home."

He gulped a little, composed himself, and spoke again.

"And Mr. Davion, I'm hoping all the best for you especially."

Leo, standing behind his father who was seated on the couch, looked at Gibb somberly. Sissie and Mrs. Davion both looked at the floor as an uneasy quiet engulfed them all, no one knowing what to say.

Finally, Mr. Davion spoke up. "Thank you, son. Thank you for your help today."

The light caught his eyes, the same remarkable blue-green eyes as his son's, his gaze cutting right into Gibb as he continued.

"And thanks for bein' there for Leo. The boy needed a good friend like you, comin' up here to this unfamiliar place and all. I can tell you been real important to him and we're all glad you been around some. So, thank you."

Gibb swallowed hard, trying not to get emotional, trying to think of what to say before the silence became too obvious and awkward.

"Yeah, well, uh…that's no problem," he said with an awkward catch in his voice. "Gonna miss him. But I'm glad I'll see him one more time tomorrow before he heads back down south."

He glanced over at Leo who was now staring down at the floor himself. Gibb grimaced, gave the family an awkward wave goodnight and walked out into the dark mid-April evening.

## Chapter 18

# OF ROCKS AND ROSES

What time was it? Gibb woke up more exhausted than when he'd gone to bed. Through the night, sleep lost out to paranoid dreams of crouching low behind a tree in the dark, rain beating down as a police helicopter hovered high above, its searchlight sweeping down to expose him to the authorities on the ground. He woke up sweaty and hollering after a wild foot chase right into Leo's yard where Mrs. Davion stood tall and silent, a mean, smug look on her face as a cop tackled him from behind.

Eyes wide and his breath coming in short pants, Gibb stared at the ceiling trying to get his bearings, first calmed by the realization that he'd only been dreaming and then hit by the wild anticipation of what today would bring. It was Friday, the thirteenth, the last day of spring break, and the last full day before Leo had to leave to head back to Bache. He glanced over at his beat-up little digital clock. Seven a.m.

Stretching and yawning, he looked out of his tiny dormer window just in time to see something that made his heart hammer harder in his chest. The Davion family sedan was slowly making its way up his street.

Without a thought, Gibb ran barefoot and shirtless towards the rickety steps to greet Leo at the front door. He immediately turned around and ran back up to his room to don a shirt in case any nosy Eislertown neighbor might see him answer the door half-naked. And, *ugh*, he needed to brush his teeth. He hurried back down the steps and into the bathroom, squeezing too much toothpaste, some falling into the sink, using his finger to move the glob toward the drain, frantically brushing to get rid of his awful morning breath and now trying to get the stupid toothpaste off his finger.

He heard a knock on the door. Hurriedly wiping his hand on a towel, he caught a look at himself in the mirror and sighed. Oh well, he'd done his best. He told himself to relax and, pretending to do that, Gibb opened the front door with a big smile.

And there he was. Leo Davion, the most important person in the world, standing on the crumbling step with a smile big enough to match Gibb's. For a moment they just stood there like that, smiling at each other. Then, without a word, Gibb opened the door wider and stepped behind it, allowing Leo easy entry into the house.

The moment after Gibb closed the door, Leo gave him a look.

"No one's home," Gibb murmured with a grin.

In less than a second the two of them were in each other's arms, the intensity of their kiss fueled by the unspoken thought that they might not ever be together again after this day.

Moments later, they were back upstairs in Gibb's room, Gibb wondering why he'd bothered to put the shirt on in the first place. Friday the thirteenth be damned, this was already shaping up to be one of the best days of his life.

An hour later they were on their way over to Leo's house to wait for the moving truck. Gibb couldn't believe his luck. Except for the time with the movers, and until Leo took off out of that driveway early tomorrow morning, the two of them were going to spend every last minute alone together. Gibb left a note for his mother telling her he'd see her some time tomorrow. He wondered if she'd even read it.

The moving truck arrived promptly at ten a.m. and with their crew of three, plus Leo and Gibb, the truck was packed up and on its way to Bache by noon. The Davions hadn't brought a lot of their belongings up north, Leo explained as they sat on the floor in the empty living room, because his parents had to first figure out if they even liked living up here before paying to bring everything else up.

"Looking back, that was kind of a smart move on their part, wasn't it?" Leo asked, his voice bouncing of the bare walls. "But I know they never expected they'd be leaving under circumstances like these."

Gibb took Leo's hands in his. "You doing OK?"

"I don't know. Maybe. Or maybe I'm just in denial," Leo said with a shrug. "'Cuz things look bad. Daddy got himself Stage Four cancer of the pancreas. All by itself, that is supposed to be really bad. But now they're not sure if it has spread to other parts of his body. He's gonna get checked out first thing Monday mornin' and they're hopefully gonna find out."

"Well, what happens then?" Gibb wanted to know. He didn't know a lot about cancer, but this didn't sound good at all.

"I'm not 100% on that," Leo said with a frown. "They might be able to do some surgery to get rid of it, but if it got spread around, he might be in a heap o' trouble. Like dying real soon. Within months."

Leo stopped and took a deep breath. When he spoke again, it was with a quaver in his voice.

"Nobody really knows. So, I don't how to react to all this 'cuz I don't know what's real right now. I just know I'm hopin' and prayin' for a miracle."

He wiped the corner of his eye.

"How's your mom?" Gibb had to ask, knowing full well it was a loaded question. Leo grimaced again.

"She's tryin' to deal with it, but Lord knows. Daddy's cancer would be a lot for a *regular* person to deal with. Let's face it, she's not what you'd call a regular person. But bless her heart, I can see she's really tryin'."

Gibb shook his head slowly, a gesture of quiet admiration.

"Man," he said softly. "How do you do it? How do you make it all OK like that?"

A look of resignation came over Leo's face.

"I don't make it *OK*," he replied. "'Cuz she's not OK. But I think guys like you and me, it's easier for us to deal with people who don't quite fit the usual definition of 'OK' and 'normal'. Mama is not a bad person, she just gets lost sometimes and then things get dark, and sometimes they get real wild. But if our family doesn't do our best to help her, who will? Nobody, that's who, and we all know that. So, we try harder.

"Plus, I learned a long time ago there wasn't anything I could do about it. I know it isn't my fault. God bless Honey, my grandmother. I've told you a little about her. When Sissie and I were kids, Honey always made sure to tell us that Mama's problems were Mama's problems. That it wasn't our fault. And Honey has always deeply loved Daddy for staying with Mama and us through all of it.

"See, with Daddy in the picture, Mama has had someone to be her rock. He's been a champ, he really has. So together, Daddy and Honey could most of the time keep Mama in check. That's why this is extra tough right now. 'Cuz if somethin' happens to Daddy, then who's she gonna turn to? It ain't gonna be me, I can tell you that. I'm always trippin' her trigger...just by bein' around."

"That's what I don't understand," Gibb broke in. "You never give your parents any trouble. Why is she like that to you?"

"Well, I believe there are two main reasons," Leo stated matter-of-factly. "Mama would prob'ly never admit it, and I'll never ask her, but the first one is Honey."

"Why Honey?" Gibb asked.

"Well, I was Honey's first grandchild and she doted on me like nobody's business. She still does. Treats me like the sun rises and sets with me. Plus, 'cuz of Mama's troubles, Honey stepped in to help out, *a lot*, when we were little kids. I think Mama has always resented her for that, and then me too because of it.

"No matter what, Mama's relationship with Honey has always been loud and complicated. That's 'cuz Honey never put up with her shit. Plus, Honey's a big girl, too, OK? Whenever Mama would get wild and start talkin' about beatin' Honey's ass, Honey would remind Mama that if she went off, it wouldn't be a fair fight. Trust me when I say that Mama don't want no part of Honey, 'specially if Honey just happens to have a cast iron fryin' pan in her hand."

"I would love to meet Honey someday," Gibb said with a smile. "She sounds awesome."

"She *is* awesome," Leo agreed, "and a right handsome woman, too."

"Handsome?" Gibb asked, a curious expression on his face.

Leo tried to come up with a good explanation for what he'd said.

"Well, there are pretty men, and you and me know 'em when we see 'em. We wouldn't rightly call 'em handsome, because they're good-lookin' in a pretty way. 'Pretty like a girl' is what we say down south, and it really isn't meant as an insult.

"On the other hand – there are some very good-lookin' women that you just can't call 'pretty'. You'd call 'em handsome. They just have handsome features, like a strong jawline and brow. That's Honey. She is a *handsome* woman and when you meet her, 'cuz by God you will someday, you will see what I mean. I wish we still had our pictures here in the house or I'd show you now."

"Then you get your looks from her," Gibb said, completely sincere, before doing a bad job at aping Leo's accent, "'cuz you're a right handsome man."

"Gawd, the things you say," Leo said with a bashful smile. "You really think so?"

"Ha! Now you're just fishing," Gibb said. "Dude, as if! Every girl in school wants to be with you. If you'd wanted to go to the prom, do you even know how many chicks would have jumped at the chance to be your date?"

"No, I don't, and I don't care. 'Cuz I'm not going to any prom. If I could take you, then maybe I'd consider it. Right now, that isn't possible but I predict that maybe in about thirty years, a couple of boys who ain't even born yet will be able to go to a prom together and no one will care. Maybe right here in New York State. Till then, the rest of us will either fake it with a girl or stay home with their boyfriend and make a night of it."

He winked at Gibb, poking him and tickling him as he did. Gibb laughed.

"Yeah, tonight's our prom night!" he said, grabbing Leo's shoulders and playfully wrestling him to the floor. "Let's make this Friday-the-thirteenth a night we'll never forget!"

They wrestled around, playfully making out for a minute until Leo pulled away and said, "I like this whole prom idea. What do we wanna do to make it special?"

Gibb gave Leo a funny look.

"You really need to ask that?"

"Ha ha. Sure!" Leo laughed. "But what else? I have the car, we can pretty much go anywhere we want. Hell, let's just go find us a justice of the peace and get married!"

He was only half-kidding. Gibb did a double-take.

"Get married? Yeah, I wish." He wanted to make sure Leo knew he was serious as he looked him straight in his blue-green eyes. "I'd definitely marry you."

"Would you now?" Leo said, pulling Gibb close again.

"You have no idea," Gibb half-whispered, their joking around halted for a moment, "how much I'd marry you. I'd marry you a million times if you wanted."

"That's a whole lot of times," Leo said softly. "But how awesome would it be if we could do it just once?"

"I'm trying to picture it," Gibb murmured, looking at the ceiling, "I don't know who the hell would come, other than our immediate families. But we could really make it amazing, and it could be hilarious."

He snorted as he laughed out loud.

"First, we could have the Dead play at the reception and bring the whole Wall of Sound. Whaddya think about that? Can you imagine? That would blow some minds. Then stupid Jack would be there, only out of curiosity of course, asking us," Gibb aped a nerdy voice, "'Now... which one of you is the *woman?*'"

Leo burst out laughing, only encouraging Gibb to continue describing their whacked-out fantasy wedding scene.

"And you can bet there would be plenty of smoke in the room, too, but not the kind you'd wanna find at a Dead show. It'll all be coming from my mom. Perpetual cigarette hanging out of her mouth, two cartons worth of butts piled up and spilling out of the ashtrays in front of her, pretending she's happy for us but she's totally staring at the door, hoping she can leave soon 'cuz she doesn't wanna miss 'Scarecrow and Mrs. King.'"

Leo howled and clapped at Gibb's depiction of Lily.

"Then there's *your* Mom threatening to beat my ass, secretly giving me the finger when she thinks no one else is looking, 'til Honey sees her and starts chasing her around the hall with a cast-iron frying pan.

"Meanwhile, the Dead is playing an hour-long "Dark Star" for our wedding song while we're all hugged up on each other out on the dance floor, and your dad and Sissie keep trying to find a way to dance and clap along. Ten minutes in they finally give up and stand there slack-jawed and bug-eyed, all pissed off, wondering what the hell kind of music this is while they boo the band and start throwing shit at 'em. The band just laughs while Bobby Weir reminds the hecklers they're getting paid good for this gig, dodges whatever they throw and asks 'em to take a step back. 'And another step back! And take one more step back!'

Then we head off to our honeymoon in Hawaii. Fuckin' A, tell me that wouldn't be the best wedding ever!"

By the time Gibb was done, Leo was laughing so hard he was coughing.

"Oh man, it has to happen. It HAS to! Honey with that fryin' pan. Bobby tellin' Daddy and Sissie to take a step back! Gawd! Gibb, you kill me sometimes."

He paused for a moment to let his breathing come back to normal.

"But back to tonight…."

Gibb contemplated a few scenarios. He took a deep breath and held Leo tight for a long moment. When he started talking again, he was serious now.

"Well, since two guys can't marry each other, at least tonight, how about this? I'm gonna be honest – I'm kinda freaking out that this is our last night together for a long time. We don't need to go anywhere. Let's just order pizza and stay here. I just wanna be with you."

"That's very cool," Leo replied, smiling.

"OK, awesome. We'll pretend what we're wearing are our tuxes," Gibb said, running his hand down his T-shirt and jeans.

"Call 'em a tux if you want. They're just gonna end up on the floor anyway," Leo remarked, his grin turning sly.

Gibb grinned back, shaking his head, a little stunned at his luck at being able to be here alone with Leo tonight. Not in a car. Not in the woods or shivering in some ramshackle abandoned barn wishing they'd brought a blanket. For the first time since New Year's Eve at the Tranquilla, they would be alone together, inside, finally, where it was warm.

Leo suddenly jumped to his feet.

"But nothin' happens tonight until I give you something."

He hurried down the hall to his all but empty bedroom. Gibb was intrigued when Leo returned a few moments later wearing a light jacket.

"What's up?" Gibb asked.

"C'mon," Leo said. "Put on your jacket. We need to be outside when I give this to you."

## Chapter 19

SHADOWS IN
THE VALLEY

"What you got there?" Sam asked.

"Something Leo gave me the night before he left." Gibb held up the rose quartz crystal for Sam to see, then clutched it in his fist again.

"What is it?"

"It's called rose quartz. Stained with the blood of the Greek god and goddess who fought for love. That's what Leo told me, anyway."

Sam shook his head.

"Gods and goddesses," Sam mumbled bemusedly to himself before turning to Gibb. "How do a cat get that heavy at the age of eighteen?".

Now it was Gibb's turn to shake his head. He squeezed the crystal tighter.

"You wanna stop somewhere and call him to let him know you'll be there later today?"

"I actually tried from the gas station back there," Gibb said, chagrin in his voice, "No one answered. When he left in April I never got his actual phone number, so I hadn't talked to him until he called yesterday. Weird, right?"

Sam shrugged. "I don't know...is it?"

"Yes!" Gibb declared. "Because when he lived up home, his mother would just hang up on me if I called his house. We figured she'd for sure hang up on me if I ever called him in Louisiana, so we planned for him to just call me at my house. Which he didn't do until yesterday."

"Why his Mama hang up on you? She heard you callin' her names or somethin'?" Sam asked, only half-seriously.

Gibb pursed his lips in annoyance.

"No! I only met the lady once and it was when I helped them pack up their house to move in April. She probably just hated me because she hated the fact that Leo's gay. He never once told her anything about us, but she figured Leo out a while back and it pisses her off. I was just one more reminder that what she didn't like about Leo wasn't going away just because they'd moved up north.

"So, Leo and I said 'Screw it, let's just write to each other' with him writing first because my letters were bound for the trash can if Mrs. Davion picked up the mail. But then he didn't write. The whole plan was dumb. I should have gotten his number anyway," Gibb mumbled absently as he stared out the window, rubbing his thumb along the crystal's surface.

"I guess," Sam said. "Sound pretty tricky to have a relationship on the down-low like that," Sam said.

"It is for sure," Gibb replied. "And it's stupid. Why should we be expected to keep it a secret? But you hear it all the time from the good people of the world: 'Why can't *they* just keep *that* to themselves?' We're a 'they' to all those 'good' people. Something other. Something alien. And our relationships are a 'that'.

"What are they even talking about when they say 'that'?" Gibb went on, clearly irked. "Keep *what* to ourselves? Sex? No one's having sex out in public for the world to see. Love? Yeah, so two guys kissing in a public place is a horrible thing, but two guys shooting each other in a war movie or fighting each other is awesome. OK, I get it now. As long as it's a girl-guy kiss out in public, everyone can be happy and relaxed because they get to see a society that's just so...*normal*. Whew!'"

Gibb was indignant now. To Sam's obvious amusement, he began to mimic a caricature of the voice of the general populace. He sounded like an uptight, middle-aged white lady.

"'Oh my gosh, I'm so happy for that cute couple!'" Gibb mocked with a nasal whine. "'Aren't they a *neat* couple?' 'Oh look, they're going to the prom!' 'I wonder if they're gonna get married'. 'Isn't it wonderful to see only *normal, heterosexual* couples around here holding hands and giving each other little kisses?' 'Tee-hee-hee.'

"But make it two guys or two women kissing in public and it's all 'Faggots!' 'Dykes!' and 'Why do *they* have to flaunt it?' or 'I don't want my children exposed to *that*.'"

Gibb wasn't mocking anymore, he was ranting, and now Sam could only arch his eyebrows behind his dark sunglasses as he quietly drove on.

"And then people, mostly guys, use that shit as an excuse to physically hurt us. Imagine if I started throwing rocks at straight couples holding hands or kissing in public or beating them up or worse. Just imagine! They'd arrest me for sure and I'd deserve it, wouldn't I, because people aren't hurting anybody when they do that! They're just out having a nice day together and showing their affection to one another.

"But gay couples? Forget about it. Just by existing we seem to be hurting someone. But *we're* people, too! Somehow, that gets overlooked. Somehow, it's wrong. 'Take your lumps because you *chose* to be this way, faggot. God hates you, and so does everyone else, so that makes it OK for us to call you names, beat you up, incarcerate you, deny you a job. Even kill you.

"It's unreal that they boil it all down to what they imagine we're doing in private. They call *us* freaks. Geez. Trust me, we don't see a straight couple holding hands and imagine how they're gettin' it on. Seriously. They're just people out in public holding hands, for God's sake. So are *we!*"

"Why people wanna mind other folks' business all the time is beyond me," Sam said quietly.

"Right?! What the hell kind of thinking is that?!" Gibb fulminated on. "What *choice* are they even talking about, anyway? You think I *chose* to be gay? Look, I don't hate being the way I am. It's just life, my life, the way it just…is."

He paused, determined to stop his tirade, but he couldn't stop more thoughts from tumbling out of his mouth.

"But I damn sure didn't choose it. I just chose to accept it rather than pretend. As beautiful as so many girls are, why would I *choose* not to be with them? Caring about somebody isn't a bad thing, no matter what anybody says," Gibb said, remembering Ms. Mullan, "and if it's someone of your own stupid gender, then that's that. Can't help it."

"Makes sense to me," Sam replied thoughtfully.

"Leo has a good way of looking at it," Gibb said. "He said some people want to live next to the ocean. Others like to live in the desert. Is there anything wrong with that? Are people 'wrong' if they want to live near the ocean? What if they were born there, like in Hawaii or along the coasts here, and they love it and they're just naturally happy there?

"But then what if someone came along and said, 'No, no. This is all wrong. In order to be a good person, you have to pick up and move to the desert where there's dry heat and cactuses and no water, the exact opposite of the place where you were born and raised. There's only one way to live on Planet Earth. In the desert.'

Sam nodded, following Gibb's logic.

"And that's the whole analogy, see? Gay people are the 'ocean' people here and straight people are the 'desert' people. Good for the desert people and all, but that doesn't make us ocean people any less human or any less worthy of our relationships. Just like the ocean and the desert themselves, we're only the way we are. If it's in our nature to live by the water, that's what we're going to do. By the hand of Mother Nature, the Hand of God, the Universe, whatever. Doesn't matter what some shyster TV preacher or slimy politician running his mouth has to say about it. They might be able to shame us into moving to the desert, but that doesn't mean we'll ever thrive there. We belong where we belong. By the ocean.

"I think once a person realizes that about themselves, *everything* becomes different. Maybe a little unrecognizable from before, maybe a little scary, but better. 'Cuz then you know a little something about something: just because you happen to be a 'desert' guy, you're not somehow a better person than me. You're just some dude who lives in the desert. And I'm just some dude who lives on the coast and no, I don't think I'm any better than you. We're both just people, living our lives the way nature intended."

"I'm hearin' you, I'm hearin' *both* of you, loud and clear, man," Sam said, glancing over at his now self-conscious passenger.

Gibb looked over at Sam ruefully.

"Sorry to go on and on like that," he said with a baleful shrug. "I'm just sick of stupidity and for some reason I'm seeing it everywhere. Well, mostly from people in our own families. It's ingrained in them that somehow we're inferior, and that's what we have to deal with every day."

Sam nodded.

"I know what you mean...sort of, but it's different. When I was a young guy like you, I had a lot of the same kind of feelings. Not about being gay, even though it's a good point about 'ocean people' and 'desert people' and all that stuff. It make perfect sense. But that's not where I'm goin' with this.

"I've never been attracted to another guy, but...being a *black* man in this world...well...I'll put it this way - you might just get angry sometimes about the way you're treated. And it don't stop once you get sick of it, I'm sorry to say, no matter how old you get. And when I was your age I started to realize that, and then I became really angry."

"I wanna hear about it," Gibb said.

"I was angry because, what I saw from my perspective as a black boy and as a young black man, there is never no way to escape the spotlight. You know what I'm sayin' about 'the spotlight'? Sam made air quotation marks with his index fingers over the steering wheel.

Gibb shrugged.

"You have experienced it just a little bit yourself with Leo's mama. So... before I continue...I just wanna tell you that I know being gay ain't no choice. I got that. But you *do* got another choice, OK? *You* can avoid the spotlight if you want. How? By not doin' nothin' with Leo in public – no holdin' hands, no kissin', jus' sneakin' around and stuff. It don't sound like a good way to go, but that's up to the individual and lotsa gay people make that choice. Don't they?"

"They do," Gibb said.

"Yep. Because it's safer that way. If nobody know about 'em, then they don't get hassled." Sam said. "But try bein' black. You visible. You *always* visible. And trust me. You feel those eyes on you wherever you go – in the store when the shopkeepers payin' extra attention to your every move. On the street when you see a white woman move over some and clutch her purse tight or just hurry into a doorway you know she ain't headin' for. The white faces turnin' in your direction when they thinkin' you and your family bein' too loud at the restaurant table. Like, 'Really? What are y'all lookin' at?' Please.

"You start seein' it when you a kid in school and mouth off a little like your white friend do. Totally different punishments. Mouthy white kid get a little talkin' to. Mouthy black kid get yelled at in front of the entire class, sent to the principal and then suspended for a week.

"That mouthy black kid was me, by the way," Sam said, "just in case you thought I was talkin' theoretical.

"There are a million more examples, but for now I just wanna point out... when you black... wherever you go...the spotlight is on you and there ain't no turnin' it off. I know it sound kinda paranoid when I say it, but I know that uneasy feelin' in the air when that spotlight start glarin'.

"White folks just waitin' for you to step outta line and then 'BAM!'" Sam shouted, slapping the steering wheel for emphasis, "they gonna be the good people they are and shut that darkie down! Make a example out of him. Show the other white folks that things is in control 'round here! 'Up against the wall, motherfucker!', big public shows of authority. All that shit."

Gibb sat quietly, giving Sam his full, sleep-deprived attention.

"I'll give you a very mild example from my young life," Sam added. "Train tracks run right along the river in New Orleans. Freight trains get long and they stay stuck on them tracks right between the river and the city for a *long* time sometimes. If you on the wrong side of the train, you in for a long wait. But if you ain't got that kinda time, you climb between the stopped cars and hop on over to the other side. No big deal. That is...unless a cop who don't like folks like you just happen to be on that other side.

"This one mornin', when I was about twelve years old, I'm stuck on the river side of the tracks because of this long-ass freight train. So, I do what everybody else is doin' – I follow all these other people climbin' between the cars to get to the other side.

"As soon as I jump down onto the city side of the tracks, there's a white cop right there, pointin' at me and sayin', 'No! Not you. You go back on over to the other side and wait for this train to pass!'

"I say right back, 'What about all them other people walkin' right past you? They jus' done the same thing!' There was like a dozen people strollin' right past him as he go pointin' me out. You know what he said?"

Sam was chuckling.

"Was it something funny?" Gibb asked.

"It's funny now, only because I choose to laugh at it," Sam said with a scornful smile. "But it wasn't funny then. Cop say, 'I'm not talkin' 'bout them. I'm talkin' 'bout *you!*'

"Can you believe that shit? 'I'm not talkin' 'bout them, I'm talkin' 'bout *you!*'," Sam repeated, in an irritated, sing-song voice. "Those other people crossin' the tracks that day? All white tourists. Every last one of 'em. Me? Just some good-for-nothin' local black kid wit' no money and nuttin' else to do. Basically, 'Take yo' ass back to the other side of the train 'cuz you got time to wait. These other people's time is important and yours ain't.'

"So I went back over and waited. Like a half hour. Cop never called me no names, never threatened no violence or nothin', but he said a helluva lot in just a few words."

"That is *bull*shit," Gibb exclaimed, sincerely taken aback by Sam's discriminatory tale.

"*Dude,*" Sam sneered, "that's one of the most *benign* examples I could give you. But it prepped me for what was to come. I don't want to scare you too much with the worser ones, 'cuz they get a lot worse.

"Anyway, when I got home that day and told Mama what happened, I got a ass-whoopin' from her for even tellin' her what I said to the cop. She told me, 'Next time, and there's gonna be a next time, don't you dare say nothin'! You don't never talk back, you do what they say. No matter what. Your entire life depend on it, wit' yo' stupid ass.'

"Even though I was pissed off at her, she knew what she was talkin' about. Now stuff like that don't happen *every* day. But if you black, you know that every day it *can* happen. And that's when I feel that familiar anger, that anger

I first felt when I was a kid getting singled out in class and the whole train tracks thing."

"Well, what else happened?!" Gibb exhorted Sam, outraged on his behalf. Sam just shook his head.

"A lot of stuff, man. Not just to me, but to family and friends, too. I don't wanna talk about it because it will put me in a bad mood. I'll just put it this way – I know it's a tough row to hoe when all you tryin' to do is live and someone else decide they have a better idea about how you should be *allowed* to live. You seein' it from your angle now. And I *been* seein' it from mine, for a lot longer than you been alive."

"But that's exactly the problem. It doesn't *have* to be that way, so why *is* it that way?" Gibb asked indignantly.

"Why you askin' me? A lot of dumb shit exist with no explanation for it. Hunger. Disease. Poverty. Any of it. It exist because it exist, I guess. I don't have no other answer. When enough people want to work together to change things, they'll change."

"But why, though?" Gibb persisted. "Not just 'Why do all these terrible things exist?' but even more than that. Like, is there a purpose to human life? Or is it just some sort of, I don't know…like, a mistake? Are we just marking time here and then we die like any other animal by some awful disease like Leo's dad? Or in some terrible accident, like my dad? And then what if there's nothing afterwards, not even love?"

"Well…" Sam rubbed his chin and glanced over at Gibb, "shit. If I knew the answer to *those* questions, why the hell would I be drivin' this piece of shit with some ate-up kid I just met up north prattlin' on and on? I'd be makin' a ton o' money bein' one of them shyster TV preachers you mentioned."

They rode along in silence for a few moments before Sam spoke again.

"I guess if life have a purpose, we gon' find out. If life don't have a purpose, we gon' find that out, too. You young. You got a long way to go with a lot of shit, good and bad, comin' your way. Focus on enjoyin' the good! Don't worry about the bad. You know you can't see around no corner when you only halfway up the street."

"I have a hard time doing that sometimes," Gibb replied. "Every time I try to like, be happy, something happens that hurts me or makes me feel stupid or embarrassed. Actually, everything seems to embarrass me.

"And now I start to expect it, like something bad really *is* right around that corner up there," he said, taking Sam's analogy further. "It makes me dread walking further up that 'street', even if the weather and the scenery are nice. That's what makes me think that everything might be pointless anyway. I mean, why keep trying when all you do is feel like a weirdo or an idiot?"

"You feel like a weirdo or a idiot right now?" Sam asked.

Gibb paused before he replied, wondering why Sam was asking.

"Not really," he said. "It's pretty easy to talk about your deepest, darkest secrets with someone you don't even know."

"You just proved my point, man," Sam replied. "See? You don't feel embarrassed or stupid *all* the time. So, pay attention and appreciate the times you don't. That's what everybody gotta do, because *everybody* feel like you, OK? You ain't unique.

"Look, you think I wasn't embarrassed by the cop sendin' me back to the other side of the train? Or when the teacher tore me up in front of ever'body that day? You think I'm not embarrassed when I get pulled over for going five over the speed limit and told to get out the car and put my hands on the trunk so I can get frisked and the car can get searched for no reason? That's real life for me, bro, and it's scary as hell sometimes."

Gibb just stared at Sam in silence.

"Well, I was doing more than ten over," he finally said. "And nobody pulled me over, even when I saw a cop."

"Man, that is what I was trying to *explain* to you earlier," Sam spoke deliberately now, pronouncing each word slowly and emphatically. "Now you might see it better. You not gonna get pulled over for being *gay* while speeding. But you might very well could get pulled over for bein' *black* while goin' one mile over the limit.

"This is why I'm sayin' – you, YOU, Gibbon-the-gay-white-monkey, can be invisible if you choose to be. Jus' speed on by if you want, keepin' your gay life secret. That's called privilege. Me, Sam the big seven-foot black man? No chance. Dark as a chocolate roux, shinin' bright as the daggone sun wherever I go…whether I want to or not."

The things Sam was saying were exasperating Gibb. It wasn't because he couldn't imagine they were true – of course he could. It was the whole question of *why*. *Why* did people have to be that way? *Why* did people need to deem others inferior somehow?

And why did they need to feel superior in the first place? Because they weren't and how could they be? Maybe some were smarter in certain areas or had an aptitude or a determination that set them apart from the rest of the crowd. But that didn't make them superior to anybody else, not when they needed the exact same basics – clean air, clean water, nutritious food – just to survive. People were essentially all the same at the physical level, weren't they? Wasn't every human skeleton the same grey-white set of 206 bones?

Sam hadn't answered Gibb's question. So he framed it differently and asked again.

"OK, let me put it another way. Why do you suppose people think they're superior to other people and that people like you and me are inferior? Ever wondered?"

"Dude, of course I've wondered," Sam said, furrowing his brow in consternation. "I been on this Earth more than twice the time you been here. I've had a little time to think about it. But I don't have no real answer."

"Do you have a guess?"

"Do I have a guess?" Sam asked, impatient. "Well," he capitulated, "sort of. But the way you carryin' on, I know you not gonna like it."

"I still want to hear it. You're already giving me a lot to think about," Gibb said.

Sam shrugged.

"Told you already. Things just got to be the way they are until enough people say it's time to do things the right way. There's been some great civil rights work done and some gay rights work, too. If you payin' attention to either, you know it's just the beginnin', though. There been some successes, but the work got to continue.

"But… hey look there," Sam paused, suddenly raising an urgent finger to point at a big green sign welcoming them to 'Alabama the Beautiful.'

"Cool!", Gibb said as he read the sign. "This is the sixth state I've been in today!"

"Yeah…funny we here in Alabama just as we start talkin' bout civil rights. You at the place where it all began now. Montgomery, Selma, Birmingham. Rosa Parks, Dr. King, the boycotts, the KKK, the fight against people like Governor George Wallace. You know about him?"

Gibb shook his head.

"Dude was a hard-ass segregationist. When he was governor in the sixties, he got up in front of a crowd on Inauguration Day and declared some bullshit like, 'Segregation now, segregation tomorrow, segregation forever!' And that white crowd went wild. Scary shit to watch, let me tell you. The fifties and sixties was a crazy time 'round here in Alabama. But shit got changed see? People worked hard, they sacrificed, they *died* for it. Shit got changed. So as hard as it is, it's up to us to work to change folks' perspective…if we ain't too scared or lazy to do it."

"But that doesn't answer *anything*," Gibb complained dismissively. "I asked *why* things are the way they are, *why* people think they're superior in the first place, not about how people can change."

"I don't know, man," came Sam's frustrated reply. "A lot of it might be because people learn and copy behavior from people they love and respect. So, if you love your Mama and Daddy…and they believe black people ain't as good as white folks or gay guys are sinful…and they raise you that way…you might just take on that belief yourself. You know, 'Well, Daddy thought that, and he was a great father and husband. I want him to admire and respect *me* the way I admire and respect him, so I'm-a act like him.'

"So, it can become learned behavior, but all sorta innocently based in love and loyalty to someone important to you. A lot of jacked-up belief systems in this world have they roots in love and respect, see?"

"I do see," Gibb said. "That doesn't make it OK, though. Plus, the whole idea of group superiority started somewhere before even that, I think. That's what I'm asking. Why is someone prone to believe it in the first place and then be so…I don't know…hardcore about it?"

"Look man," Sam huffed, "I don't know who you think I am or what I'm s'posed to know about. I know a lot about some stuff but I *don't* know a lot about most stuff, see? Jus' like you. Unless you special or somethin', but I already know you ain't, so don't go tryin' to pretend you are wit' all your damn questions."

Gibb smirked.

"Yeah, that's what I thought," Sam said. "Anyway, you askin' me to guess about why this kinda shit has been goin' on forever, and all I can tell you 'bout is what I *think*. I don't *know* nothin', really. So it still ain't gon' amount to jack for you, OK?

"I don't care," Gibb said. "Just keep talking."

"OK, then. I *think* – and this is just me havin' an opinion 'cuz I don't speak for no one else – people think they're superior because they think they're superior. That's it. They jus' do. They was either born into a situation and a structure that supported the idea that they better than everyone else - like Daddy had a lotta money or political connections or maybe they was just naturally the smartest kid in the class and the teacher and the other kids reinforced that idea every day.

"Or…look at it the other way. Maybe they was born into a situation that made 'em feel like they wasn't worth nothin'. I'm talkin' places where there wasn't no money but a lot of drinkin' or druggin' or abuse in the house. Not a lot of love around. Those people can still feel superior to everyone around 'em."

Gibb raised his eyebrows.

"Mmm-hmm," Sam hummed. "Sound backwards, I know. Them ones who felt like they wasn't worth nothin' felt cut off from everybody else around 'em, like the shit they was dealin' with at home was unique, somethin' that nobody else could *ever* understand. So, they felt like they had no choice but to 'go it alone'. So they did and, somehow, they survived and that happened because of three things: their determination, a couple of lucky breaks, and yep, privilege.

"But…" Sam held up his long, mocha-colored index finger, "when they think about they survival, it's only the *determination* part they remember. They don't remember that lucky break or the privilege that come from a bein' a certain skin color or gender as they made their way out of a tough situation.

"So now them 'self-made' folks spend a lot of time waverin' between either feelin' like God's gift, 'cuz they believe they made it out all on they own, or feelin' like they don't meet up with nobody else's standards because they got hurt pretty bad on the way up and nobody gave a damn about them. Actin' superior on the surface, feelin' inferior and wounded underneath.

"And let me tell you, those are some pissed off people. Their confused feelin's give them the potential to be very dangerous out there in the world. However they feel – like they either better than or worse than everyone else in the world – can cause a lot of harm when they bring them angry feelings into a situation. Angry 'cuz people ain't showin' 'em the respect they think they entitled to, or angry from the memories of being beaten down. Just angry!

"So…that's my only answer to your dumb question. I'd say the people who be makin' the most noise about gay folks or black folks or any other kinda folks they think is different…is either those angry, wounded kinda people or the ones whose Mama and Daddy told 'em how great they are and who never once wavered from the way they parents thought about the world. Angry on one hand, loyal little sheep on the other."

Gibb sat still, struck by Sam's insights. "Wow! How do you *know* all that stuff?" he asked incredulously.

"I told you I'm jus' *guessin'*," Sam replied, mildly irritated. "I don't *know* jack shit."

"No, no. No way. You *know*," Gibb said, holding up his hand. No way was he letting Sam off the hook.

Sam had in the space of a couple of minutes sort of just explained Gibb's whole experience of people – his mother, his stepfather, his whole freakin' town and, appallingly, even Gibb himself. Now Gibb wasn't sure whether he despised everyone even more because he knew their secret, or if he was actually thinking about having some compassion for their situations back up there in rundown Eislertown. For now, though, he only knew he felt different about it somehow.

"You just explained pretty much everybody I've ever met, except maybe one," Gibb told Sam dismally.

"Oh yeah? Who I miss?" Sam said, chuckling. "You?"

"I wish," Gibb replied. "No, not me. The only person I can think of who isn't like that is Ms. Mullan."

"She the teacher, right?"

"She is," Gibb said with a nod. "She actually *is* special, as far as I'm concerned. But...nah...wait. I guess she's like everybody else, because now that I think about it, she does feel superior to other teachers who make their students diagram sentences and stupid stuff like that."

"Yeah...well...you lucky she been there for you. We all seem to need that one person who can show us the world ain't all bad."

*You're helping me see that right now*, Gibb thought to himself, smiling blankly as he wrestled with the idea of actually saying that to Sam.

"Well, I sure appreciate you talking to me like this," Gibb said instead. "I guess I should tell you that I've never once had a conversation like this with a grown man. Never. Can you believe that? The times I've talked about anything important were only with Leo or Ms. Mullan. Well, my mom a little bit too, when she would tell me about my dad and stuff. But I don't need to rehash my whole relationship with her. You know that story."

"Boy, don't be all tryin' to all butter me up," Sam complained, "after you forcin' me to talk all this whole time. I coulda been ridin' in blissful silence and enjoyin' the lovely scenery 'round here in Alabama the Beautiful."

"No, I'm serious," Gibb said. "You don't have any idea. The adult men I've known in my life have either been abusive – physically to their kids, like my Uncle Bill was - or emotionally to their wives, like Jack is. Either that or they were just sort of...detached...like the teachers at my school.

"I always imagined if my dad had lived, he would've been a good person to talk to and we would've been friends. The opposite of Jack. And I think everything would've been different for my mom if he'd lived, too. Maybe that's why I don't hate her – I think maybe she's just lost.

"But…" Gibb paused for a moment to think about what he was going to say. "I guess after hearing your thoughts, I'm definitely one of those people you talked about, the go-it-alone person. And I must be a hypocrite because I actually *do* feel superior to people where I'm from, because I think their beliefs are stupid and so are they."

"Yep," Sam said.

"Yep, what?" Gibb asked.

"Yep, you a hypocrite. We all are, though. Just takes a while to see it and some guts to admit it."

"But isn't there a better way to think about and behave towards people, one that isn't filled with so much…contempt?" Gibb asked.

"Sure, there is!" Sam said. "Now you go on back up to Eiffel Tower or whatever the name of that town is where you from and be that way to your Mama and stepdaddy."

He chuckled to himself. Gibb glared at him from the passenger seat.

"It's called Eislertown," he grumbled. "And I told you I'm not ever going back there."

"Why not?" Sam asked smugly. "Thought you said people shouldn't be actin' superior to nobody else."

"Yeah, but this is different!" Gibb said. "They're a hundred percent wrong and it's pretty clear. I don't *ever* need to change my attitude towards them."

"Fair enough," Sam said. "But there it is."

"There what is?" Gibb asked.

"The gris-gris cast upon the human race at the beginnin' of creation," Sam replied.

"We all lookin' for understandin', but *we* don't wanna try to understand no one else. That's 'cuz *we* got our pride, right? *We deserve* that respect and understandin' after all we been through, right?"

"That's exactly right!" Gibb exclaimed before thinking deeper into what Sam just said. "But wait, if everybody thinks they're right," Gibb went on, "and they think they're better than the people they disagree with, then nobody's right. And that can't be, or else no problems would get solved and nothing would ever get done!"

"You right," Sam agreed.

"Then how does anything get done when people always disagree about everything?!" Gibb groused, exasperated now.

"Prob'ly because smart people, and only smart people, understand that the only way to get anything done is to face one fact. A fact that won't never change.

"Much as we may not like it," Sam said, looking over his sunglasses at Gibb, "we stuck with each other. That's it. And at some point, in order to make a disagreement pass, we gotta recognize the other side ain't nothin' more than a bunch of people with a different perspective, sometimes as awful and wrong as you could ever imagine. But smart people always find a way to work together to find a solution. Because we stuck with each other."

"So that's it?" Gibb said, pursing his lips. "We're stuck with each other. Really? That's all you got?"

"Yep," Sam said. "That's the answer to all of life. Mark it down."

He threw his head back and guffawed, his laugh as loud as the one that first shocked Gibb awake this morning all the way up in Maryland.

Gibb, more confused than ever, could only stare in wonder. How could Sam be laughing at an answer so dull and basic? Nothing about what he'd just said was funny at all. But Gibb did have to consider that maybe, just maybe, it was totally true.

*Chapter 20*

# FALLING DOWN
# LIKE RAIN

Their last night had finally crossed the dreaded midnight dividing line, winding down to their last few hours together in the Finger Lakes. In the darkness of the barren living room, Gibb and Leo huddled together under an old sheet and a wool blanket, each watching the red numbers on Leo's clock mark the moment, neither of them mentioning it. Gibb uncurled his middle finger and discreetly raised it to the clock.

He felt silly and stereotypical as he envisioned poor Dorothy frightened and crying, staring at the blood-red sand running coldly through the neck of the Wicked Witch of the West's hourglass in the Wizard of Oz. Silly or not, it was an accurate reference point. They were almost out of time. He was frightened himself at the possibility that he might not ever see Leo again. He shivered and snuggled up closer to Leo.

*What's next for us, really?* Gibb thought.

He opened his eyes to stare at the back of Leo's head, taking a moment to listen to his shallow, dozing breathing, moving his palm up to Leo's chest to feel his awesome heartbeat.

Leo stirred and rolled over to look at the clock. Already three a.m. now. In the dark, he reached for Gibb's face, running his fingers along the stubbly jawline.

"Hey," he said sleepily. "You awake?"

"I am," came Gibb's croaky, wee-hours reply. "I can't really sleep. Too much on my mind."

"Yeah, me too. But I been tryin' – long day of drivin' ahead for me and I have *never* driven that far alone in my life."

"You're gonna do great," Gibb said. He pulled Leo as close as he could and kissed his neck.

At five a.m., Leo was gripping the wheel of his parents' station wagon, his handsome face somber and unsmiling as light rain caught him through the open car window. He and Gibb had kissed each other goodbye about twenty times inside the house before he'd forced himself to walk outside and get in the car. Gibb leaned down through the open window, his face equally stoic, to tell Leo one more time to be careful, to write, that he would love him forever.

"Forever's not just time, y'know," Leo said, staring straight ahead through the windshield at the light mist dancing lightly through the car's headlight. He turned to look at Gibb.

"It's a whole lot more than we can imagine. Think about that."

Gibb didn't know how to respond to whatever it was Leo was trying to communicate, especially at that early hour. He just stood there stone-faced, his face and clothes dampening as the mist became heavier. Leo put his hand over Gibb's and looked up at him.

"I promise you, Mr. Gibbon Mulcahy, I'm gonna love you forever, too. You really sure I can't give you a ride home?"

Afraid he'd break down if he spoke, Gibb declined with a wordless shake of his head. He leaned down, wishing for some sort of magic to happen to make this whole scene just a dream.

Once again, he whispered, "I sure wish I was going with you."

And then their longest last kiss through the window before Gibb finally pulled away. Nope, this was not a dream.

Ignition. The engine sneezed and roared to life and then, grudgingly it seemed, the white sedan and its handsome, grim-faced driver backed slowly out of the driveway. The exact same way Gibb felt he was moving. Backwards. Back to being alone. Back to figuring everything out on his own. Back to having no one to talk to, no one to laugh with, no one to love, no one to love him. He used to know how to manage that kind of life and he knew he'd get through it, but he definitely didn't want to go back to nothing after experiencing something as big as loving Leo.

The meteoric enchantment of those last twenty-four hours with Leo spat, sputtered, and finally spent itself as Leo's car shifted into Drive and rolled away in a huff, disappearing into its own mist-grey destiny, driven by the only person in the world who mattered.

The only sound now in the grey, wet dawn was the cheery chirp of a robin and the empty, sad thump of Gibb's heart pounding mallets against his eardrums.

There was a reason Gibb declined Leo's offer of a ride home. Before he resigned himself to his old life in that Eislertown hellhole, there was somewhere else he needed to go first.

⌖

Rain, falling hard now in harsh and drenching intermittent showers, hampered the long climb up the crude wooden steps, turning them slick and slimy, as they spiraled and slanted upward and upward in direct opposition to Gibb's worsening mood. The punishing thousand-stair climb up Blue Rock there at the north end woods of Rogers Park was bad enough on a dry day. In the rain, it felt like a three-thousand stair climb.

As calf muscles and quadriceps groaned against the abuse this impulsive hike was heaping on them, Gibb's simmering frustration gave way to the hard boil of anger. His mind began cursing him for bothering to even try to make this trek, especially this early in the morning on almost no sleep. He quickened his steps in spite, marching heavily, his face tight, his mouth open wide to gulp in the air he only wanted to exhale in shout after louder shout into scream after vocal cord- shredding scream.

As he finally reached the thousandth step, the top of the rock, he tripped, falling palms first onto the sharp and muddy gravel. Blood trickled from both of his hands as he jumped up like a madman, shouting angrily and unintelligibly at the top of his lungs. Choking on rain and pain, his fists clenched in almighty rage, he stood ready to take down anyone who even dared to look in his direction. Of course, at six a.m., there was no one else up there. No one but Gibb... and Leo's massive absence.

Gibb could truly feel his own insignificance here as he surveyed the expansive green valley below set starkly against the silvering, frown-faced sky. Nothing he cared about mattered. Nothing he wanted ever came true. The Universe was a bully, and Gibb made the effort to be here this morning to let it know he knew just that.

With both middle fingers aimed towards that cheerless sky, that dark-grey barrier between him and whoever was up there pulling the miserable levers of his life, Gibb bellowed a sound he could have never made before, transforming himself into his own storm of rain and wind that twisted up, down and sideways across this mount of misery, his gloom trying to expend itself in one terrible and terrifying eruption.

On his bloodied hands and knees now, Gibb howled like a wild animal, his cries of pain coming from the deepest recesses of his memory. His father's death, his mother's indifference, Jack's racism and gay-hating comments, every uncelebrated school success, Billy's life and death, every feeling of worthlessness he'd ever had, from being gay to just being invisible in the eyes of his mother, his teachers, his classmates. And just when he'd finally met someone who understood him, who could relate to his struggles *and* love him anyway - and who, by God, should be going with him to the Grateful Dead concert in Rochester on Monday night - the Fates, the Universe, God, whatever it was - all conspired to not just take it all away, but to hurt Leo and his whole family in the process. What a terrible joke life was.

Gibb, exhausted, lay back on the gravel and rocks, cradling his head in his hands, welcoming the rain now to help wash his face and, maybe, his spirit.

He took a long deep breath through his nose, thankful that only the ancient pines and the birds within their branches bore witness to the agony and despair that had just confronted them on this ordinarily peaceful crest.

He'd done what he came to Blue Rock to do. His throat was sore, his leg muscles burned, streaks of blood marked his palms. He was truly embarrassed by the formidable display of his deepest grief, but even though his body and pride hurt like hell, Gibb was glad he'd gone through with it. He needed to freak out, all by himself, and that's just what he did.

Now he needed sleep. He stood up, dusted himself off, and with one last look at the valley below, began his slow descent down the slippery steps to begin the short, wet trek back to his old worthless life in Eislertown.

## *Chapter 21*

# CRACKS

The hardest part of Leo's absence was the sneaky way it would casually drain away the color his presence had poured into Gibb's life. Day by fading day, each vibrant hue dripped slowly out of Gibb's memory. Two months after Leo left, the world had returned to exactly the way it looked before he'd arrived: an excruciatingly familiar palette of safe, sad grey. Just like today.

Today was like walking around in a black and white movie. Light grey June sky. Dark grey clouds. Muggy grey air and oyster-colored streets and sidewalks. Dirt and grass greyed out somehow, too. Gibb's summer landscaping job had started again just before Memorial Day and today he'd been out working in the humid drab until even the weather got bored and exploded into a thunderstorm to finally break the monotony.

He walked into the house wet and dirty and alone, the mid-afternoon squall only adding to the unshakeable bland, grey feeling of boredom and restlessness that takes a person nowhere but into the kitchen and back to his room.

Gibb's mother and Jack were at some farm picking strawberries this afternoon, leaving Gibb mercilessly alone with his thoughts. With no one else there to occupy his attention he couldn't help but run through everything again.

Hadn't he and Leo made an agreement? So what the hell, then? Hadn't Leo had said he'd write first? Then why hadn't he written or called? Two months!

Hadn't Leo asked Gibb not to write to him until he'd received a letter from him? Gibb never even questioned that plan and worse, he'd never even asked Leo for his address. Worse, Gibb hadn't even gotten Leo's Louisiana phone number! What had he been thinking? And to put the finest of fine points on the whole sorry scenario, when exasperated Gibb finally called Directory Assistance, Leo's family's number wasn't even listed in Bache's white pages.

This was the annoying part, the silly part, the frustrating part of being in a relationship with Leo. The guy would just disappear. No real warning that it was coming. He'd just vanish, exactly like in the weeks before he'd told Gibb about Mr. Davion's cancer. Then he'd show up again like nothing happened and Gibb would pretty much play along. It was weird and it hurt, too. If he didn't want to try to do this thing long-distance, then just say so. That would be tough to face, but at least it wouldn't be as bad as wondering if he'd even made it back to Louisiana two freaking months ago.

He'd had no reason not to take Leo at his word, and Leo sure had a way with his words. But what if he was dead? Seriously, he could be. Who knew? Who does that anyway - drives away saying he loves you, and then never writes or calls once he gets to his destination 1,300 miles away?

Gibb had gone from hopeful to concerned to resentful to angry to, now, just plain baffled. At this point, any news would be an improvement over no news. One thing was for sure though, he was sick of thinking about it. Sick of caring about it. Prepared to pull the plug and detach from it if he had to. Maybe the life he knew before Leo, the one where he didn't attach himself emotionally to anyone, was really the best preparation for whatever came next.

The more Gibb thought about it, maybe simply by staying out of touch, Leo had freed him somehow. Freed him from needing to believe that connecting with another person was really ever necessary. Or important. From now on, why not just have fun and leave all the deep stuff out of it? It sure would make things a lot easier especially considering that tomorrow, finally, he, Gibbon Mulcahy, was graduating high school.

At last. Four years of doing his best to sneak under the radar and out the back door into the world, taking not a thing with him from his books or classes other than the simple power of the lesson he'd learned from Ms. Mullan ("You can't hide from your truth, Gibb."). Well, that and now, maybe, this whole thing with Leo's disappearance.

Maybe there really was another lesson in all of this. Maybe what he was supposed to learn was that a deep bond with another person was amazing and powerful and life changing. Humbling. And then, just like an icicle or a snowfall, something comes along, something you can't control, and makes it go away.

That was it and there it was. On a humid and stormy June strawberry afternoon, simply by envisioning a melting layer of snow, Gibb was able to see he had no choice but to let Leo go. It was over.

For whatever it was worth, whatever it was meant to teach, their relationship was beautiful and amazing while it lasted. Their discoveries of each other and the world around them, those memories would only ever be theirs alone. No one else could share them – no one else was there. Only Leo. Only Gibb. That was as beautiful a thought as Gibb had ever had, and it made him smile a little.

Ironically, for someone who talked as deeply as Leo, it was without words that he was making his clearest point here. By never writing or calling, Leo was saying loud and clear that whatever they'd had couldn't last. There was no other choice but to face that fact.

For a while now, Gibb thought Leo was the answer to whatever needed answering. But it turned out that Leo was just another question. A question with his own questions, likely as unsure of the point and worth of his own life as Gibb was. Gibb and Leo couldn't rescue one another from whatever forced them both to call for rescue. No matter how much he loved Leo, and he'd meant it when he said the word "forever", they were each on their own now.

He had to let it, let Leo, go. He had to let it all go. And today, in the tiny, dirty kitchen of this neglected Eislertown house, he *would* let go, but on one condition. He would make this promise to himself and not break it: never get too carried away again by the illusion of anything that looks like permanence. In love. In life. Anything.

Nodding to himself, affirming the silent words he spoke in his head, Gibb caught his mopey reflection in the cracked pane of the dusty kitchen window and just…laughed. Out loud. How perfect. There was a crack in everything – this house, this family, this town, this whole life up to now. This mean, stupid world. The lame idea of a forever marriage or partnership.

It had just taken Gibb a little longer but, thanks to that crack in the windowpane, he got the picture. And just in time, really. After all of the unanswerable questions life had posed to him so far, where his only response was a torrent of hidden, awkward emotions– it turned out that the answer to everything was, simply, time. Time. Wait long enough and things will change.

As he was leaving, Leo had said "Forever is not just time". Gibb thought he'd understood a little of what Leo had meant by that, but now he was pretty sure. And somehow, it was going to be, it was going to *have* to be, OK.

*I'll figure it out,* he thought to himself as he reached for a glass in a nicked-up cabinet next to the sink. Suddenly, he jumped backwards in fright, his free hand clutching his chest as the jangle of the telephone cut through the quiet of the kitchen like a machete. The glass tumbled from his hand, performing a perfect mid-air somersault in front of Gibb's astonished face just a half-second before it smashed in shards across the kitchen floor.

"What the hell?!" Gibb whispered, eyes wide as they raced across the glinting glass splinters, vexed at the startled mess he'd made, surprised at how jumpy he was. His heart raced and his chest heaved from the alarm of the phone's intrusion.

He grabbed the receiver in mid-clang.

"Hello?" he almost hollered in frustration. The next second, he almost joined those fragments of glass on the floor. He steadied himself against the wall as he listened to the voice on the other end of the phone.

Leo. Of course, it had to be Leo.

*Chapter 22*

# WIDE-EYED
# AND SLEEPY

G ibb and Sam rolled across the rest of Alabama without saying much. After their animated discussion on race, sexuality, and the meaning of life, both men instinctively retreated into their own worlds. Gibb was a little rattled, feeling like he'd said too much. Maybe Sam was, too.

Gibb didn't realize it at first, but somehow it seemed like the entire world had begun a slow tilt the moment they'd crossed into rural Mississippi, all bright and humid with dripping, draping Spanish moss, beautiful and mysterious, hanging everywhere. Gibb noticed that Sam was even quieter, tense, as they drove through Mississippi. Gibb could guess why, and it wasn't just road fatigue.

Now, less than 250 miles later, they'd nosed their way into Louisiana where wide-eyed Gibb finally felt the world stop tilting and come suddenly to rest…completely, unapologetically upside-down.

Twenty hours after their fluke meet-up in the Finger Lakes, Gibb and Sam finally made it to Louisiana. Sam limped the little station wagon southbound across Lake Pontchartrain as Gibb, exhausted now, could only stare in happy disbelief at the setting sun. The longest bridge across a waterway in the world, all twenty-four miles of the Causeway, welcomed them to the Pelican state as it bumped beneath their tired wheels.

Every moment of Gibb's and Sam's lives had brought them to this here and this now: legendary New Orleans, one of the most important cities in the early history of the United States, still extraordinary and world-famous today.

*Nawlins!* That was the charming way Leo and Sam both pronounced the name of the town where they both were born. Now Sam was back home, Gibb was finally here and, for the first time in his life, he felt like a foreigner.

At this exact moment, he should have been in his high school gym accepting his well-earned diploma instead of rolling roughshod into the Crescent City, but nothing anyone could have said would have changed his adamant mind. Yes, he'd been impulsive, but as far as he was concerned, he'd made the right choice. Here is where he needed to be tonight, not there.

Taken as Gibb was by both the novelty and the significance of where he found himself at the moment, none of that really mattered right now. He still had to get to Leo. It was another hundred miles to Bache. He didn't want to ask Leo to come to New Orleans to pick him up, not when his family needed him as much as they did right now. To Gibb's amazement, Sam offered to let him take his car over to Bache by himself.

"How the hell else you gon' get over by there if he ain't comin' to get you?" Sam snorted.

"You can't *walk* no hundred miles. And your good hitchhikin' luck prob'ly done run out by now. Bring it back full and don't hit nobody."

Gibb could only muster a grateful grin as he thanked Sam, again, for his generosity.

Meandering the car through the streets of New Orleans, Gibb saw things he'd never seen before: street cars full of people bumping along a track right next to them, palm trees both lanky and squat shading the manicured front yards of huge southern mansions facing the street and, for some reason, shiny beads of every color dripping off the limbs of every tree lining this road. Too tired to react but still excited, Gibb promised himself that one day he'd come back to check it all out again.

Without a word, Sam pulled up in front of a house – no, rephrase that. Sam pulled up in front of a *mansion* and parked on the street right in front of it. Unfurling himself from the car, he stood up, extending his long, long arms into the orange sky above them as he shook his head and yawned.

"Good to be home!" he exclaimed. "I'm..."

His thought was quickly interrupted by the sound of a Hispanic man's voice.

"Hola, amigo!"

Gibb turned to see a paunchy, middle-aged man with coal-black hair calling down from the top of a ladder tilted against the second story balcony of the grand home on the other side of the fence.

"What's up, man?" Sam called back. "Y'all miss me?"

"You ain't been gone that long, man," the ladder man said with a laugh. "But your sister owe me money!"

"Man, gimme a minute to get inside and put my things away before you start hittin' me up," Sam groused. "Why you not askin' Char anyway? She not home yet?"

"Yeah, she home," Ladder Man said. "But she don't say nothing to me when she walk inside and I no wanna chase her into the house like some kind of crazy person."

"All right, man. Hold up," Sam said, resignation and fatigue in his voice. "I'll get with Char in a minute and we'll get you straight. Gimme a minute, OK?"

So, Sam lived with his sister? In this prepossessing, deceptively large three-story lemon-chiffon painted mansion with window-length black shutters flanking every window, front and side? A giant, fat palm tree in the side yard climbed high above the roofline. It had to be at least forty feet tall. The entire yard was fenced in by a deep-green hedge, but this hedge was unlike anything Gibb had ever seen back home in Eislertown. This one was framed in – top, bottom, and sides - by a wide square fence of dark-grey painted concrete. It was ritzy and classy and intimidating and, damn it, what the hell was Sam doing living in a place like this? Not once on the long ride down here did he give Gibb any indication at all that he was rich or that he lived in such a fancy home.

Except in a movie, Gibb had never seen a house like this in his life. In fact, as he stood there on the sidewalk and looked around him, he saw nothing but elaborate houses like this one, lining the entire block as far as he could see. The white-painted mansion across the street was even bigger than this one. Every yard on the block was perfectly landscaped and there were white and pink and purple blooms wrapped around every wrought-iron fence and balcony he could see. What was this?

Wasn't this New Orleans? They'd driven right past the Superdome and all these tall buildings just a little while ago. Gibb had seen a city with his own eyes. Where was it now? Where were the skyscrapers, the crowds? And what about the noise? So far, save for the occasional car creeping by and one ambulance siren, this place was almost as quiet as Eislertown. But Eislertown sure didn't have houses like this, or palm trees, or balconies, or guys on ladders painting those non-existent balconies.

Eislertown didn't have this kind of humidity, either. Gibb yawned, scratching at a trickle of sweat trying to sneak down his neck and under his T-shirt. He was so tired and for the first time he thought maybe he'd just call Leo and promise to join him in Bache in the morning. He really needed to sleep, and he was badly losing that fight.

Sam's voice jolted him.

"Boy, come inside. You fallin' asleep standin' up in the middle of this street."

Carrying his backpack, Gibb followed Sam through the heavy black wrought-iron front gate and up onto the white-columned black-painted porch, too tired now to be intimidated by the elegance of Sam's home.

"Char, where y'at?!" Sam called out. He turned around.

"Do me a favor, dude. Take off them shoes and have a seat on that sofa over there for a minute. I need to go find my sister and talk with her."

Gibb did as he was told. He slipped off his sneakers, then padded across a gorgeous braided rug to get to a soft, overstuffed blue sofa. *What an amazing place this is*, he marveled as he sat down and looked around the splendid front room. Gorgeous flower-painted pottery decorated the shelves and tabletops as vivid framed flower paintings watched over the proceedings from dark-grey and white-wainscoted walls.

"Wow!" Gibb whispered aloud. Ten seconds later, he was asleep.

## Chapter 23

# ONE ROOM OUT
# OF TWENTY-ONE

"Who's this li'l stray red dog sleepin' in my house?" Gibb heard a woman's soft voice say.

He opened his eyes to sunlight glaring through a window and with no idea where he was. His blurry eyes couldn't make out anything in the room. Instinctively, he started to fumble around for his glasses.

"They're on that high table, honey," the voice said from the doorway. "Wasn't anywhere else to put 'em. You're gonna have to sit up to reach 'em."

Gibb sat up squinting, still dressed in the same exact clothes he'd been wearing since he left Eislertown. Why was it so light in this room? What time was it?

*Holy shit! Leo!*

He had to get to Leo! Frantic, he threw on his glasses and faced the direction of the voice.

"Umm...hi," he said, trying to be polite in spite of his growing anxiety as he swung his legs off the bed.

"Hi yourself," the very attractive fifty-something woman replied kindly. "Did you sleep OK?"

"Err...yeah," Gibb replied, still trying to wake up as he regained his memory of everything that led to his sitting on this unfamiliar bed in this amazing room, stammering as he gawked at this beautiful woman.

Gibb could only guess that this was Sam's sister, Char. In his life he had never seen anyone so...so...put-together. Save for the single strand of pearls resting comfortably above her rather ample bosom, this woman was an elegant two-tone portrait in black and gold. Her head was crowned by beautiful jet-black braids spiraled into a bun at the nape of her neck. Expensive-looking glasses framed her long-lashed eyes in black and gold. A smart black business dress showed off her body without being too suggestive and look at those perfect, glossy gold-painted nails. Her shoes, shiny black flats each adorned with a little black rose over the closed toes, finished the look with quiet flair.

Roses and pearls and black and gold. Wow. Gibb took a deep breath. Something smelled like vanilla and warm cinnamon. Was that her perfume? This woman was, in a word, Fabulous. That's right, with a capital F.

"SamWell tells me you have somewhere you need to be this morning?" the woman said, her voice shaking Gibb out of his awed semi-reverie.

Ack. It *was* morning?! Oh. My. God. How did he just sleep through the night like that? He had to get down to Bache! How did he even get to the room he was in right now? He didn't remember anything after sitting on that sofa last night and now...what the hell?

Whatever, it didn't matter. He had to go! He had to get down to Bache to be with Leo! Dammit, he'd meant to call Leo as soon as they got to New Orleans and now it was the next morning. Leo was probably thinking he was never going to show up!

"Uh...yes. Ma'am," Gibb added quickly, visibly flustered. "And I'm really late. I was supposed to call last night to let him know I was in New Orleans and would be there soon and I didn't and I've gotta go another hundred miles or so down to a town called Bache. You know it? Bache?"

"I know it," the woman said, her succinct reply a stark contrast to Gibb's rambling.

Gibb, still only half-awake, continued to stare openly at those shiny gold fingernails. He never saw nails like them. He wondered if they were fake.

"They're real," the woman deadpanned, reading Gibb's face as he looked her over. Gibb was embarrassed – he hoped she knew he was looking at her nails.

"Shower down the hall that way," she said, pointing to her left, "towels in the bathroom closet. Please clean up after yourself. No maid comin' here today.

"Also, SamWell left his keys on the kitchen island downstairs and he wrote some directions how to get over by Bache," she said. "It isn't hard to get there. Highway 90 all the way to the Bache exit, then follow the signs on the back roads. You'll find it."

Gibb sat, still sort of dazed.

"Well, whatcha lookin' at?" the beautiful woman prodded. "Get going!"

"What is your name?" Gibb said, completely fascinated and wanting to know more about her.

"My name is Char," she said. "Short for Charlotte, but don't ever call me Charlotte or I'll have to break one of your legs off. Good luck today," she said, turning on her flat heel to leave.

"Wait…uh…Char," Gibb stammered. "Where is Sam?"

"Sleeping," she said. "He always sleeps till noon or so. Musician's hours, you know."

Gibb nodded. "Yeah, he mentioned that on the ride. Can I ask you one more question?"

"Don't you need to get moving?" she replied, looking puzzled behind her stylish glasses.

"Well…" Gibb stammered. "I'm a little blown away right now. This place you live in is unbelievable. I've never met you before in my life and still, you're letting me crash in your beautiful home and letting me take a shower here and Sam's letting me borrow his car. Why is everyone being so nice to me? It's… well, I don't know…it's like…how can I even thank you?"

Char smiled.

"SamWell says you're all right, so I'll take him at his word. That's about all I've got to say about it. And I've got to go now," she said sweetly.

"Well…thank you a million times over," Gibb said, meek but sincere.

"You're welcome," she said kindly, but dryly. "Safe travels."

Gibb hurried down the hallway, barely noticing the handsome hardwood floors and the beautifully framed artwork marching down its walls. A quick shower, an apprehensive glance in the mirror and a toweled dash back down the hall to find his backpack and his one change of clothes. He was going to see Leo today. HE WAS GOING TO SEE LEO TODAY!!

After a shower and a full night's rest, he felt great and he was more than ready for the most spectacular reunion of his entire life. He hoped he didn't crash Sam's car in his rush to get down to Bache.

Without any warning, he began to tear up a little. Not from sadness, just from relief and happiness mixed in with a lot of anxiety. For a moment he thought about death and the afterlife. People who believed in Heaven always talked about looking forward to seeing their departed relatives and friends when they died and went there. This reunion with Leo was going to be as intense as that, he thought.

He would be there in less than two hours. He wiped his eyes on the sleeves of his T-shirt and, grabbing his backpack, he rushed down the hall again. Running down the gorgeous spiraled steps of the staircase like a sprinter, he blasted into the kitchen a second after his feet hit the floor of the great living room.

He stopped in front of the phone. For a second he was intimidated, knowing what would happen if Leo's mom picked up the phone. He dialed the number anyway. His heart raced in the dead quiet kitchen as he waited for it to ring. Suddenly…a busy signal. A loud one, too. Ugh.

*Why were they so loud sometimes?* Should he wait a minute to call back and then get going or should he just go now?

Noticing Sam and Char's phone number on the white label centered in the phone dial, Gibb looked around for a pen and paper to write it down, just in case. He hung up the phone and scanned the expansive kitchen, unbelievably bigger, by far, than their whole living room back home in Eislertown.

Aha, there they were – Sam's keys and the directions to Bache on the kitchen island. And look at that, Sam had already written their phone number on the paper.

*Imagine having a kitchen big enough for something like this,* Gibb thought. *An island. Who has an island in their kitchen? Not a single person in Eislertown, that's for sure.*

One more minute. He'd wait one more minute and then call. If it was still busy…well, at least he could say he tried. He'd explain it all to Leo when he got there.

*"One thousand one…one thousand two…one thousand three,"* he counted urgently to himself. When he got to sixty, he grabbed the receiver off the hook, dialed again, and held his breath.

Still busy.

OK, forget it, he had to get going. Hanging up the phone he looked around the kitchen once more and….wait, what was this? A still-warm strawberry muffin sitting alongside a little handwritten note.

*Lagniappe.* That's all the note said.

Gibb paused for a second just to stare at the word, and then he remembered. Lagniappe. Pronounced Lan-YAP. Sam had explained the concept on the way down here. In New Orleans, lagniappe meant "a little something extra". Just something - a little gift, a little after-dinner drink or dessert - to send a person off knowing they were cared for. Above and beyond. And that's exactly what this was. It was more than a muffin – it was an incredibly thoughtful gesture to make towards a stranger who didn't know anyone or even how to find his way around. Incredible.

Again, Gibb had to shake his head and wonder why these people would just take in a nobody like him and be so awesome to him. His eyes were still a little blurry from the tears upstairs, so he didn't want to get all cry-eyed again.

Instead, he just whispered a quiet *"Thank You"* in the kitchen, grabbed the muffin and the keys and he was off.

*Chapter 24*

# HELP ON THE WAY

Gibb only did ten over the speed limit on the way down to Bache, way too slow, but he didn't want to risk being pulled over. He didn't want any more delays. The anticipation of finally seeing Leo was getting painful now. Annoying too, like being stabbed intermittently by hundreds of tiny thumbtacks all over his body. Frustrated, he told himself to just calm down. No matter how far away Bache seemed, he was almost there.

Almost two hours later, there it was: the green and white exit sign for Bache pointing the way from Interstate 90. *Now* it was getting real. Seeing the name of Leo's town on that sign was all Gibb needed to brighten his mood. Gibb hoped Leo was as stoked for this reunion as he was.

Even though Leo had described the bayou perfectly – brackish water, blue sky, green rushes, purple and white flowers floating all over the water, Gibb had never known what *bayou* really even meant until he saw it now for himself. Beautiful for sure. Right now, though, all he wanted was to find St. Denis Street. Once he got there, maybe Leo would show him around and tell him what all these amazing trees and plants were.

Gibb slowed down so he could read the street signs. It seemed they were all named after saints. St. Mary, St. Genevieve. St. David, St. Paul. Where was…hold it…was that it…yep…there it was. St. Denis. *ST. DENIS!*

His heartbeat quickened as he slowly turned the car onto Leo's street. Two blocks to the dead end and he was there. Gibb sat still for a moment to breathe a sigh of relief and to just take the place in, although sitting in the car out in this heat was abominable.

Through the open window, the ungodly humidity frizzed his hair and made his head itch, like a couple of mosquitoes had buzzed their way right down to his scalp. Just in case, he swatted each side of his head before taking off his glasses to attack the annoying drop of sweat trickling down the left lens. It was like this all the time down here? Poor Leo. Poor everyone who lived around here.

He perched his glasses back on his face and blinked. Only two things mattered now: he was here and there it was. 212 St. Denis Street in Bache, Louisiana. Leo's childhood home. And it was not at all as he'd imagined it.

An expansive grey-painted covered porch hugged the house front, its refreshing shade and cozy furniture offering visitors a place to make themselves at home for a while. The pine-green shutters framing the eight-foot-tall front windows offered the illusion that this house, gleaming white in the sun, was much bigger than it actually was. Size notwithstanding, "the ol' home place", as Leo had called it, looked more like something out of a Civil War movie than the ramshackle farmhouse Gibb had somehow gotten used to imagining from Leo's tales of his Louisiana travails.

There were no trees to speak of in the front yard, allowing the June southern sun to beat a merciless assault on anyone who lingered there at mid-day. But Gibb couldn't help himself. He had to stand there and just appreciate what he was seeing. This was where Leo grew up. This was the place where it all began, where his parents had brought him to live before he'd even turned two years old. This was where the promise of his young life had really started.

This is where Leo had begun to become himself, to establish his strongly held positions that so often ran counter to the accepted norms of this town, this state, the entire country, really. His belief that queer people were just as good as anyone else. The belief that being gay was a gift from God, not a sin to incur the wrath of the Rougarou, the legendary bayou-dwelling werewolf that would hunt down and kill bad Catholics.

This was where Leo's dream of embracing his differentness began, the starting point of a brave journey once he realized that, around here at least, he would have to go through life as nothing more than a misunderstood oddity. How Gibb could relate. Standing here in this front yard and imagining Leo's childhood and youth, Gibb felt an even stronger connection to him.

At a fundamental level, their experiences had been so similar, despite the obvious regional and cultural differences they'd encountered on the way to this moment. Leo somehow *got* it earlier than Gibb did, though. And it was because of Leo - his wise perspective, his gentle demeanor, his patient understanding and his love - that Gibb began to see for himself a life of pride and openness about who he was. A queer person in America in the 1980's. The future wasn't bleak at all. Not with Leo in it. Well, just as long as Leo didn't disappear every time he got in a mood.

As Gibb stood there, though, he began to wonder if Leo was even home. The house looked quiet. Lifeless. A sweltering breeze danced quietly across a front yard badly in need of mowing. There wasn't a single car in the driveway.

He took another deep breath and, feeling a little dizzy and more than a little out of place, Gibb made his way towards the front porch. His mind began racing with each plodding step.

*I promised Leo I'd be there for him, but does he really want me to be now? Did I take too long? Why did I have to fall asleep in New Orleans last night? What if Leo's mom freaks out and throws me off their porch? What if I made this trip and it was all a big waste of time? I still don't know how the hell I'm gonna get home. I feel like an idiot.*

Up the steps and across the shady grey porch he went, his steps sounding extraordinarily loud to his own ears.

*Oh my God, yes this was stupid. I am an idiot. I shouldn't be here. This is too weird.*

He took a deep breath.

*OK, stop it. Leo asked you to come down here.*

He knocked, feeling foolish, the redness in his face only partially caused by the heat and humidity. He listened for footsteps. Nothing. The twitter of a couple of birds. The hum of a truck engine on the street behind him.

He knocked again, louder this time. This time, he heard a faint female voice.

"Hold on, hold on! I'm comin'!" came a soft shout from inside the house as the woman neared the door. He saw movement, a big shadow, through the window.

*Uh-oh. Mrs. Davion?*

Hopefully not. With his bashful heart pounding and his mouth too dry to even swallow, Gibb unconsciously crossed his fingers as he wished for Sissie, Leo's younger sister, to be the one to come to the door. He shook his head, still not believing that he was actually standing on the front porch of some house in friggin' *LOUISIANA*, out of his mind, stupider than he'd ever been in his life. In love. For love.

The door opened a crack. Gibb didn't recognize the big brown eye, because that was all he could see, of the woman peering at him through the small opening.

"May I hep you?" she asked sweetly. Her drawl seemed to eliminate a consonant and somehow the word "you" sounded so long she may have added a syllable.

"Umm...hello," Gibb stammered. Then he coughed. And coughed again. Suddenly, he erupted into an all-out, bent-over coughing fit on Leo's porch, right in front of this complete stranger. His face was red and his eyes watered as he tried to stop coughing, making the situation even worse.

Meanwhile, the woman, who turned out to be much taller, stouter, and louder than Gibb could have imagined, decided to throw open the door and suddenly start pounding on his back, shouting things like "Lord have mercy!" and "You gon' be awright, boy. Stand up! Stand up straight!"

Gibb complied, completely mortified and wishing she'd calm down and lower her voice.

*What is happening right now?* He only wished a TV camera had been there to catch the whole scene. What a freak show. He didn't know whether to laugh or bolt for the car. But the look of concern and curiosity on the woman's face kept his feet right there on the porch.

Slowly regaining his composure and his breath, Gibb smiled at the woman and tried not to laugh about their train wreck of an introduction.

"I'm so sorry about that," he said. "Dry mouth."

The wide-eyed, large and hyper stranger looked at him with concern.

"I'm jus' glad you're awright. I thought you come here 'cuz you was chok-ing to death or somethin'. God knows you put me in a state!"

"I really apologize…umm…ma'am. I'm actually here to see Leo," Gibb stated matter-of-factly. "I've come all the way down from New York to meet up with him."

"You come all the way from New York to see Leo?" she asked, surprised. A second later the woman's face registered recognition.

"Wait a minute, are you Gibb?" she asked, her voice dropping to a con-spiratorial whisper.

Gibb, suddenly ill-at-ease, cocked his head and stared at the woman from the corner of his eye. Mouth half-open, he could only nod. Finally, he found his voice.

"Yes. I'm Gibb. Is everything OK?"

"Child, come inside where I got the air on," the large woman said, turning on her heel and marching into the house. Gibb followed her inside into dim-lit air-conditioned relief.

"After all that, you're gonna need somethin' to drink? You want some sweet tea?" she called over her shoulder.

"Water would be great, thank you."

While he waited, Gibb looked around the living room. He didn't know what he expected, but it was clear the Davions hadn't done much to unpack after their move back to Bache. There were boxes everywhere, empty picture hooks on grey-and-pink flower-papered walls, the living room furniture, and not much else.

The woman came back with a tall glass of cold water. Handing it to Gibb, she smiled and pointed him towards the couch. Once Gibb sat, the woman started speaking.

"I'm so sorry I haven't properly introduced myself. I'm Honey. I'm Leo's grandmother."

"Ohh, wow! It's really nice to meet you!" Gibb exclaimed. "Leo has told me a lot about you. He told me that even he calls you Honey."

"He does," she said, smiling. "Ever'body calls me Honey. But then I call ever'body honey, too. So, I guess that makes us even. Honey."

She laughed and swatted Gibb on the leg.

Leo loved Honey. Gibb could see why – she seemed like such a nice, genuine person and he'd only known her for five minutes. Gibb stifled a chuckle as he sat there. Honey had no idea how hard he and Leo had laughed at the idea of her chasing Mrs. Davion with a frying pan at their fictional wedding reception. It was great to put a face with a name. Now that he was seeing Honey, he could understand why Leo was laughing so hard. She *was* a big, handsome woman.

The room grew quiet as Honey's face became quite serious again.

"Now you know Mr. Davion had been very sick, right?" she said to Gibb.

"I do know," Gibb said. "Leo called me a couple of days ago to tell me Mr. Davion died last week."

"Yes, Mr. Davion did pass. I hate that it happened but at least he ain't sufferin' no more. He was *so* sick, bless his heart, there really wasn't nothin' them doctors in Atlanta or anywhere else could do for him. I don't believe Leo really knew how bad off his Daddy was when they was fixin' to come back down here."

Gibb fought back tears. Why hadn't Leo called him sooner? He would've been here as fast as he could get here. Just like he was doing now.

"I'm so sorry," Gibb whispered hoarsely, flustered he didn't have anything more insightful to say. He paused to wipe his eyes.

"How is Leo handling it?"

Honey grimaced and shook her head.

"He went all to pieces. He was strong for his mama and Sissie for a while, but…well, his mama is my daughter and I love her dearly, but…"

Gibb could imagine where Honey was going with this, but he didn't want to pry.

Honey hesitated for a second before simply telling Gibb, "Anyway, Mrs. Davion is where she needs to be right now, gettin' some rest over in Morgan City. She's been through it these past few months and she just couldn't take no more."

Gibb nodded his understanding.

"It's good she's getting help, right?" he asked.

"It's *great* that she's gettin' help!" Honey declared. "But I don't know, the stress of all of it...well..."

Honey hesitated, an odd look on her face. Gibb stared at her quizzically.

"What?" he half-demanded of Leo's grandmother, a person he'd just met.

"Well, this is the hard part," Honey said quietly. "I hate to have to tell you this, but the day his Mama went into the hospital, Leo run off somewhere. And baby, I don't know where in this world he is."

Gibb almost rolled his eyes as Honey broke the bad news to him.

*Of course he ran off,* Gibb thought. *And now no one knows where he is. Perfect.*

"He didn't tell nobody where he was goin' and he ain't called us to tell us where he is. I'm all tore up about it. I was hopin' that maybe he got a wild hair and drove back up north. To see you," Honey said, looking Gibb straight in the eye.

"Me?" Gibb asked innocently, his face reddening. "Why would he go all that way to see me, especially with everything that's going on here?"

Honey pursed her lips for a second, her mouth crooked in doubt at Gibb's disingenuousness.

"Give me your hand, son," she commanded. Gibb slowly complied. Honey's hand was rough-skinned, but her touch was gentle. She gave Gibb a comfortable smile.

"Now, I know a question ain't an answer, but I'll ask it anyway and then maybe you'll get the answer to the question *you* just asked, OK?" she said, nodding her head to get Gibb to assent. He nodded back, slightly confused.

"So why would *you* show up here in that junk heap in the driveway, all the way from way up north?" she asked, her dark eyes boring into Gibb's. "Maybe you was jus' passin' by the bayou on your way to California or somethin'?

Gibb looked down, mortified. Honey squeezed his hand and then reached over and took the other one, rubbing her palms against his as she spoke.

"Look, baby. I know about y'all. I know about y'all the way Leo's Mama knows about y'all. His daddy knew too, but he never said nothin' because he never said nothin' about nobody, least of all his own son. And I think Sissie knows, too, even though we ain't never talked about it."

Gibb couldn't bear to look up and back into Honey's kind, steely eyes. He swallowed hard, trying to distract himself by mentally counting the number of rings in the oval braided rug on the floor of the now-chilly living room. That air conditioner was working hard. He shivered a little bit as Honey continued.

"Son, look at me." Gibb looked up. Honey's unsmiling face was resolute as she squeezed Gibb's hands again.

"You don't need to be ashamed, hear? Let me tell you somethin' about Leo. That boy has been on an island all by himself his whole life. He was always on his own, over yonder somewhere, no matter where he was. Every situation he found himself in, he just could not fit in. *Could* not, not *would* not. There's a big difference between them two words. He *wanted* to be liked and accepted, but he was always just different. Gentle. Quiet. Sweet, too! I'm sure you seen them qualities in him.

"He became an easy target for the boys around here. He was always gettin' his feelin's hurt or gettin' pushed around and beat up and stuff. He wasn't no fighter, put it that way, so he did whatever he could to hide himself away from having to deal with it. But, beautiful as he is, well, that didn't work so good neither. The way he stands out just by *standin'* there," Honey said, her voice a blend of sadness and grandmotherly pride.

"I know you seen it. Hell, ev'ry girl in Loozeanna just about loses her mind when they see him. But you know he just don't *like* that kind of attention. He never did, from the time he was a young'un."

Gibb nodded his head in agreement. That was the Leo he knew. Honey frowned and shook her head.

"The attention made him miserable because he knew there wasn't nothin' he could do about it. About them girls. About anything like that. 'Cuz he was wired different. And around here, that don't sit well. Some folks worry 'bout whether you're right with the Lord and talk about Hell and the Rougarou comin' to getcha and all that stuff.

"Others want you to be just a regular guy. 'Just fit in, why don't ya?' Leo also seemed to get a lot of unwanted attention from boys who wanted him to act like he was one of them. But how could he? He was who he was, and he is who he is today. Nothin' they said or did changed him. Because nothin' could, nothin' *can* change him. Just *bein'* him made him a target. It sure did."

Gibb swallowed hard, a little awestruck that Leo's sixty-something southern grandmother could acknowledge, without naming it, that her grandson was stuck with his sexuality. It seemed like she was accepting that he didn't choose it, the way so many people seemed to think.

"So, you've known about Leo for a long time, then?"

"Oh, baby. Yes, I did. Between you an' me, I know Leo don't like girls in the regular sense of the word and that was plain from the time he was a child. Don't get me wrong now…he *loves* girls. As friends. He had lots of girl *friends,*" Honey said, making quotation marks again, "not *girlfriends.* You know what I mean.

"When Leo was about eleven, their cousin Wanda was over and Sissie and her played dress-up. They come up an' ask Leo to play with 'em. They put make-up and lipstick on him, a wig, high heels. Leo was grinnin' like a possum eatin' a sweet tater the whole time. He wore that make-up on his face the whole day and didn't care who said what. He always liked playing with his trucks and he loved cars and things a boy usually likes, too, but there was somethin' about how comfortable he was doin' 'girl stuff' that made us all think…yeah, that boy's a little sweet."

"And we wasn't wrong. But Leo grew tall and so handsome. The girls loved him. His Mama ripped the phone out of the wall one time because them girls wouldn't stop callin' the house lookin' for Leo."

"Leo told me that story," Gibb said. "He told me he couldn't blame her."

"Yeah, it was messy. I don't know what else to say. The boy was a square peg, the girls loved him, and folks 'round here seemed to want to round him out, make him fit. It didn't work. That's why I just want to tell *you* that when Leo come back from up north a couple months ago, it was the first time I seen him so happy. Even though his Daddy was so sick, he was at least happy because he'd found himself a special friend. You."

Honey's words made Gibb emotional again and he looked back down at the floor. Honey went on to explain that throughout his life, she and Leo had

had a special bond. Not only because he was her first grandchild or because he needed her more than ever as Mrs. Davion's mental health unraveled. She just knew there was something "queer" about such a gentle boy and she felt extra-protective of him.

"And so, baby, that's why I think Leo disappeared." Honey sounded weary as she began speaking in a half-whisper. "He jus' got so tired of fightin'. He felt like the whole world was against him and he took off. He loved his Daddy and losin' him so young is terrible. His Mama's troubles. Havin' to leave you up north to come back down here. Dealin' with the stress of his Daddy's cancer treatment and then havin' to graduate high school with his tormentors. All of it."

Her voice broke.

"He don't deserve all of this foolishness. I pray the dear Lord is takin' care of him, wherever he is."

She rubbed her eyes and looked at Gibb.

"Child, I am scared out of my damn mind right now. I ain't got the faintest idea where my Leo is, where he's goin', or how he's gettin' there. All I know is I love him and I want him home. Right now!"

Gibb held Honey's hands as she finally broke down. The sofa shook as she sobbed. Gibb could only trace the pattern of the sofa fabric with his eyes, trying to detach himself from the emotional scene confronting him.

He'd come to Bache for a joyous reunion with Leo. Now he had no idea where, when, or – the thought was almost too much to consider – *if* it would ever happen.

*Chapter 25*

# SALTY MAGNOLIA

G ibb had no idea how or where to even begin searching for Leo, but he had to try to reassure Honey, and himself, that everything was going to be OK. Whenever Leo disappeared he always showed up again, didn't he?

"Y'know…ma'am…" Gibb said awkwardly, still not comfortable calling Honey by name, "I never even asked. Where's Sissie?"

Last summer, Sissie had gotten a summer job at Little Dan's Grocery right on the corner of Main and Caffery in Bache's brick-faced and tidy downtown. When she got back to Bache they hired her back right away.

Gibb had passed right by that little storefront on the way here to Leo's house, remembering it distinctly from a couple of letters missing from the sign on the building's weather-beaten face. To passersby, it appeared that Little Dan was telling them to G-OC-R-Y. He'd snickered at it as he drove past. It wasn't so funny now. He was so frustrated with Leo, crying was exactly what he felt like doing.

*He called me and practically begged me to come down here. And now he's gone. Again!*

"I'm just wondering if Leo talked to Sissie about anything before he took off. Maybe she has *some* clue where he might be headed."

Gibb was more thinking out loud than conversing with Honey at this point.

"No, baby. Sissie don't know nothin' about where he's at. She's as tore up about it as me."

They just stood there and looked at each other for a moment in silence. Gibb grimaced and scratched his head. Honey cracked her knuckles with an unintentionally loud pop, breaking the tension in the room. For a quick second, each of them smiled.

"If it's OK with you, Honey," Gibb said, finally using her name but still feeling weird about it, "I still want to go over to see Sissie and talk to her."

"Go, child, go!" she urged, waving her hands towards the front door. "Y'all two can put your heads together. Go on and find Sissie."

As he hurried out, Gibb suddenly realized he was really excited to see Sissie. She was loud and funny, a big personality to go with that big hair and big body. Sissie loved Leo so much and every time Gibb had met her, she'd always treated him great, too. She was a good person.

Gibb broke into a run, arriving breathless and sweaty at Little Dan's door just in time to see the back of Sissie's pony-tailed head moving towards a beaten-up old door marked with a fading "Employees Only" sticker.

"Sissie!"

No response. He'd have to yell louder before she got to that door.

"Tara Lynn Davion!"

He saw Sissie stop, then slowly turn around as he moved closer to the deli counter. As her mind slowly registered who she was seeing, Sissie's eyes grew wide. She slapped her palms to her cheeks and just...screamed. Gibb stopped in his tracks, mortified, looking around to see if anyone else was in the store.

"Oh, my Lord!" she shouted. "It's Gibbon Mulcahy!"

Next thing Gibb knew, there were bags of chip snacks scattered all over the floor and his back kind of hurt. A powerful leap and then a hug from Sissie had set them both off balance and careening backward into an endcap, sending the bags flying and Gibb's back and behind smarting. They couldn't stop laughing.

"Gibb! My lands, boy, what on God's Earth are you doin' in Bache?!"

She suddenly stopped.

"Oh my God, you found Leo! You found him! Please tell me you've found him!"

He pulled out of Sissie's embrace and put his hands on her shoulders, moving her back so he could look her in the eyes when he was talking to her.

"First of all, hello. Second of all, no, I didn't find Leo and I don't know where he is. I only just found out what happened. Honey told me when I went to your house."

"Oh Gibb, it's terrible. I keep tellin' myself he's all right, but now I'm really scared because he just up and left and we haven't heard from him at all. I was hopin' maybe he somehow got himself back up north to see you after all this insanity down here! But now you're down here and you don't know about what's goin' on with him, either. That just crushes me inside 'cuz now I know he didn't go up north! Oh Lord, Gibb. Now I'm really scared."

Gibb nodded and looked Sissie reassuringly in the eye.

"We're gonna find him, Sissie. We have to. He's too important to us not to."

"Oh Gibb, my God, I'm so happy you're here. You don't have any idea! I just believe you're gonna save the day!"

Her eyes welled up with tears as she reached out to hug Gibb again.

"Well…thanks. I'm happy to see you, too," Gibb stammered, awkwardly returning her hug. He felt unworthy of her confidence, afraid he would let her down no matter how hard he knew he was going to work to find Leo.

He dropped his voice as the bell attached to the front door rang the announcement of other customers entering the snug but orderly little market.

"And I'm very sorry to hear about your dad."

"Hey y'all," Sissie smiled as she called over Gibb's shoulder to the young man and woman who had just come into the store. "Let me know if I can help y'all find anything, OK?"

With Gibb's body blocking the customers' view, Sissie's face instantly grew serious and her eyes grew teary again as she whispered, "Oh Gibb, you just don't know! I'm mixed between being sad, scared as hell, and now so pissed off at Leo all at the same time. Why does life have to be so insane all the time?

"We lost Daddy so quick and I never expected that. I knew it was bad, but I thought he had a lot more time. It hurt like hell to lose him, but he was in so much pain there at the end that Leo and I were feeling it along with him. It was excruciating. I don't believe that I'll ever recover from it. I truly don't.

"Then Mama. I don't mean this ugly, but she has always been crazy as a damn moonbat and she'd been barely hangin' on for the past few months. I'm so glad she agreed to go into the hospital for a while. Truth be told, Honey was about ready to snatch her bald. And," Sissie looked to the sky and made praying hands, "God forgive me, I'd been thinkin' the same thing. My own mother!"

Furiously wiping away two tears of frustration rolling down her cheeks, Sissie couldn't stop herself from apologizing.

"I'm so sorry, Gibb. Sorry about this, you havin' all this dumped on you. And I'm sorry I've felt so ugly towards Mama. Lord knows we all try. But, bless her heart, she should be OK for a while. Me and Honey try to get over to Morgan City to see her every day."

"Does she know about Leo?" Gibb asked.

"We haven't told her about Leo. I don't know how we could. I honestly can't believe him! He disappears! Just disappears, like some kind of terrible magic. 'Now you see him, now you don't'," Sissie said, irritated, imitating a sideshow announcer.

"Don't I know it?" Gibb said in solidarity, shaking his head defeatedly.

Sissie stepped back behind the counter to ring up the young couple, the only customers who'd come in since he arrived. Once they left, they were free to talk aloud again.

"Did you guys file a missing person's report with the police?" Leo asked.

"Not yet, but we tried. They say after someone's been gone for three days you can do that, so we have to wait until tomorrow. But you know what? Even when we do, no one's gonna do anything. He run off like that on his own. He's eighteen, goin' on nineteen years old, a grown man, and it wasn't like he committed some crime. They ain't gonna look for him no matter what they say.

"We go see the fat-ass sheriff with his big ass hat and this fat-ass cigar and all he kept askin' me, in the most deepest, annoying, country-ass voice, 'Now ma'am, do *you* suspect *foul play?*'

"I wanted to ask him, 'Who are you, Boss Hogg?!,'" she grumbled angrily. "This ain't the Dukes o' Hazzard and I ain't Daisy May! Find my brother, you fat son of a bitch! That's what you need to be doin'! I wanted to jerk a knot in *his* fat tail, too. Dumb as a bag of hammers, he was. It was really like we were on some damn TV show! I ain't lyin!"

Gibb burst out laughing, making Sissie giggle in spite of herself. She was hilarious when she was exasperated, but the gravity of the situation quickly brought both of them back down to their fear and uncertainty about what to do next. Gibb rubbed his hands down and around his face, as he always did when he was nervous. For a long few seconds, just like when he was with Honey, he and Sissie could only stand and stare at each other in silence, completely out of words.

Gibb finally spoke.

"Look, I know you're working, and people are going to be coming in and out of the store all day, but rack your brain. You know Leo better than anybody. If he didn't go back up to New York, where else do you think he'd go? *Any* ideas, no matter how crazy, let's just throw them out there and see. Like, don't you guys have an uncle in Atlanta?"

"We do," Sissie nodded, "Cecil. And his wife Penny. And that's a good idea because they have always been good to Leo. But we called 'em to check, and he ain't there. If he shows up there they promised to call us. They're real concerned, too."

Sissie grimaced and shook her head, her blonde ponytail tickling her shoulder blades.

"Gibb, look. Once Leo run off, you were the first person I thought of. I didn't know how to get ahold of you, though. There's no listing for a Mulcahy up there in Eislertown. Trust me, I called Directory Assistance three different times and talked to the same lady. I know she must have thought I was crazy. And I didn't know your house address to write to you. I know Leo prob'ly has all that, but that don't help us none if the guy with the info is the guy we're searching for. So Cecil and Penny were the next best choice. He wasn't there. Other than that, I don't have a clue. Maybe New Orleans, but he don't really know anybody over there."

She took a deep breath and sighed.

"Can you think of somewhere?"

"I was trying to come up with something on my walk over here from your house, but I just can't think of anything right now," Gibb muttered, frustrated.

"Where are you staying, baby?" Sissie asked, her tone both curious and incredulous. "I seriously cannot believe that you are all the way down here in Bache," she said, shaking her head and squeezing his shoulder to make sure he really was standing there.

"I stayed in New Orleans last night," Gibb replied, "but I don't know where I'm staying tonight. That's a whole 'nother story and not important now."

"Where in New Orleans?" Sissie wanted to know.

"In the most beautiful house I've ever seen," he said. "It's on Edward Street – I only know that because I saw the street sign when I was leaving to drive down here today. It's beyond amazing - there's all these mansions and palm trees and flowers and big fat trees."

"Ohh, you're in the Garden District," Sissie said excitedly. "That's what that neighborhood is called, you know. It's the most beautiful neighborhood in New Orleans, to me anyway. You know Honey lives there, right?"

"What?!" Gibb exclaimed.

"Born and raised," Sissie replied. "Mama too. And Leo too, for a little while, because when he was first born, they lived with Honey. But he prob'ly told you all that. Wait…" Sissie looked confused all of a sudden.

"How on God's Earth did you end up in the Garden District of all places?"

Wide-eyed, Sissie listened to Gibb relay the story of the wild way he met up with Sam, and then Char this morning, their kindness, Sam's humor, Char's stylish beauty.

"That is the craziest story, Gibb," Sissie said once Gibb finished talking. "Wonder if Honey knows the folks you're staying with. You should ask her."

"Wouldn't that be weird?" Gibb asked, almost a statement rather than a question. "Wait, do you think Leo would have gone there to her house for some reason?"

"To Honey's house?" she asked, surprised. "Nah. Well, I mean, maybe. But I really doubt it. Isabelle is there – she's Honey's housemate. She'd-a called Honey right away."

"OK, well, I just figure that anything's possible at this point. So, you and Leo have *never* had a conversation that would make you think he'd head out to a specific location?" Gibb clarified.

Sissie got quiet, first looking at Gibb, then staring at the ground. Gibb had to ask.

"Sissie, why was Eislertown the first place you thought Leo would go? It's almost 1,500 miles away."

Sissie wiggled her index finger along the bridge of her nose and then along the corner of her eye, like she was trying to catch a tear before it fell. She looked up and she definitely had tears in her eyes.

"Not Eislertown, Gibb," she whispered. "You. I thought he was runnin' back to *you*. Look, baby, I know a lot of stuff about Leo, OK? And because of that I'm real protective, 'specially if I think someone's out to hurt him. And I know you would never hurt him. That's why he loves you so much. No, let me re-word that. That's why he's *in* love with you so much. He *finally* found his other half, and he couldn't even believe it. He told me those exact words just before we lost Daddy but, tell ya the truth, I already knew the whole deal."

"So…you're OK with it?" Gibb asked, not quite sure how Sissie took that news.

"*OK* with it?!" Sissie exclaimed. "I *love* it! I am *thrilled* Leo found you. And the idea you come down here to be with him like that…oh my Lord… I'm gonna cry. Gibb, I don't wanna cry again."

"You can cry if you want," Gibb replied. "I've been crying or feeling like crying all day."

Sissie gave Gibb a tearful smile. Suddenly the store phone rang, slightly startling both of them. Sissie rolled her eyes and frowned.

"There's Leo now, callin' us to tell us everything's OK. Hold that thought!" she said, holding holding up her hands with fingers crossed on both of them. She picked up the phone.

"Good afternoon, Little Dan's Grocery," Sissie said sweetly, her back to Gibb.

As Gibb heard the caller's tinny voice squawking unintelligibly from the receiver, Sissie turned to face him as she spoke into the phone.

"Do what now?" she said impatiently into the phone. "Slow down! I didn't hear a word you said."

The voice began again. Gibb could tell now that the caller was unmistakably female. Sissie's eyes grew wide as she listened, looking Gibb in the eye the whole time.

"Where?!"

She put her hand over the receiver and whispered to Gibb, "They found him!"

"Yes!" Gibb whispered back, clenching his fist.

Suddenly, Sissie burst into tears, crying as she listened further.

"What?! Oh my God!"

"What?!" Gibb whispered urgently. "What?!"

Sissie turned away, ear pressed to the phone.

"Oh my God!" she exclaimed again. "Who the hell *is* she? And where was this exactly?"

Sissie's voice was blurry with tears. As the dire voice squawked even louder over the phone, Gibb was only able to make out one word.

*Dead.*

# Chapter 26

# STAND ON IT

Gibb's head hurt. His eyes, swollen with tears and tight with frustration, had trouble staying fixed on the road in front of them. With Sissie crying softly in the passenger seat of Sam's station wagon, they were speeding east on Interstate 90, following closely behind Honey on the way back to New Orleans.

"All I wanna know is how it happened," Sissie kept repeating over and over again. "And who the hell was the girl or the woman who was with him?"

The call Sissie received at Little Dan's might as well have been a cannonball shot right through the front window of the store. The explosive news it brought had the potential to wreck all of their lives.

It had been Honey on the phone. The Louisiana State Police, acting on a tip from a passing motorist, had found Leo's overturned 1974 Ford Maverick car deep in the wood line off State Highway 70. A few more feet to the right and the cab of the car would have been submerged right in the dark blue-brown waters of Lake Poularde over near Morgan City. Two people were found inside: Leo, badly injured and unconscious, but still alive. The other person was female, her age and identity unknown at the moment. She was dead and had been for more than a whole day.

Leo's injuries were too severe for the local hospitals to deal with – he was rushed to the trauma center at University Medical Center in New Orleans where they were being recklessly led by Honey right now at speeds of eighty to eighty-five miles per hour. Honey had the right idea. If she hadn't floored her own accelerator, Gibb would have whipped past her and done it himself. Sissie could navigate.

They'd rushed out of Little Dan's after a flurry of activity – Gibb frantically turning off lights, pulling shades, turning the sign to "Closed" as Sissie frantically wrote a note to "Little" Dan, the store's owner, about what had happened. She'd tried to call his house but no one answered.

"He ain't gonna fire me," she wheezed as they ran the seven blocks back to her house. "If he does, tough shit."

By the time they'd run the short seven-block distance back, Sissie was crying more from exertion than emotion. There wasn't a second to rest, though. Honey had backed her car out of the garage and was out in the front yard hollering and gesticulating at them to hurry up and get in the second she saw them.

"I am gonna beat her ass!" Sissie gasped as they crossed into the yard. She bent over and put her hands on both of her knees, breathing hard. Honey wasn't having it.

"Tara Lynn, get your tail in this car!"

"I'm goin' with Gibb!" she hollered breathlessly, shaking her fist at Honey as she climbed into the passenger seat of Sam's station wagon. They backed out of the driveway, waited for Honey to back out in front of them, then tore off behind her to race through the sleepy streets of Bache and out to the interstate.

Sissie rubbed her eyes as her breathing returned to normal.

"I'm sorry, Gibb. I'm so freaked out right now. And that woman drives me insane. As if we weren't movin' fast enough! She always feels like if she just yells and hollers enough she'll get everyone and everything under control. Like her yellin' could really make this big body move faster. We know how urgent this is, dang it, Honey!"

She looked at Gibb through raccoon mascara-smeared eyes, her hair disheveled and face streaked with tears, then turned the rearview mirror to look at herself.

"Good God!" she gasped. "I look like the loser of the $1.98 Beauty Pageant. You ever see that show? Where the winner gets the crown with the missing point and a whole bouquet of carrots? That's me right this minute. Shit, they'd give me a bouquet of dead rats with hair like this."

Automatically, she reached into her purse for a brush, looked at it for a second, then just threw it back in her purse and started sobbing.

"Oh my God, who cares if I look like hell in the middle of all this? What the hell is going on right now, Gibb?! I swear if Leo dies I'm not gonna be able to go on. I'm serious, I won't be able to take it. I can't stop squallin' as it is!"

"He's not gonna die!" Gibb said, as much to reassure himself as Sissie. "Just keep telling yourself that. He's gonna make it."

Gibb felt like he was in a car chase movie as he tailed Honey speeding along the interstate. He had never driven like this before, but his fear, frustration, and his downright anger kept his adrenaline pumping and his foot heavy as he motored around the slower cars on the road. He glanced over at Sissie and scowled.

"You know why he's gonna make it? Because he needs to hear how freakin' pissed off I am right now! What the hell does he mean by disappearing like that and putting us through this?!"

Sissie's eyes grew wide, but she nodded her head in agreement.

"Hell yeah! That's exactly right. I'm scared as hell but I'm pissed, too! And I need to know..." she said again before raising her voice in a holler, "WHO THE HELL WAS THE WOMAN??!!"

Gibb could only wonder himself. He'd never imagined this scenario, recklessly chasing his boyfriend's grandmother across southern Louisiana in an almost-stranger's car as his boyfriend's sister bawled and hollered in the passenger seat on the way to an intensive care unit at some hospital in New Orleans, a city he'd only ever laid eyes on for the first time yesterday, where that same boyfriend was now fighting for his life in critical condition. Plus, they still didn't know how it all happened. *And* all of this after Leo hadn't even bothered to call him for two months after he'd left the Finger Lakes to move back down here! And yeah, *WHO WAS THE WOMAN?!*

*What kind of a wet mop am I, putting up with this shit?* Gibb thought angrily before catching himself and feeling guilty for not being more compassionate right now.

*Look at my sorry ass. Here Leo is possibly close to death and I'm thinking about myself and how pissed off I am. I gotta think positive. He can't die. He can't.*

Gibb chanted those words over and over in his mind, not really hearing what Sissie was even saying now, occasionally looking over at her to nod and pretend he was paying attention to her.

How could this be happening?

They'd made it to the city limits, still barreling down the interstate right alongside downtown New Orleans now. With no warning and no turn signal, Honey suddenly whipped three lanes over to the right and screeched off the exit for the Superdome. Gibb had no choice but to follow. A chorus of honking horns and gesturing hands from his fellow motorists laid bare their truth: they were driving like maniacs.

Three minutes later, though, through the miracle of five steady green lights, they made it. University Hospital. There it was. It had taken Gibb almost two full hours to get over to Bache today. They were now back in New Orleans in a little more than half that time.

Honey screeched into the emergency room parking lot. The entire drive had been so wild, Gibb imagined he saw smoke coming from her tires as he slammed Sam's station wagon to a stop on the steamy New Orleans black top. They didn't see a single patrol car the entire hundred-mile drive.

"Glad y'all made it one piece," Honey said roughly as she grabbed her purse and broke towards the hospital door.

"Well, come on!" she urged them, stress in her voice. "Sissie, you move any slower you're gonna be movin' backwards, girl. Move!"

Sissie looked at Gibb as if to say, *"Can you believe her?!"* As they hurried behind Honey under a blazing hot sun, Sissie angrily gave her the finger behind her back.

Gibb wished he was anywhere else but where he was. He wished the same for all of them as the electronic door slid open and they stepped into the air-conditioned emergency room.

# Chapter 27

# HURTS MY EARS
# TO LISTEN

Hospital rules only allowed immediate family to visit patients in the Intensive Care Unit, but Honey lied glibly to the hospital staff, telling them that both Gibb and Sissie were her grandchildren and had come with her to see their brother.

A nurse led the three of them to Leo's room. Gibb took a deep breath, steeling himself for the shock of what he was about to see, then entered the room behind Honey and Sissie. Aside from the constant beeping and whirring of all of the monitoring equipment in the room, there was the non-stop murmur of serious voices out in the hallway – nurses, doctors, family members of other patients in similarly critical states – and the deep breathing sound of the ventilator that was helping to keep Leo alive.

Nothing in his life up to this point could have prepared Gibb for what he was seeing there in that room. That was supposed to be Leo over there in that bed, the only person he loved in the world and the only one who'd ever loved him back, the entire reason he'd dropped his whole life to run down here. What he was actually seeing might as well have been a ghost.

All he saw was white: white bandages covering Leo's head, white plaster casts on both arms and one elevated leg propped up by some ghastly metal suspension system hanging from the ceiling. White sheets, white pillowcases, white cabinets in the room and worse, the white skin of Leo's closed eyelids. Would Leo ever open his eyes again?

Dizzy, Gibb held on to the footrail of Leo's hospital bed, feeling like he was either going to pass out or throw up everywhere. Honey and Sissie stood in the room weeping, Honey clutching Sissie's arm, Sissie with her hands at her side, frozen in place, unable to bring herself to reach out and touch the motionless figure laying in the bed.

"Leo, baby, we're here," Honey said through tears. "Honey's here, Sissie's here, and y'ain't never gonna believe it, but Gibb is here too, all the way from up north. He come down here to be with you, too."

Too stunned by what they were seeing, neither Gibb nor Sissie could bring themselves to say a word.

One of the monitors in the room started beeping, loud, much louder than Gibb would have expected in a hospital room. Wasn't this place supposed to be quiet for people to rest and get better?

All three of them looked at each other, bewildered. What did the beeping mean? What was wrong?! Sissie looked terrified, but before Gibb could say a word she moved, almost stomping, to the hospital room door and called out to no one in particular, "There's somethin' beepin' loud in here, y'all!"

In the next instant, a very pretty but serious-looking young nurse in blue scrubs and a dark brown ponytail stepped into the room and slipped past Sissie without a word. She calmly walked over to the machine and pushed a button. The beeping stopped.

"Y'all, don't be alarmed when that starts beeping," the nurse said with a genuine smile. "I know it's loud, but it's to get our attention when we're with another patient in another room or down the hall. Dr. Dresbach will be here to visit with you shortly, OK? Wait, here he is now…"

As if they'd rehearsed this scene for some hospital drama on TV, a handsome young doctor wearing studious-but-stylish glasses and a white doctor's coat walked through the hospital room door right on cue.

"Good afternoon," he said to Honey, with only a quick glance over at Gibb and Sissie. "Are you Leo's mother?"

Honey blushed a little and Gibb suspected she was flattered by the young doctor's question, but she wasted no time in answering, throwing a casual lie into her reply.

"No, sir. I'm Leo's grandmother. He's my first. These other two here, Gibb and Sissie, are mine, too. Leo's brother and sister."

"Hey y'all," he said, nodding curtly to them as he turned back to Honey. "What is your...?"

"Honey," she replied, cutting him off. "Honey Cormier."

"Nice to meet you, Ms. Cormier. I'm Dr. Dresbach. I was here when your grandson was admitted last night."

*Last night?* Gibb thought, anxiously looking at the terrible vision in front of him. *That means I was either on my way here or crashed out at Sam's house when they found him. And they'd already been in that rolled over car for a day when they were found? I really think I'm going to be sick.*

The handsome doctor paused, glancing over at Gibb and Sissie again. "Can we go out in the hallway and talk?" he asked Honey.

Honey looked over at Sissie who was clearly irked. Gibb continued to register no emotion, just a blank, white-faced stare.

"Go on, y'all," Sissie said bitterly with a dismissive wave of her hand. "Can't let the bad news fall on the children's ears."

Honey shot Sissie a look and walked out into the hallway with the doctor. Gibb walked around to her side of the bed and put his arm around her. She buried her face in his chest and cried quietly, her body wracked with sobs. Gibb led her over to a chair so she could sit. He found another one across the room and sat in that one. They said nothing to each other as they waited for Honey to return, and neither of them spoke to or touched the apparition in the bed.

When Honey walked back into the room with the doctor, they were accompanied by a third person, also a doctor based on the white coat, but clearly female. Young like Dr. Dresbach and equally good-looking. Gibb scratched his head.

*If looks are a requirement for some kind of medical career, I'm in a lot of trouble,* he thought miserably.

As they came in, Gibb could clearly hear Honey telling the female doctor, "I had no idea they had woman doctors here in New Orleans. I knew they had 'em up north, but this is a first for me!"

The doctor hardly paid Honey any attention as she headed to Leo's bed with a clipboard and a chart, conversing with Dr. Dresbach. She looked around at Gibb and Sissie.

"Hi y'all. I'm Dr. Tracey. I'm taking over from Dr. Dresbach this evening and I want to make sure you know we're gonna take the best care of your brother."

"Y'all," Honey piped up, almost cheerily, "the doctors say Leo's doin' better and he might soon be able to come off that…thing…that…whatever it's called."

"Vent," Dr. Tracey said, a note of consolation in her voice, "Or ventilator."

Sissie stood up.

"Really?! He's gonna get better?"

"There's some hope he will," Dr. Dresbach said. "His injuries are significant, but his vital signs have stabilized enough that we think it'll be OK to take him off the vent. If he's able to breathe OK on his own and his oxygen levels stay up, then we'll go on from there. If not, he'll have to go back on it. We needed to get your grandmother's permission to try to take him off the vent and she agreed."

Gibb and Sissie looked at each other, each grateful for the news they were hearing. Gibb's eyes filled with tears. As the doctor continued speaking. He looked down at the floor.

"He's young," Dr. Tracey said reassuringly. "And he has a very strong heartbeat. He's really fortunate that he wasn't the one driving that car."

Gibb and Sissie's eyes widened.

"What?!" Gibb exclaimed, his head snapping back up. "But it was his car!"

"Maybe so, but the young woman he was with was the driver," Dr. Dresbach said.

"Unfortunately, she didn't survive the impact. And based on where the state patrol said the car was found off the road, Leo here is extremely fortunate to have been found at all, let alone found alive."

"Who was the girl?!" Sissie demanded. "I've been freakin' out tryin' to figure out who it was since we found out about the wreck."

The doctors both hesitated, but Honey broke in and delivered the news.

"It was Marie, Sissie."

Sissie's mouth dropped open as Gibb screwed up his eyes in confusion.

"Marie?!" Sissie asked, incredulous. "Not Marie Guidry."

Honey just stared at Sissie, her lack of a response all the confirmation Sissie needed.

"Oh my God," Sissie exclaimed, looking dumbfounded as she sat slowly back down in her chair, rubbed her hands down her legs, then bent over at the waist and put her face in her hands.

Gibb, not wanting to give himself away in front of the doctors, said nothing. He was supposed to be Leo's brother, so supposedly he should have known who this person was. But the voice in his head was screaming, *"Who the hell is Marie Guidry?!"*

"Please don't make that public at this time, y'all," Dr. Dresbach requested. "The police, to my knowledge, are still trying to notify the young woman's next of kin."

Sissie sat back up.

"Yeah, good luck with that," she said bitterly. "Doubt that trash even got a workin' phone in even one of that mess o' trailers they got strewn all over their land. Marie Guidry. I never would've guessed. Wait…yes, I would. Honey, that scrawny li'l haint ain't never left Leo alone since he was ten years old."

Her voice dripped venom as she looked across the room at Gibb and shook her head.

"Sissie," Honey said, her voice saccharine as she glanced embarrassedly over at the doctors, "let's try right now to focus on your brother and him gettin' better. That's the most important thing. And please remember yourself. We're lucky, 'cuz Leo is still alive and the doctors here are sayin' he has a chance. The Guidry family is gonna have to deal with somethin' terrible when they find out what happened to Marie. Let's be hopeful, not hateful."

Given Sissie's mood all afternoon, Gibb was afraid she was going to explode and tear Honey apart right here in Leo's room in front of the doctors.

This time, thankfully, she seemed content to only shoot Honey a glare and then silently nod her agreement.

*Here we go again,* Gibb thought, turning his gaze to broken and bandaged Leo lying in the bed. *Leo and his secretive life. And who knows where the hell this leaves things between us now? Has he been messing around with girls since he got back down here?*

Dr. Tracey spoke up.

"Just to be clear, y'all, this doesn't mean that Leo is out of the woods. Oh my goodness, please pardon the awful pun," she said self-consciously. "This is one positive step in what could be a journey filled with some big setbacks."

The doctor explained that removing the ventilator was not a simple process and that it would take some time. If Leo was able to breathe on his own, he would eventually be moved out of the ICU to another wing of the hospital. For now, she asked, would they mind leaving while the staff removed the vent?

Gibb followed Honey and Sissie out of the room. He could see both of them quietly jawing at each other as they headed down the hall towards the waiting room, wisely keeping his distance from the hostile murmurs he heard coming from both of them. By the time they got to the waiting room, neither of them was speaking to the other.

All three of them sat down in uncomfortable silence, Gibb next to Honey, Sissie almost on the other side of the room.

"Leo never mentioned anyone named Marie Guidry to me," Gibb said perplexed, loud enough for Sissie to hear, too, if she wanted to join in the conversation. "Can someone please tell me who she is and why she would've been in the car with Leo? Was she an old girlfriend of his?"

Sissie snorted from across the room.

"Ha! As if. Hell no, she wasn't his girlfriend! She wasn't nothin' to him. That's why I'm tryin' to understand what the hell he was doin' with her and why the hell she was drivin' his car. It don't make any kinda damn sense!"

She fidgeted in her seat. "How long did they say it was gonna take before we know Leo can breathe on his own?"

"It'll be at least an hour before we get any news," Honey said. "Maybe longer if they get backed up and can't get down here to give us an update."

"In that time, then, maybe one of us can go with Gibb so he can drop his car off and then give him a ride back here in yours," Sissie said. "The guy who owns it lives somewhere near you in the Garden."

Gibb sat up straight and looked over at Sissie, suddenly impressed by her take-charge attitude. That sounded like a great plan. He needed to get out of here for a little while, that was for sure. Honey fished around in her purse and found her keys.

"Y'all two go," she said. "I need to be here in case something happens and they need somebody to make a decision. Sissie, can you run by the house and let Isabelle know we're here and ask her to please come sit with us?"

Sissie just took the keys out of Honey's hand and stalked out of the waiting room without a word, leaving Honey to stand there, mouth agape, looking to Gibb for some sort of explanation. As if he had one.

"Why is that girl so ill today?" she asked incredulously. "She's mean as a damn snake."

Gibb could only shrug, bewildered himself.

"I don't know...I guess she's just dealing with...her own feelings or whatever."

"Yeah, well, so we all are. She's lucky we're out in public," Honey murmured to herself as she watched Sissie disappear down the hallway. She turned to Gibb.

"How you doin', honey? You doin' OK?"

*Actually, no. I feel like I'm in a weird and awful dream. I'm in a completely unfamiliar place and right now, I'm somehow in the middle of a moody fight between my gravely injured boyfriend's grandmother and sister. I'm really scared and I keep thinking more bad stuff is gonna happen if I stay asleep, but I can't wake up.*

"I'm doing OK," Gibb replied. "Just a little dazed with everything going on."

Honey took hold of Gibb's hand, the second time she'd done that today, and looked him the eye.

"He's gonna be OK, you know," she said emphatically. "He is."

"I sure hope so," Gibb replied, his tone skeptical as he averted his eyes from her gaze.

"Look at me, boy," Honey calmly commanded. Gibb did as he was told.

"He's gonna be OK," she repeated. "Those are the words y'all need to be repeating over and over to each other and in your own heads. You tell that ill granddaughter of mine what I said here. Her brother needs all the good thoughts and prayers and love we can give him right now, not some moody sourpuss actin' like she's the center of the universe. You can tell her I said that, too, when y'all are together in the car!"

Gibb gave Honey a sad smile. "OK, I will," he said half-heartedly.

*Actually, no I won't. This nightmare is already too twisted for me to be your carrier pigeon.*

He hurried out of the waiting room and down the hall to find Sissie.

*Chapter 28*

# STANDING THERE, DREAMING

G ibb couldn't wait to show Sissie the gorgeous home where he'd slept the night before. What a welcome distraction from the horrible reality of Leo's hospital room. He steered Sam's station wagon slowly through the narrow, occasionally cobblestoned streets of New Orleans' Garden District, following close behind Sissie in Honey's car. She knew the area much better than he did, so when he described the route Sam took yesterday, she knew exactly how to get there.

"Dear God. That place is beautiful!" Sissie exclaimed as they stood in the street gawking at the formidable lemon-chiffon mansion, the porch now illuminated in the fading light by a handsome, flaming gas-lit lantern.

"But just to let you know before we get over by there," she said wryly as she looked over at Gibb, "Honey's house definitely ain't no mansion like this place. She just got a li'l shotgun up there between Pleasant and Harmony."

"A what between what?" Gibb asked, confused.

"A shotgun. Shotgun house?" Sissie asked, noting Gibb's bewilderment. "You ain't never heard of a shotgun house?"

Gibb shook his head.

"I gotta remember I'm talkin' to a Yankee," she laughed. "I guess you ain't got shotgun houses up north. It's just a narrow li'l house with each room kinda behind the other from the front till you get to the back of the house. No hallways. They used to say if you shot a bullet through the front doors, it could go right through the back without hittin' any other walls. Shotgun. See?"

"Hmm...never heard of that," Gibb said. "But what was the other thing you said... pleasure and something...harmony? What's that mean?"

"Oh, those are just street names. She lives between *Pleasant,* not pleasure," she giggled, regarding him with eyebrows raised in mock dis-approval, "wherever your mind is at, young man. Pleasant and Harmony – they're both streets. I'm confusin' the hell out of you tonight, ain't I?" she laughed.

There were lights on in Char and Sam's front room – hopefully, somebody was home. If not, Gibb could just return the key tomorrow or something. As Gibb and Sissie stood there on the street talking, a clearly drunk couple stumbled past them, drinks in hand, almost tripping over the uneven side-walk in front of them.

"I almost spilled by goddam drink," the woman rasped too loudly, her other hand holding a freshly lit cigarette.

"Careful – too far to go back there to get you another one," her male com-panion slurred. "And I ain't sharin' mine."

The woman noticed Gibb looking at her.

"What the hell are *you* lookin' at, Red?" she griped at him as she stumbled up the street towards her consort. "Did that motherfucker look like Archie from the comic books or what?" Gibb heard her mutter once she caught up to the guy.

Gibb winced. *Like she was any great prize. Must be Jack's long-lost sister,* he thought to himself.

Sissie wasn't having any of it, though.

"What'd you just say, skank?!" Sissie belligerently called out after her. Gibb's mouth dropped open. He never knew Sissie could be such a hothead.

The drunk woman, easily only half Sissie's size, turned slowly back around. Wisely taking stock of the situation as she stared at them, the slatternly woman took a slow drag off of her cigarette, then waved her drink at them. She didn't want any part of Sissie.

"Y'all have a nice night!" she hollered.

"Yeah, that's what I thought, bitch!" Sissie yelled back.

She turned back to Gibb. "You go on, Gibb," she said, her demeanor sullen now. "I'll just stay out here and wait while you go and return the keys."

He sighed as he walked up the two steps to Char and Sam's front porch and knocked. Suddenly the door swung open and there was Sam, all seven feet of him, smiling down at Gibb.

"Where *y'AT?!*" he half-hollered.

"I'm right here!" Gibb exclaimed. "I tried to call…"

"Dear God, boy, you a slow-ass learner. Oh, hello, young lady," Sam said, noticing Sissie on the street.

"That's Leo's sister, Sissie. Sissie this is SamWell, but you can call him Sam. If you're cool, that is," Gibb said jokingly.

"Hello," Sissie called unenthusiastically from the sidewalk.

"Come on inside," Sam said. "Come on back to the kitchen. Why she not coming in?" he said over his shoulder as Gibb followed him through the house, as overwhelmed by its grandiosity as he was when he arrived last night.

"It's better this way," Gibb said dryly. "Trust me."

"So, how'd everything go?" Sam said once they got to the kitchen.

"I'm afraid to tell you," Gibb said quietly.

"Did you mess up my car?" Sam demanded intimidatingly.

"No," Gibb said. "The car is fine. But I didn't get a chance to put gas in it. I'll give you money, though. Once I tell you what happened, you'll understand, but I'm afraid I'm gonna start crying. It's been a terrible day. Do you have a few minutes?"

"Only a few, 'cuz I need to get where I'm playin' tonight. But tell me the important parts."

Gibb tried his best to be brief, only telling Sam that Leo had been in a bad wreck, that a girl named Marie had been driving and lost her life and that Leo was at University Hospital fighting for his. He said they were there right now only to drop off the car before heading right back to the hospital to be with Leo. Other than that, he didn't know what to say or do.

Sam looked like he didn't know what to do, either.

"That sound like a lot to deal with," he finally said. "Boy, you been through it today, ain't you?"

"I guess I have," Gibb said, rubbing his eyelids as he moved his hands down his tired face. He looked back at Sam, his face drained of color.

"And right now," he went on, his voice shaking a little as he took off his glasses and rubbed his eyes again, "I'm so upside down, I'm not sure if I'm even in real life anymore. Is this some long, weird nightmare I can't wake up from? Nothing makes any sense! Hell, just a minute ago I was standing on your street here in the middle of freakin' New Orleans, Louisiana, ready to see Leo's sister throw down with some drunk chick out on your street over a stupid comment she made as she walked past. It's surreal! I'm just some lame douchebag from Eislertown, New York. I don't belong here!

"I guess I'm feeling just like your old car out there," he said, gesturing towards the window. "I'm running out of gas."

Sam looked towards the window and back towards Gibb.

"But you love him right?" Sam asked matter-of-factly.

Gibb nodded.

"Then don't be dumb. This ain't no dream. Especially now – you got a lot to figure out. If you feelin' like an old car, you still can't just run out of gas in the middle of the road and then be there for everybody else to worry 'bout. Like it or not, you gotta man up and deal. Leo's sister and grandma gonna need you and you gonna need them too, for sure.

"Remember I told you in the car I was impressed that you was takin' on some real adult shit by comin' down here? Well now, here it is, right in yo' face. Don't let it beat you. You come a long way just to turn around and run home a day later. And sorry. I didn't really mean to call you dumb."

"It's OK," Gibb said. "It actually helps to hear you talk like that to me, believe it or not. Another thing I'm beginning to see is that I have a bad habit of avoiding things by telling myself this could all just be a dream. While I'm doing that, I'm stalling. Just stalling. It's fear, I guess. Fear of not wanting to be too emotionally involved."

He shrugged. To his amusement, Sam shrugged back, a goofy look on his face.

"Too late for that now, ain't it? Look here, I gotta get goin'. Y'all got a lot goin' on, but I'm givin' y'all a open invitation to our big crawfish boil next weekend. That's if your boy is doin' better and all that, of course. Which I hope he will be. Anyway, it's a big party and it's fun. Come for a hour, maybe two. Just to give y'all a break. We gonna play some music out there in the yard, Char and her friends gonna boil up the crawfish, and folks will bring all kinda food. We gonna have beers and other stuff to drink if y'all don't drink beer."

"That's really cool of you to offer, Sam," Gibb said, his mood lightened a bit. "Definitely not sure if I can do it, but I'd love to be there if I can. I'd probably bring Leo's sister with me. As you can probably tell from her attitude, she needs a break for sure."

"Bring his grandma, too. Bring whoever you want. We do this thing every year in June," Sam said. "It's how we mark the end of crawfish season…which mean the end of the good weather. We do it to try to get people ready for the hell of a New Orleans summer. Stick aroun' here long enough, you gonna see exactly what I mean by that."

Gibb had never had crawfish, had no idea if he would even eat them. He didn't know of anybody back home who actually cooked and ate them. But the idea of hanging out in Char and Sam's beautiful yard with music and food and people was something to look forward to in the week ahead, even if they ended up not being able to attend. It all depended on what was going on with Leo.

Sam accompanied Gibb to the mansion's front door and opened it for him. As Gibb stepped out onto the flame-lit porch, he turned back towards to Sam.

"So, when you say you're gonna play some music at the party, like, are *you* gonna play your sax?" Gibb asked.

"Hell yeah, I'm-a play. I ain't no DJ. Come on by and check us out."

"If I'm around, can I help do anything, like set up for the party and stuff?" Gibb offered.

"Hmm…" Sam said, scratching at his cheek. "It's next Saturday. Tell you what, Red. If you still around, bring yo'self over by the house aroun' ten, eleven in the mornin'. Char will put you to work."

Feeling better than he had when he'd gotten there, Gibb jumped off the top step of the porch and hustled to the street. Regrettably, the light-hearted moment lasted only as long as it took to open Honey's car door and climb into the front passenger seat. Sissie was crying quietly in the darkened car, her bowed head resting against the steering wheel.

Gibb silently took in the pitiful sight for a moment before patting her on her shoulder.

"You want me to drive? Just tell me how to get there," he offered gently.

"No, I'm OK," she said. She tried to smile at him through her tears as she wiped her eyes and cleared her throat. She turned the key in the ignition.

"Just another day in the wonderful life of Sissie Davion."

Gibb didn't say anything, allowing them both the space to breathe and think in silence for a moment. He could only imagine what Sissie was going through right now. Her father had just died, her mother was in a mental hospital, and now her brother was fighting for his life in a New Orleans hospital. Add to that her contentious relationship with the only family she had left, her grandmother, and Gibb could understand why she was crying.

"Man, life is fucked sometimes, isn't it?" she said as she pulled away from the curb. She probably wasn't looking for a reply, but Gibb gave one anyway.

"Yeah, it is. But I guess I have to admit it, there's always something that's OK about it, too. Like, all the time."

"What? Ugh. Don't blow sunshine up my butt, Gibb," she replied, waving her hand at him in irritation. "There ain't nothin' OK about anything right now."

"Yes, there is," Gibb objected. "How about this? You could be in this car by yourself right now and I could still be up in Eislertown without either one having the other here to support us. But life made sure we ended up together today. *We're* what's OK about life right now. You and me. That counts for something, no matter how small."

Neither one of them said another word as they drove the last few blocks to Honey's house.

## Chapter 29

# TESTY, TESTY

"Marie Guidry is...or was...a flat-out nobody, God rest her soul," Sissie said. Her attempt at sounding compassionate was entirely unconvincing.

It was getting close to midnight now and after a chaotic and frustrating night of deciding with Honey who was doing what and where, Gibb and Sissie now sat in Leo's darkened hospital room, talking in hushed tones. Honey and Isabelle, her housemate, would come back early in the morning to give the young people a chance to take a nap. They'd need one, Gibb thought, because the way Sissie was talking now, he doubted he'd be able to even get a chance to doze tonight.

Leo was still in pretty serious condition and even though he was now breathing without assistance, he was still semi-comatose and heavily sedated, lying motionless in his bed. They'd given up on talking to him for now, but they'd been encouraged by fluttering eyelids and the occasional grunt or slight moan when they spoke or when he moved.

Gibb was uneasy with the way life just had to carry on around Leo's bed while he lay there not knowing anything that was going on. Here was Sissie, talking up a storm, completely aware of the gravity of her brother's injuries but, just like Gibb, walking the razor's edge of denial about them. Hoping for the best, not daring to think the worst. Every lull in their conversation made them turn their heads back towards the bed and the re-reminder of why they were there.

Even though he was beat and having a hard time paying attention, Gibb figured that the more Sissie talked, the quicker time would pass. One minute at a time they were getting closer to Leo's total recovery and the amazing moment when they would all walk out of here together. He looked over at the bed again.

*Or not.*

As the night went on it was clear that Sissie truly had nothing nice to say about Marie Guidry. She kept telling Gibb that she didn't mean to be ugly or disrespectful, but she couldn't fake it. As far as Sissie was concerned, Marie was just bad news. She had just graduated high school with Leo, and Sissie was surprised she'd made it. She was just one of those girls who was always making trouble and she had a small group of girlfriends who were all the same as her.

"She called me a fat bitch one day…no, she *mumbled* 'fat bitch' behind my back one day downtown, and then I heard her and her li'l meth-head friends laughin'. So I turned around and jacked her skinny ass up against a wall and told her to say it again, with my hand around her throat. She never said it again, I can guarantee you. Not out loud, anyway."

Gibb's eyes widened. It was clear that no one should ever even consider messing with any of the women in Leo's family. Wow.

"Her and her skinny li'l haints, all trailer-trash. You know the type – I saw 'em at your school when we were up north, too. Skeezy little cigarette-smokin', druggie, li'l-goin'-nowhere bitches. Anyway, Marie always had her eye on Leo and she wasn't happy that he didn't have his eye on her."

"Was she pretty?" Gibb asked. He wanted to know.

"If you like your girls skeezy, skinny-assed, flat-chested, and fake streaked-blonde, yeah. I guess she was," Sissie said sarcastically before relenting. "Nah, I guess you could say she was pretty. Leo still didn't want nothin' to do with her, though.

"But she was persistent. She's prob'ly the main reason Mama ripped the phone out of the wall that one day. That li'l girl just called Leo all the time! All the time."

"Well, if she was calling all the time, wouldn't it be because she was picking up on some kind of signal he was giving her? Maybe he wanted her to call," Gibb said softly.

"No!" Sissie hissed. "He did *not* want her to call. He's just too…I don't know what the word is…he's nice, yeah…but no. He was too *intimidated* by her to tell her to stop callin'. He couldn't bring himself to tell any of that little band of harlots to leave him alone."

"So why do you suppose he and Marie were together that night, then? And why was she driving his car?" Gibb asked for about the millionth time.

Sissie looked over at her unconscious brother hooked up to his IV and monitoring machines in the midnight half-light of the hospital room.

"Only he can tell us that," she said sadly.

❧❧

Right on time, at seven o'clock the next morning, Honey and Isabelle showed up at Leo's hospital room to sit with Leo for the morning, allowing Gibb and Sissie a chance to go back to Honey's house for a nap and a shower, a routine they all fell into over the next few days. Gibb would go to Honey's house to take a nap for a few hours, then come back to the hospital to sit with Leo. Sissie or Honey would leave the hospital at noon every day and drive over to Morgan City to visit Mrs. Davion in her own hospital surroundings, returning irritable and exhausted six hours later.

In and among all of the angst and fatigue, there was good news, though. Awesome news, in fact. Leo had begun to open his eyes, and he was beginning to try to verbally respond to them, too, further encouraging all of them, his doctors especially. Recovery was coming slowly, but it was coming.

Gibb was happy about Leo's progress, but wasn't sure why he wasn't more excited about it. Maybe it was because he'd expected it all along, assuring himself that there was just no way Leo could succumb to his injuries or be permanently disabled by them.

Maybe Gibb was just trying to stay calm in the face of all the uncertainty, not getting too up when things looked good or letting himself get too down if there was a setback. Whatever it was, his approach helped him keep his emotions in check. He'd get excited if Leo started talking soon, though. That would be the one thing to make all of this anxiety worth it.

Gibb had to admit the monotony of this daily routine was wearing on him, though. Being around people, especially stressed-out people, was getting tougher every interminable hour, especially when he was used to spending so much of his time alone. He'd been here for a whole week now, but aside from a short jaunt over to Magazine Street to buy a couple new T-shirts, underwear, and jeans, he'd seen nothing of New Orleans except the route they drove between Honey's house and the hospital. He knew the way well enough now to walk the short three miles, and that was just what he was doing today before he had to spend the rest of it cooped up in that god-forsaken hospital room.

In his right hand, Gibb clutched the rose quartz crystal, his thumb noting the contrast between the rock's flat faces and its craggy, blunted edges as he walked. Despite the upheaval of the past week, the crystal was still his most prized possession, maybe now even more than the night they'd stained it with their own blood. Something about the uneven surfaces - alternating so naturally between the perfectly smooth and the jaggedly imperfect - exactly mirrored his current situation. He made a face as the metaphor registered in his mind, sticking the rock back in his pocket so he could focus on other things for the rest of the walk.

Ambling along Camp Street towards downtown, he was becoming more enamored of the architecture here in the Garden District - the eight-foot-tall windows, the long sets of stairs from the lawns up to the front doors of many homes, the distinctively different shapes and heights and colors of these amazingly well-preserved mansions, many over a hundred years old. The wrought-iron railings patterning across the verandas and balconies of the neighborhood's ritzier homes splashed like grand and orderly black fountains of grape vines, angel wings, and dark, mysterious hearts. They looked like they could be adorning homes he'd seen in pictures of old Paris, frozen into the forever of yesterday, today, and probably a million tomorrows.

Walking these streets really was like stepping back in time, a time foreign in both culture and language. Just given the name of the town, New Orleans, it was the influence of old France that was most obvious to anyone who had ever read about the place or visited here. But many cultures helped form the cultural heart of the present-day city: African, Native American, Spanish, Caribbean, German and Irish, too.

In the past few months, Gibb had read a lot about this unexampled American metropolis: its inhumanity as the epicenter of the slave trade in the Deep South, its horrifying yellow fever epidemics in the 1800's, its hurricanes and daily afternoon thunderstorms and the Great Flood caused by failing levees along the Mississippi River back in 1927. On the brighter side, though, there was this all this amazing, artful architecture, all the amazing food he had yet to try, and stories of the festivals and parades that supposedly packed the streets with revelers of all ages all day and night.

Stories of New Orleans piqued Gibb's interest over these past few months mainly because it was the town where Leo had made his own grand entrance into human existence almost 19 years ago. Yet the more Gibb read about the city, its history and culture, the more he realized that New Orleans couldn't have been a more perfect setting for an event as blessed as Leo's birth. It was a city as beautiful, and complicated, as he was.

Leo's peculiarities couldn't be pinned solely on the unique nature of his birthplace, however. Nurture definitely played its part in his development, too, and Gibb was now seeing that first-hand as he spent all of his waking hours with Sissie and Honey. It gave him a little more compassion for Leo's unpredictability. If he'd had grown up with Leo's family, Gibb would have wanted to disappear anytime he got the chance, too.

All week, the tension between Honey and Sissie had gone from being mildly amusing to irritating to unbearable. As soon as one of them walked into Leo's hospital room, the other would bristle or just stop talking and walk out of the room. Then the one who'd just come in would use Gibb as a sounding board for all of the issues she had with the other one. He did his best to tune it all out, but he wished the two of them would just shut up and grow up.

Earlier today at Honey's house, Gibb grit his teeth hard as he listened to Sissie blather on and on about a note Honey had left them, asking them to do a couple of things around her house before they returned to the hospital for their sitting shift. It was Honey's day to go over to Morgan City and she needed a little help with household stuff. It was no big deal...to Gibb. Sissie couldn't stop talking about it or Honey, though. Gibb finally got fed up.

"Why does she bug you so much?" he asked, frustrated. "She just wanted a little help."

Sissie shot him a look across the little pink-rose wall-papered kitchen.

"Well, isn't that it?" Gibb asked, vexed and perplexed.

"No, that ain't it," Sissie said sarcastically. "I don't mind doin' stuff around her house. I just don't like the way she asks. Or should I say, *demands*. She acts like she's all superior and knows every damn thing all the time. I'm just sick to death of her shit."

Suddenly she stopped.

"Look, I don't know what all Leo has told you about Honey, but you know about her and Isabelle, right?"

"Uhh, what about them?" Gibb stammered, his look blank. Sissie cut him off.

"They're *together* together, OK?" she said impatiently, making finger quotes in the air. "And they have been for a long time, most of my life anyway. There ain't nothin' wrong with that as far as I'm concerned, and as you can tell, Isabelle is a very nice woman. The problem is Honey. She has never once been honest with our family about any of it, always callin' Isabelle her *house-mate* and stuff like that. She's a straight-up liar.

"They're not jus' sleepin' in the same bed because I happen to be sleepin' in 'Isabelle's room' right now. Isabelle don't have a different room. Her and Honey sleep in that same bed every night and they have for the last fifteen years, at least!"

*Well*, Gibb thought to himself with chagrin, *I asked the question*. As the vitriol continued pouring from Sissie's mouth, he was really sorry he hadn't kept his mouth shut.

"She got some real nerve hidin' her true life from us, actin' all high and mighty, tellin' me and ever'body else what to do all the time. She's loud. And obnoxious. Mean as a damn snake sometimes, too, especially to Mama, who's just as mean back to her. And she don't even try to hide how she favors Leo over me. Always has, always will. From the minute Leo was born, he was the slice of King cake with the baby in it. To her, I was always the end slice that missed the damn frosting, the one ever'body leaves behind in the pan."

Sissie looked almost triumphant as she ended her rant.

"So, you asked me why she bugs me, now you know. She can kiss my ass all up and down the Quarter for all I damn care."

*Oh God,* Gibb thought, rubbing his hands down his face as Sissie whirled away from Gibb and trudged out of the kitchen. *Wait, I'm in a shotgun house, right? Then please, can somebody just shoot me now?*

He stood there for a second rubbing his face, pondering what Sissie had just told him. He was actually surprised by the news, not just because he'd never thought about people as old as Leo's grandmother being in a lesbian relationship, but also because she was in a lesbian relationship with a woman of color. Isabelle was black. "Coming out" in their situation could cause them real trouble and Gibb knew it. Sissie's resentment towards her grandmother didn't seem to allow her to understand that.

"Hey, Sissie," he called after her. "Hold on a minute."

Sissie stopped in the front room and waited for Gibb to catch up.

"Look, just so you know," he said as he reached her, "I've never 'come out' to *my* family, either. My stepfather is a real piece of work and he'd have the potential to be a real asshole about it. My mom's no prize, either, but it's him I don't really trust. He's not a good guy. I would never just give him the power to throw my sexuality in my face or my mother's face while I lived there, you know what I mean?"

Sissie glowered at him.

"Seriously, you have to think about what I'm telling you here," Gibb went on. "Keeping that secret to myself for now doesn't make me a liar or unwilling to face reality. It's the same with Honey and Isabelle. Hell, I'm in a relationship with your brother and we're both 'out', you know, to ourselves and each other. And now you and Honey, too. It's a process, every day in a gay person's life. It's not just some major announcement and then suddenly everything's cool and everyone's all right with it.

"Try not to be too pissed off at Honey about it. We all have to be able to share that information ourselves. That's our right, 'cuz it's kind of a big deal, even though it really shouldn't be, and we could get hurt pretty bad if we share that info with the wrong person.

"Just because *you* want Honey to acknowledge her relationship with Isabelle doesn't mean that she's *obligated* to do it for you, for your mom, for anyone. We all have to do it in our own time and our own way. She probably has real fears about your mother's reaction to her news, the same as my fear about my stepfather's. It's delicate. I'm saying this as a friend – just leave it up to her, that's all.

"And besides," Gibb concluded with a smirk, "I refuse to believe that you're such a dull person that you don't have some secrets yourself."

Sissie stared hard into Gibb's eyes the entire time he spoke. He could see she was a little chastened as she squeezed his arm.

"No, you're right," she conceded. "You're a hundred percent right. Just like you were right about needin' to try to focus on what's good in life when we were in the car last week. You got the right idea about things, Gibb, and I'm sorry. I really am. It's their business and, you're right, I'll leave 'em to it."

Her dark eyes sparkled mischievously in the late morning sunlight dancing through the room.

"But Honey's still a bitch."

Gibb shook his head in resignation at the memory, marveling at the scenery around him as he stepped up his walking pace. The colossal trunks and twisting limbs of the Southern live oaks adorning the genteel side-streets of this neighborhood suggested a petrified line of tornados, a long row of killer storms stopped in their tracks by some powerful local voodoo, their swirling winds transfigured into branches, like brawny bouncer arms, blocking windows, balconies and upstairs glass doors from the curious eyes of casual passers-by.

Gibb had never seen such trees until he got here to New Orleans; their mighty presence and majestic beauty awed him. As he walked, his mood began to lift, similar to the way those trees' roots robustly lifted up the slabs of the concrete sidewalks under his feet in jagged, bumpy patterns. He was beginning to feel much better. It was so good to be able to get some fresh air and take a good look around. Maybe he'd do this walk tomorrow, too. Why not?

Lost in thought and staring at an enormous pink mansion with a perfect front lawn shaded by a grove of three handsome palm trees, the toe of his sneaker suddenly caught the edge of an uneven slab of pavement and he stumbled, hard.

Flailing his arms to keep himself from falling down on the sidewalk, Gibb, like most human beings, was no match for gravity. Fortunate to land his fall hands-down, he still scraped his palms pretty raw. Worse, his unplanned pratfall caught the eye of two landscapers working in a yard across the street.

"You OK, man?" one of the workers called over to him, laughing.

*Really?* Gibb thought. *Yeah, I'm OK, asshole.*

"Yep, everything's perfect. Thanks, dude."

Instinctively, he reached down to pat his right front pocket. The crystal was still there.

⊣⊢

Scraped-up hands and bruised ego notwithstanding, Gibb was glad he'd walked over here to the hospital. A little time alone had made all the difference – he wasn't dreading the rest of the day as much as usual. He still had to gird himself for the Honey/Sissie onslaught, though.

He took a deep breath as he approached Leo's hospital room door, not sure what he was going to find on the other side, but when he walked in, there was Dr. Tracey talking to Honey, Isabelle, and Sissie. All four of them turned to him with big, happy smiles on their faces.

"Hey there," the doctor said brightly as Gibb entered the room. "Guess who's making more than a little noise today? In real word form."

"W-what?!" Gibb exclaimed as he hurried over to the bed. "He's talking?!"

"Yep," Honey said, her beaming smile a mixture of joy and relief. "But he's asleep right now."

"What did he say?!" Gibb demanded.

"He's very disoriented right now," Honey whispered, "but he was able to say 'hey' to us and he said mine and Isabelle's names. He said y'all's names too and asked for y'all just before Sissie got here. Ain't that hopeful?"

Gibb's head whipped over towards Dr. Tracey, his eyes wide with excitement.

"Is that true? That's amazing!"

"It really is kind of amazing," she said. "Like your grandmother just said, it's hopeful. Just keep talking to him and doing what you're doing. At some point, if he can hear you, he'll probably try to respond somehow. It'll help him focus when he recognizes your voices talking back to him. Ask him questions, too, and remind him of stuff y'all did when you were kids and even recently. It'll help his mind and his memory piece things back together."

Gibb didn't need any further encouragement.

"Leo, it's Gibb," he said softly, leaning down to kiss Leo's face. "I'm here. I love you and I'll be here when you wake up."

But just as that tender moment was happening at Leo's bedside, another less loving moment was happening right across the room. It was almost noon, time for Honey to head to Morgan City to visit Mrs. Davion. But now that Leo was beginning to really form words, Honey wanted to stay here in his room this afternoon. She wanted Sissie to go to Morgan City in her place. She was cold about it, too. Pushy. Basically, she was telling Sissie it was more important for herself to be by Leo's bedside today instead of Sissie and wouldn't Sissie like to go be with her Mama today, anyway?

Sissie wasn't having it. She'd made the long drive to visit her mother yesterday and she wasn't about to go today. If Honey didn't want to go, she could just call the facility and ask the staff to tell Mama she was sick or something. Mrs. Davion still knew nothing of Leo's situation, and they weren't planning on telling her until they had a clear understanding of Leo's chances for recovery, so what did it matter?

"Somebody needs to go visit your Mama," Honey groused. "It ain't fair for her to not have someone come in and see her."

Used to this daily folderol, Gibb and Isabelle exchanged glances. Isabelle gave him a slight, knowing smile. Gibb rubbed his temples, the never-ending feud feeling more every day like a long, cold ice pick being jammed through his eardrums.

Dr. Tracey broke the tension.

"It's unlikely that Leo's going to be sitting up in bed and talking in full sentences this afternoon. He's still going to be groggy from the traumatic brain injury, the medication, all of it. I don't think you'll be missing anything this afternoon, Honey."

That was all Sissie need to hear. She grit her teeth, angrily snarling through them at Honey, trying to keep her voice down.

"See there? You can go see Mama now. Just go, woman. Go! Go! Go!" she barked at her grandmother, pointing wildly towards the open hospital room door, her face red with anger and embarrassment.

An audible moan came from Leo's bed, interrupting Sissie's tirade. Every head in the room turned towards the sound. Engulfed in quiet for a second, they were all surprised when the next voice they heard was the mellowest one in the room. Isabelle.

"Y'all two, please stop fussin'," she said softly. "Sissie, come on over here and stand next to your brother. Gibb, baby, get that chair there and pull it up to the bed so Honey can sit by her grandson. There you go, that's it. Honey, you sit down right there next to Gibb. Gibb and Sissie, y'all two can take turns sharin' Gibb's chair."

Isabelle turned to the doctor.

"Dr. Tracey, may I use the phone at the nurse's station for a quick minute?' she asked sweetly.

"You can use the phone in my office," Dr. Tracey offered. "I'll walk with you there now."

Isabelle turned back and looked at the three of them huddled silently now around Leo's bed. When she spoke, her voice was gentle, but firm.

"Y'all got one focus today and it's not each other," she said, looking first at Sissie, then at Honey as she gestured towards sleeping Leo. "He's in that bed. Me and Gibb don't wanna hear another bad word from either of y'all today. I got voodoo dolls of both y'all in my purse. For y'all own good, don't push us. I *will* start stickin' 'em with pins."

Sissie grumbled dismissively, turning to glare at Isabelle. "You ain't got voodoo dolls in your purse."

Without a word, not taking her eyes off Sissie, Isabelle reached into her big brown-leather purse and casually pulled out two female peach-colored yarn dolls, one with short grey hair, the other with a long, blonde ponytail. Gibb's smirk turned into a huge dopey grin as he watched Sissie's mouth fall open in disbelief.

"Y'all two best remember yourselves or I'm-a start with the pins," Isabelle said, looking hard and unsmiling at Sissie and then Honey as she held up the dolls. She turned to Dr. Tracey who was watching the whole scene unfold in quiet amusement.

"I'm callin' Morgan City and tellin 'em," Isabelle said, more for Honey and Sissie to hear, "ain't nobody goin' by there today."

# Chapter 30

## DEATH AND
## NO MERCY

Gibb sat in the hospital waiting room engrossed in a National Geographic, lost in the world of aboriginal people somewhere in the Australian outback, as nurses changed Leo's bedding just down the hall. A sudden baritone voice broke his concentration, startling him.

"Gibb, he's asking for you," Dr. Dresbach said with a smile. "Clearest he's spoken since he started coming to."

Yesterday, Leo had begun to make some real progress. He had begun to speak real words and respond to the voices of the people around him. He'd said their names and squeezed their hands. Gibb had been holding Leo's hand at one of the moments his eyes fluttered open. Leo had mostly looked dazed and fearful as the light in the room hit his pupils but yesterday, as his eyes adjusted to his surroundings, it was clear that he recognized Gibb. And when he did, he gave Gibb a faint smile. Gibb's chest felt like it was going to explode as it often did when he saw it. It was a remarkable moment, most notably for the whoops and shrieks emanating from Leo's sister and grandmother and a young nurse running in at top speed to first admonish them, then share in their joy.

Gibb had said nothing when it happened but, true to form, silent tears streaked his glasses and his face as he squeezed Leo's hand, then got down on one knee next to him and rested his face on Leo's chest. It felt miraculous, and in many ways it was.

Both of his doctors were clear that it was still hard to tell what the long-term effects of Leo's injuries would be. They'd been honest when they said they weren't sure if he would ever wake up, but from the moment his eyes recognized Gibb, Leo seemed to be progressing at an exponential rate.

Yesterday morning, Leo's speaking had become intelligible, but he spoke in a hoarse and barely audible whisper Most of what he said hadn't made sense at first. He could barely form sentences and he was dealing with some real hallucinations. He looked over at the bare white wall and asked Sissie to take a non-existent book from an invisible shelf and hand it to him. He asked a nurse to bring in some bug spray to kill a line of invisible ants marching across his covers. And he asked, slurring the question over and over, if the Yankees had left New Orleans yet, a reference to the Union occupation of New Orleans in the Civil War. Gibb reassured him that he himself was the only Yankee in the room.

Leo's delusions had scared everyone at first, but the doctors and nurses assured them that Leo's situation was actually pretty normal for someone just waking up from a coma. As they dialed back his pain medication, Leo's mind became noticeably clearer and, thankfully, so did his speaking. By the time Gibb and Sissie left late last night, Leo was making much more sense when he spoke.

With Sissie gone on her way to Morgan City - with no struggle today, thank God - Gibb made his way into Leo's room alone. Leo's eyes lit up when he saw him, amazing Gibb. These past twenty-four hours had given everyone so much more hope for Leo's future.

"Hey!" Gibb called with a wave, turning to grab a chair to pull up to the bed. He sat.

"I love you," Leo said raspily but clearly.

"Oh man," Gibb said. "I love you, too. I came all the way down here to hear you say those words, you know that? Feeling pretty lucky right about now."

Gibb fished around in his pocket, then pulled his hand out with the treasure he'd sought: the rose quartz crystal. He held it up for Leo to see, then kissed it and silently clutched it to his chest.

Leo smiled wearily, but then his face fell.

"I'm really sorry," Leo croaked in his rough whisper.

"It's OK now," Gibb said, gently touching Leo's face. "You're gonna be all right. Do you know what happened to you?"

"Accident," came Leo's reply.

"Right. Accident. But do you remember how it happened?"

"Stupid. I was stupid," Leo said.

"Right, but you weren't driving. You were the passenger," Gibb gently reminded him.

"No. Drunk. I drove and I was drunk."

Gibb, thinking Leo was confused, tried to correct him.

"No, no. Marie Guidry was driving, remember? Remember Marie?"

Leo furrowed his brow in confusion. Or was it consternation?

"Yes, I remember Marie."

"Marie was driving, remember?" Gibb nudged again.

"No, me. Drunk and driving when I saw her," Leo said haltingly. "Pulled over and I picked her up."

Gibb got a lump in his throat.

"What made you do that?"

"Drive drunk?" Leo slurred slowly.

"Yes, that. And what made you pull over to pick up Marie?"

"I don't know," Leo muttered.

"You can tell me," Gibb said. "I came a long way to be with you. What made you do it?"

Leo stared at him blankly for a second.

"Daddy, I guess," he finally mumbled.

"What?" Gibb asked, confused.

"I did it for Daddy," Leo said, more definite this time.

"You drove drunk for your dad?" Gibb asked, unsure that was what he'd heard.

"You're confusin' the hell out of me," Leo mumbled crossly.

"Sorry. Take your time."

Leo gave Gibb a stern look.

"I was sad about Daddy and I was pissed off at Mama," he stammered hoarsely.

"OK...so that's why you drove drunk. But why did you pick up Marie?"

"'Cuz that's what Daddy woulda wanted."

"Why would your dad want you to pick up Marie, of all people?" Gibb asked, a little bewildered based on everything Sissie had said about Marie.

"Not Marie," Leo murmured thickly. "A girl. A girl."

Leo swallowed hard and closed his eyes, his brow still furrowed.

"Daddy wanted to see me happy with a girl. He knew about you and me."

Gibb's eyes widened in surprise.

"What did he say about it? You know, about us. Was he angry?" Gibb wanted to know.

"He didn't say anything about it."

"Then why are you so sure he wanted you to be with a girl?" Gibb asked.

"C-Come on, Gibb," Leo said, stuttering slowly but speaking more clearly now. "Every dad wants his young'un to be normal. Just have a...a...normal... a normal, everyday life. Get married – to a girl. Have grandkids. Be proud his kid is...not...some...weirdo.

Gibb was bewildered as he listened to Leo. *Weirdo?* So, they were weirdos now? What Leo was saying was the exact opposite of everything he'd ever said when he lived up north.

"No dad wants his son... to grow up... to be a sensitive... li'l...introvert... who likes to play... dress-up... and dreams... of a happy-ever-after life... with another boy," Leo said, haltingly, but emphatically.

Gibb could feel his face reddening in frustration as he glared at clueless, helpless Leo.

They sat there in silence for a moment. Leo turned his face away, gazing towards the hospital room window.

"You're not gay because of anything your dad did," Gibb finally said quietly, but through gritted teeth. "Neither am I. My dad died before I even turned four. It has nothing to do with them."

"But Daddy never really knew that," Leo said slowly. "He just wanted me to be like all the other guys whose sons were chasin' after girls, havin' a high ol' time, cruisin' around and gettin' themselves in trouble. Daddy was quiet, but he raised some hell when he was young. He got a kick out of tellin' me those stories. I know for sure he was hopin' somehow they'd make me wake up and change into a normal, regular guy. He just wanted me to be like him. For my own well-bein'. I know he blamed himself."

"Blamed?!" Gibb burst out before composing himself. "Leo, if your dad never said anything about it, you're just guessing," he groused. "And you're probably guessing wrong. He loved you. You know he did."

"I think he did, yes. But he didn't want me to be gay."

Gibb shrugged.

"So what? I'll bet you a million dollars your dad never said a bad word to you about any of this stuff."

"No, he didn't. But in his quiet way, he'd make his feelings known that bein' queer was something to mock a little bit. He'd see that Dr. Smith from 'Lost in Space' on TV and he'd say, 'That boy got a l'il sugar in his step.' Or if 'Soap' or 'Three's Company' came on, he'd say, 'Oh, *that* guy is on TV again? Well, y'all, I got some stuff I need to do.' And he'd leave the room. He never said anything real bad, but the signal was always clear. Always clear."

"Leo, you're the one who made me feel the best about being gay and accepting myself for who I am," Gibb said, trying to reconnect Leo to his own word. "You're the one who told me that all sexualities are a gift from God. Why are you backtracking on that now and hating on yourself?"

Leo was only half-listening to Gibb, cutting him off before he could say another word, his speech slow but resolute.

"Please," he murmured impatiently, "just listen right now. I was also feelin' bad that night because I'd been tryin' to distance myself from you and us. My feelings for you are so deep. I knew if I kept it up with you, I'd never have a chance at a 'straight' life. Not that I truly wanted that, but...I don't know, it sure would have been easier."

Gibb stared at Leo in confusion. The words coming out of his mouth continued to be a direct contrast to anything he'd ever said from the time they'd first met.

"It's hard sometimes just to accept yourself knowing that some people, people you really love, just never will," Leo lamented softly. "That's why I ran so hot and cold when we were together up north.

"Here's the whole truth, Gibbon Mulcahy. As much shit as I was talkin' about bein' myself and lovin' myself for who I really am, I was just sayin' that shit out loud in front of you to try to convince myself it was true. But it wasn't. The funny thing is, *you* were the one who was makin' *me* realize it's possible to have some kind of normal, lovin' relationship with another guy."

Gibb could only stare blankly at Leo. He wasn't sure how to put it into words, but he was beginning to think that Leo had been some sort of salesman the whole time, a big phony talking a big game with all of his deep philosophical insights and flowery, loving words. And it all turned out to be bullshit. Gibb now wished Leo had never started talking, but it was clear he wasn't ready to stop.

"But I still kept feelin' like I owed Daddy and Mama more," Leo mumbled on. "There was nothin' I could do about it, though, and I was miserable. I always felt like a failure. When Daddy died, I couldn't help but think he left this world blamin' himself for my troubles and disappointed in me too, which is even worse. I felt like total shit about it.

"Then I called you all desperate on the phone when I hadn't even kept my promise to write or call for two months. Another damn failure on my part. I got drunk on beers all alone in my car that night. And then I started drivin'. Then I saw Marie and she waved at me and I pulled over and found a place and we parked awhile. I'm so stupid."

He sighed and closed his eyes.

"Then what happened?" Gibb prodded, still trying hard not to sound angry.

"We sat and talked."

"Is that all?"

"You jealous?" Leo frowned.

"No, I just wanna know what happened," Gibb retorted, his blue eyes flashing danger. Leo got the message.

"We talked, she made a move, and I let her."

"OK…" Gibb said. "And…"

"Well, she noticed right away I wasn't, you know, that into it. She told me I shouldn't-a drank so many beers cuz now I couldn't, you know…perform. I'm so sorry about all this."

"No need to apologize to me," Gibb said flatly. "I don't have a stake in it."

"You sorta do," Leo said, confused. "Me."

Gibb set his jaw and shook his head.

"I don't have any control over you, your choices, or their consequences, dude. I just fell in love with you. It doesn't mean you have to behave a certain way on my behalf. Besides, we never really promised that we were gonna be faithful or whatever, even though that probably would've been cool. But we should at least be honest about stuff."

"That's what I'm tryin' to do, be honest," Leo said, his mood turning sour again.

The tension in the room made the muscles in Gibb's neck stiffen up. He could feel a headache coming on. Still, he wasn't going to let Leo off the hook like he usually would when Leo got flaky.

"Why was Marie driving your car that night?" Gibb almost demanded.

Leo took his time answering. Gibb could see him struggling to find the right words.

"I don't rightly know, and I'm bein' one hundred percent truthful. Marie thought we could have a little more fun if I smoked some weed with her. She thought it would make me get all horny and stuff. So, we got high. Nothing happened after that, though. Between that and all the beers, I just fell asleep."

"In the driver's seat?" Gibb asked confused.

"No, baby. Geez. We were in the *back* seat. I'm pretty sure I left the keys in the ignition when I turned off the car and climbed back there with her. But my mind is so foggy after that. I think I remember wakin' up a little when she was drivin', but I was so wasted I just fell back to sleep. I don't remember anything after that – the wreck, the ambulance, nothin'."

Gibb took a deep breath, pausing long enough to let Leo have a moment of silence before he spoke again.

"I don't know if you know this," Gibb said hesitatingly, "but Marie didn't make it."

"I do know it," Leo said, closing his eyes as the weight of Gibb's words fell on him. "Honey told me a little while ago, before you got here. She said I wasn't drivin', but I feel responsible."

"You weren't driving, so you're not responsible," Gibb said emphatically.

"I still drove drunk, I still let her fool around with me that night, basically usin' her to try to make myself feel better about not measurin' up to what Daddy…and Mama…wanted me to be," Leo said sadly.

"I took advantage 'cuz I knew she liked me that way and would prob'ly wanna fool around. And, as usual, I didn't know what the hell I was doin' with a girl and I couldn't make myself perform. I disrespected her for my own selfish, drunk reasons and I disrespected myself and my own nature. If I'd-a been true to myself, to you and me, none of this would have happened. This is what I get for tryin' to act like I could be somebody I'm not."

Tears rolled down Leo's face.

"I used Marie as a bargaining chip for my parents' love and understanding. For my dead Daddy's approval! Is that fuckin' sick or what? And now that li'l girl is *dead*," Leo said through gritted teeth, "and it's all because of me."

"She's *not* dead because of you," Gibb cried, tears in his own eyes now. "You guys could've just hung out wherever you were and slept it off. She didn't have to drive!"

"I wish it was that simple, Gibb, but it's not. If I hadn't been in that state of mind when I was drivin', sure she might've waved when I drove past, but I know I wouldn't have pulled over. I would've just waved back and kept on rollin'. It's a simple fact: if I hadn't been drinkin' and drivin' and all pathetic that night, Marie Guidry would still be here right now.

"I'm gonna carry this guilt with me for the rest of my life. I made a huge mistake and now I can see for myself what I've heard older people say a million times: it don't matter how much good stuff you've done, you only need to screw up once to ruin the entire rest of your life. I might as well have died in that wreck, too, because my life is over."

"Your life isn't over," Gibb said.

"Yeah, well I wish it was," came Leo's mumbled reply. "I am nothin' but a no-good fake."

"No, you're not," Gibb whispered.

They sat in silence for a few minutes, Leo with his eyes closed in the bed, Gibb perched uneasily on the uncomfortable hospital room chair.

Everything seemed so bleak, so hopeless. A girl he'd never met was dead, Leo was involved, felt responsible for it, and wished he was dead, too. It was going to take a long, painful time before Leo recovered from his injuries, if he really ever recovered at all. Honey and Sissie were at each other's throats all the time and being around them was unbearable. He loved Sissie and he was fond of Honey, too, individually. But he'd rather scorch his hands on a red-hot waffle iron than be around the two of them together for another minute.

Sitting in that hospital chair, grimacing his way through the inventory he was taking of his current situation, the out-and-out misery of it all almost made Gibb laugh out loud. Impulsively – with no thought, only action – he'd made the trek all the way down here with no plan, no ideas, no strategy. He wasn't sure what all he'd sacrificed to do it, but suddenly it felt like a lot. He thought he had come down here for love, like some epic Hollywood drama where he and Leo would get top billing and it would be amazing. He wanted to retch.

*I think I'm in the wrong movie,* he thought as he looked at his broken boyfriend laying in that damn hospital bed. He felt like a chump. A doormat. Way too young for this and what was he even getting out of it anyway? He didn't know what he was doing. Why had he tried to act like he did? Or that he could just easily figure things out when he got down here to Louisiana?

So, it wasn't just Leo. They both were fakes, Gibb thought. Pretenders, faking their way through life until the reality bill came due. Now here it was and how the hell would they be able to pay it?

This whole stupid trip was now only the dumbest thing he could ever imagine himself doing. Suddenly panicked, Gibb wavered between wanting to just leave the room right then and wanting to just totally leave New Orleans. Tonight.

If he'd known a week ago what he knew now…nope, he wouldn't be here. He *definitely* wouldn't be here. When Leo called him at home last Thursday, Gibb would've just broken up with him over the phone, sent him a sympathy card for the death of his father, graduated high school with his classmates, and right now he'd be working his summer landscaping job before taking off for college in the fall.

Suddenly, Eislertown didn't look so bad. He wanted to go home. Now.

"Leo, I gotta go," Gibb stated matter-of-factly. "Get some sleep. Sissie will be here in a few hours."

"Where are you going?" Leo asked, his groggy eyes now open and confused.

"Out of here," Gibb said. "I need to get out and walk around." He patted Leo's shoulder, then stalked towards the hospital room door.

"I love you," he heard Leo call out hoarsely behind him, "more than you'll ever know."

Gibb just kept walking.

## Chapter 31

# KILLING SHAME

"*I love you, more than you'll ever know.*"

*Bullshit,* Gibb thought. *Bullshit!* Who *was* that wax figure in that hospital room, melting all over the bed in that pathetic display of shame and self-hatred? Where was the amazing, confident guy who'd jumped right in and performed CPR on the glider pilot last fall? The guy who knew every incarnation of the Grateful Dead and the best versions of every song they'd ever played from every tour they'd ever done? Where the hell was *Leo*? Beautiful, intelligent, gentle, kind- hearted, philosophical, Plato-quoting, not-ashamed-of-being-gay Leo?

Had Gibb completely ignored all the warning signs this whole time in order to dream up some love story that really didn't, couldn't, exist?

The St. Charles streetcar was crammed with passengers as Gibb struggled his way through the packed aisle to the back of the car. He tried to block Leo's hoarse voice from his mind, but he couldn't. The words, the whole scene, kept replaying over and over in his mind as a looming feeling of panic began to set in. He darted his eyes wildly around the crowded street car. He wanted to get out of here. Out of this city. Out of this relationship. Out of this whole mess of a mistake.

Gibb reached into his right front pocket to adjust the position of the rose quartz crystal. At this moment it felt only like a fat, worthless annoyance.

He clutched the rock and ran his thumb along its rough face. The blood – his blood, Leo's blood – once mixed together to stain these surfaces in some sham symbolic gesture of love, was no longer visible on the crystal. Over the past few months, holding onto it as hard as he had, Gibb had unintentionally rubbed it all away. Now it just felt blank and hot in his hand, as hot as the angry tears built up behind the formidable dams hidden somewhere within the corners of his eyes.

But there was no way was he going to cry. Not over this. They could all go to hell – everyone on this street car, everyone in New Orleans, his mother, his stepfather, Eislertown, Leo's whole family, and Leo with 'em!

He was so tired of feeling this absurdly familiar mix of anger and humiliation. There had to be a better way to feel, a better way to just…*be*.

Gibb had no clue what he was doing right now, or where in this godforsaken city he actually was, but at least he knew the route back towards Char and Sam's. Maybe he'd just show up today for their crawfish boil after all. Rolling dazedly along, he watched New Orleans through the streetcar's open windows, going about its life, completely oblivious to him or his woes.

He tried to focus on his breathing. Still clenching the hot, pink-hued crystal, he took a deep gulp of air and immediately regretted it. His head hurt and he felt nauseous. Too many people aboard this thing needed a shower and why in hell was that woman barefoot on a public streetcar?

Gibb looked out the window at just the wrong time. Up above on a second story balcony, two skeletons dressed in evening clothes stood sentinel as the streetcar rolled by, vacantly staring down at the clueless passengers. Repulsed, Gibb turned away, only to see another house with skulls painted on its windows on the other side of the street. He felt his breath getting short again.

At the next stop, he anxiously jumped off and immediately realized he had no idea where he was. It wouldn't be hard to get back, though. He just needed to follow the streetcar tracks back a few blocks.

When he got to Sixth Street he made an arbitrary right turn, expecting he'd run right into Camp Street if he kept walking in this direction. What he didn't expect was to come upon his first New Orleans cemetery right at the next block, the intersection of busy Prytania and tranquil Sixth.

In his current agitated and queasy state, the aged, stern and weather-abused greyish brick wall guarding the 7-foot crucifix-crowned tombs inside disturbed him deeply. It seemed like everything in his own life was dead or dying, turning back to grey again (*again!*) and now here was this awful place. What a disgustingly literal reminder.

Gibb had learned that New Orleans cemeteries were unique in the sense that no one was really buried in them; they were entombed above ground in those snug, grim stone vaults. Placed close together like that, the vaults actually could pass for a line of office buildings or apartment houses on some ghoulish, achromatic city street.

But they weren't apartments and Gibb knew it. They were essentially ovens, baking away the putrefying remains of someone somebody loved, until all that was left were the bones. Then someone would pull the bones out and dump them down to the bottom of the vault and cram someone else in on the top shelf.

*Next.*

Gibb could feel his stomach churning in the hot sun. Trying to play it off, he casually steadied himself against the grey cemetery wall for a second, trying not to draw any attention from passersby, taking a couple of deep breaths to ward off the strong wave of nausea sweeping over him.

The odd thing was, to Gibb anyway, that this place was crawling with tourists, walking around in there, having fun. The laughter from the other side of the cemetery wall made things just that much worse, just enough that even as he willed himself to move quickly past this sad place, his defiant legs rooted him in place right where he stood. His short breaths turned to dry-heaves and then, without a chance to stop it, he finally just threw up all over the cemetery wall.

There he was, Gibbon Mulcahy, bent over and gagging, holding himself up on the wall's decrepit bricks. His red mop of hair stood on end, his ordinarily pleasant freckled face contorted in shame and disgust. Disgust not just with himself but with those…those…wide-open heathens on the other side of the wall.

*Why in hell are they laughing?* he asked himself angrily. *In a cemetery of all places. Among the remains of so many peoples' loved ones, people who would never be seen nor heard from again. Wasn't this a place of sadness? A place to show respect simply by being quiet? Or was laughing in a graveyard just another one of those weird things people did here?*

As the giggling continued, he closed his eyes to avoid, if only for a second, the truth again of where he was standing. Some random cemetery under the blazing hot sun somewhere in the middle of New Orleans, Louisiana. Completely and totally alone. He braced himself against the wall. Doubt, already haunting him like a ghost from inside one of those vaults, besieged him now.

*This whole thing…this whole Leo reunion thing.* As soon as Gibb arrived here, everything unraveled so quickly, it was as if the Universe had deliberately yanked the only loose thread holding the plan together…and then kept pulling. Just for the fun of it. And that was the most galling part of this: it felt like fate was toying with him. It hurt like hell.

Now this humiliating scene, staring down at his own vomit on the New Orleans sidewalk as he steadied himself against a freakin' cemetery wall, finally crushed his spirit. And sadly, maybe that was the whole point of this whole, stupid journey. To crush his spirit.

*I just gotta get home,* he whispered to himself.

Suddenly, right into his left ear, a baritone voice, gravelly and musical, broke Gibb's wretched reverie. Chagrined when he realized the voice was actually talking to *him*, he kept his eyes closed in a silent, vain attempt to wish the sound away.

"Hey, monkey! Where *Y'AT?*" the voice called out, laughing.

Gibb didn't move.

"He ain't down there on the ground, man. Lift that head up!"

The voice paused, then chuckled. "Lookin' like a derelic' all hunched over there."

Only because the burgeoning Louisiana afternoon sun was threatening to burn his arm off the cemetery wall did Gibb regain his posture and slowly, grudgingly, turn towards the voice. Blinking his eyes against the glare, Gibb could only see a seven-foot backlit shadow towering over him, crowned by a porkpie hat.

"Hi, SamWell," he muttered, a miserable frown pulling at his mouth as he adjusted his glasses.

"Hi, Gibb," Sam mocked with the same sad, mumbling tone. "SamWell! You all formal today! What you doin' out here in broad daylight makin' a spectacle of yourself? You on your way to the boil?"

"I don't know. I think so. I don't know what I'm doing, really."

"Uh-oh," Sam said, cocking his head and frowning as he saw not just the torment on Gibb's face, but the result of it on the grey brick wall and sidewalk.

"I'm pretty much in hell right now," Gibb lamented.

"You gon' be all right," Sam said, too casually for Gibb's liking.

"I'm not so sure about that right now. Everything is just so jacked up."

"I don't know, man – you lookin' all right to me."

"No, I'm not!" Gibb barked. "I'm standing outside this gross graveyard right next to a puddle of my own puke for the whole world to see. See that?"

He pointed angrily at the puddle. Sam winced and turned away.

"I'm a bad joke, that's what I am. Feeling like shit in a city that might as well be in a foreign country because I don't know where the hell I am and I don't understand anything that's going on. It's hot and humid as hell, the streetcar was crowded and smelled like B.O., and then I hear people on the other side of that graveyard wall laughing while they're walking around. This place is wacko!

"And even worse, Leo's in the hospital wishing he was dead, the girl he was riding with when he had his accident *is* dead and being around his family makes me wish *I* was dead. Or *them*. Somebody's gotta go! Whatever works! Just somebody make it stop!"

Sam tried to break in, but Gibb's polemic, increasingly frantic now, steamrolled that endeavor.

"Nothing makes any sense down here in New Orleans. I came down here for life. I came down here for what I thought was love!" he said, pulling the crystal out of his pocket to wave it around in front of Sam. "But the only thing I see and feel around here is death. I can't get away from it! Skull rings on fingers are cool, but skeletons on balconies and skulls laughing in windows?! It's June, it's not Halloween!

"Why is death out in plain sight everywhere? Like even right here where we're standing! Shit, the bodies stay above the ground! They're right inside that ugly little vault right next to this wall. They'll rot and decompose there, RIGHT THERE! And the stupid, giggling tourists love it in there!"

"Dude, no, no," Sam said, trying to calm Gibb down. "They don't put nobody in this here cemetery no more. Jus' empty vaults in there now."

His attempt at consolation didn't work.

"Well...they put the bodies in this kind of cemetery somewhere! Leo's Dad is newly buried – or entombed or whatever you wanna call it - in one of these sick places 'cuz you can't really bury 'em here, can you? No, you can't, because this stupid place is below sea-level! What is this, Atlantis?! How is it even possible that people can live below sea-level? At least my dad was buried properly, in the ground, where bodies belong!"

Gibb was holding forth now as Sam's eyes, hidden behind his sunglasses, looked on with increasing concern, not for the first time, over the young man's mental state.

"And look right down here, here's another thing," he said, frantically kicking at the ground.

"Look at all these stiff, dead, little brown oak leaves all over this sidewalk. See 'em? It's summer, isn't it? Those things died last fall, didn't they? Then why can't they sweep the sidewalks around here?! Why do we have to see dead leaves everywhere? And to make it all worse, right next to a cemetery!"

"They just leaves, man. Get a grip," Sam said somberly, trying to reason with him.

"Get a grip?!" Gibb fumed, kicking at the ground again. "They're just like the bodies in those vaults! Dead forever. But everyone walking past still has to see them! They'll kick the dead leaves around like I just did and then it'll be the wind's turn to toss them around and laugh at them.

"Just like those people laughing inside the cemetery," he whispered, almost maniacally. "Then it'll be the sun's turn to bake these leaves until they finally disintegrate into dust, just like the bodies in those vaults.

"There's nothing funny about that, when we're all alive outside this wall and they're all dead in there," Gibb said, frustratedly waving his arm at the cemetery, "and all the dead leaves on the ground are sitting right below those beautiful, living bright green leaves on these trees."

"Dude…" Sam tried to break in, but Gibb talked right over him.

"Maybe they're there just to remind us that we're all gonna be dead soon too?! Is that it? It's FUCKED. UP. OK?! Death is what happens when there's too much shame!"

He punctuated the end of his rant by spitting right onto the cemetery wall, then turning to glare right at his reflection in Sam's sunglasses.

Sam, about to speak again, abruptly paused as he watched Gibb drop his head to stare down at the sidewalk again, this time his shoulders shaking.

"I'm so sick of all the fucking silent shame," Gibb said hoarsely, tears in his voice. "Shame almost killed Leo. It did kill that poor girl, Marie. It's gonna kill everything!"

Silent tears began to rack Gibb's body as he bent over the sidewalk on the now quiet street.

Sam glanced down at the pitiful sight, but there was nothing he could say at that moment. Nothing that could help, anyway. The laughter from the other side of the cemetery wall rang out like a funeral toll. He leaned back against the wall, sighed, and waited for Gibb's storm to pass.

## Chapter 32

# LIKE ANY OTHER DAY THAT'S EVER BEEN

Warily, Sam looked around to see if they'd caught the attention of anyone else nearby, but only the two of them - the forty-something towering seven-foot black man, dressed in black from hat to boot, and the alabaster-skinned bespectacled red-headed young man he hoped was wearing sunscreen – remained standing there on the sunny side of Sixth Street.

Gibb took another moment to pull himself together. A grim, recalcitrant scowl set like concrete across his face. Until he glanced over at Sam. Suddenly, Gibb felt ridiculous. He reached under his glasses to rub his eyes, took a deep breath, and apologized.

"I'm sorry, Sam," Gibb said defeatedly. "I can really lose my shit sometimes. I've just never done it out in public. But seriously, fuck all this."

"Mmm-hmm," SamWell murmured. He lazily stretched one long arm, then the other, way above his head. "When you ready I got a question for you."

"I'm ready," Gibb muttered.

"What's the name of your favorite band again?"

"My what?" Gibb fixed SamWell with a befuddled stare before Sam's question registered. "Oh, Grateful Dead," he answered, his brow furrowed in confusion.

"That's what I thought. Think about that name for one second. With a name like that, you think they ain't been ridin' right alongside ol' Death himself the entire time they been playin'? Havin' a high old time, laughin' at him in they own way. And every time you listened to 'em you been ridin' and laughin' right along wit' 'em. And you wasn't even thinkin' about that, was you? So what? Jus' because you wasn't payin' attention don't mean it wasn't happenin'."

Baffled, Gibb squinted his eyes.

"What?"

"OK, maybe that don't make no sense right now. I'll try another way. Lookie here Gibb, life is tough, man. But look, dude, it's this way *everywhere* in the world, whether you believe it or not. It ain't just New Orleans. I can't tell what's freakin' you out more – death or your regrets about comin' down here."

"It's all the same to me," Gibb grumbled. "Y'know, it would totally make sense for whatever I had with Leo to die right here next to a graveyard, out in the open for everyone to see. It's all the freakin' same. The secret shame. The awkwardness. Ultimately finding out that even *he* didn't want to accept that what we had was…"

Gibb reached his right hand into his front pocket start feeling around in the front pocket of his jeans.

"Was what?" Sam nudged, watching Gibb fumbling around.

Gibb's hand popped out of his pocket with the rose quartz crystal as he answered Sam's question.

"Good!" Gibb retorted. "Legitimate! As real and important as any other loving relationship in this world. See this?" He held up the crystal for Sam to see.

"This was supposed to symbolize love or something. But it's nothing but a stupid pink rock infused with his stupid shame. Another dead, inanimate object. Just like whatever's on the other side of that wall. And now I'm gonna put it exactly where it belongs."

Gibb cocked his hand back to wing the crystal over the cemetery wall.

"Nooope," Sam said, his deep, booming voice making Gibb pause. "You throw that over that wall you gon' knock somebody in the head. Look here, give that thing to me!"

"No!" Gibb pulled his hand away. "No! No one is touching this dead freakin' thing but me."

He glared at Sam.

"Don't you see? The shame he's feeling has killed us. Not physically, but it's death just the same. Now that's all I'm seeing around here, smiling skulls and skeletons and laughing cemeteries. Making light of it all. God, I hate this place!"

"Boy, please," Sam said unsentimentally. "Every album and T-shirt of your band got a skull or a skeleton on it. Now you gon' act like you don't understand what's up."

A flash of acknowledgement disappeared from Gibb's eyes as quickly as it came.

"Mmm-hmm. You see now," Sam said. "Maybe we jus' look at it more practical down here, but death *is* everywhere, no matter where you go in the world. Two steps from the curb if a bus comin' too fast. Three inches to the left when two cars passin' each other. One stray bullet, one sharp blade, one skipped heartbeat. Death. Always there, right beside us. No mercy. Since the day we all was born."

"You're not making me feel any better," Gibb grunted.

"I'm not tryin' to. 'Cuz I can't do nothin' about it. Death is just part of *being*. You already know this, but you don't wanna admit it. Maybe we jus' deal wit' it better down here than y'all descendants of them ol' white Puritans up north."

Gibb shrugged. "Do you?"

"Think about it," Sam replied. "Some folks up North would prob'ly call it respect, the way they handle death and dying. But what it's really called is *fear*. They *afraid*. Of somethin' they gon' pretend don't exist they entire lives, until it happen. Then they try to bury it as quick as possible and get back to they little game of pretend. The difference down here, we *celebrate*."

Gibb shook his head in derision.

"Celebrate?" he muttered sarcastically. "What do you mean, celebrate? What the hell is there to celebrate about death?"

"Not death, man. *Life*! We gotta face *life*. All of it! Much as it hurts, death is one side of the coin of *being*. Life on one side, Death on the other. Can you think of one thing in this world that only got one side to it?"

Gibb looked contemplative, but Sam waved him off.

"We gon' save time by lettin' me answer that question for you: *Hell. No.* There's two sides to everything on Earth, man. And every grown adult human being also know there's a whole lot of shit in *between* them two sides. You just enterin' through that adult door now. But you learnin'."

"That's for damn sure. More than I should have to," Gibb mumbled, wiping his eye on his T-shirt sleeve.

"Nope, *as much* as you have to. Not more. You just maybe gettin' your lessons younger than a lot of folks do. But they all gonna get them lessons, too. We can learn to celebrate Death as just one big part of *being*. That's why you see them skulls and skeletons in June 'round here, or all year long on your Dead albums. Death don't just show up at Halloween. He always on the other side of somebody's wall, doin' that reapin'," Sam said, patting the grey bricks.

Gibb didn't want to hear any more. He understood, to some extent, what Sam was saying. So what that the approach to mourning physical death in New Orleans with their parades and music and noise was different from the way things were done in upstate New York? Gibb was talking about *all* death – the deaths of people and animals, sure, but then there was the death of dreams and goals and happiness. The death of Love itself and the somber, grey-walled aftermath. The end of the only loving relationship he'd ever had and all because the person he'd loved so much was actually secretly, deeply ashamed of it. Of himself. Of Gibb.

The pain of that thought felt too similar to what he'd felt as a child when his cousin Billy died. This was deep grief he was feeling and the worst part was, just like Billy's death, it was sudden and unexpected. There was no one – not Leo, not Sam, not even Ms. Mullan – who could help him get through this. Gibb was on his own. Unsmiling, he glanced up at Sam.

"I don't know what to do. Any suggestions?" he asked grimly.

"Nope...it really ain't none of my business now, is it?" Sam asked.

"Well, if you were me, what would you do? If you'd been this impulsive and you wanted to believe in someone as much as I did to just run down here...and you ran into this same situation, what would you do?"

"Run like hell," Sam deadpanned.

Gibb almost smiled. Sometimes Sam was funny even when he didn't mean to be.

"That's why I ain't the guy to be givin' nobody relationship advice," Sam said. "I ain't never cared about a woman the way y'all two are carryin' on. So…"

Gibb cut him off. "But imagine you did. Say she was the most amazing woman you'd ever met, the kind they write songs about. Wouldn't you want to follow her anywhere she went to be with her, even if she was hot and cold towards you? So, say you did go to be with her, and *then* you find out she's not really the person you thought she was at all. No matter how beautiful she is, she's now really a wreck, physically and emotionally. Would you try to figure it out? Would you stay?"

"Man, I don't know. It ain't about me," Sam replied impatiently. "Listen to yourself, though. You don't need *me* to tell you it's time to get real, dude. Seriously. You come down here for a huge reason. Maybe now you findin' out you actually come here for a totally *different* huge reason.

"You say you love that Leo cat, right? So, you gotta figure out what that means. Do love really last forever, through time and distance and all kind of trouble? The story book shit? Only you can answer that. You wanna be there for him, then you gonna be there for him. If you don't, then you won't. It ain't really complicated. You just gotta figure it out."

"I know you're right," Gibb said, pausing to think before he spoke again. "And I don't think I have it in me to stay. I'm being honest with myself – I don't know what I'm doing. I'm clueless. And I don't know how to deal with taking care of somebody. He's gonna need a lot of care for a while."

"Only one person got the answer to all of it. And I'm lookin' at him," Sam said.

"I wasn't planning on staying down here forever," Gibb lamented.

Sam scratched his chin and shook his head. He took a folded red handkerchief out of his pocket and dabbed his brow.

"Mr. Gibbon-the-Monkey-Man," he said, "I'm done testifyin'. I'm out of ideas."

The words hung in the air between them like cobwebs. Gibb's whole body drooped at the weight of them. Out of the millions of times he'd felt foolish in his life, none compared to what he was feeling at this moment. Foolish. Stupid. Sucker. Bottomless pit of need.

What if he left, went back to Eislertown and put this behind him? Leo would have to figure it out for himself. And Gibb would never again be so willing to give himself entirely to any future relationship, no matter how hot or how cool the guy was. *Or seemed to be,* Gibb thought sardonically.

But shouldn't he stay? How could he really let himself leave when Leo needed him? Leo was in bad shape. Was now really the time to go?

Yes, Gibb thought. It *is* time to go. Leo called him on a whim, got himself in some real trouble, and now needed someone to help him bear the burden of it all. Why should it be Gibb? What right did Leo have to ask, let alone expect, him to stay through the tough days ahead? For the first time, Gibb had to really ask himself, *What the hell is in it for me?*

"I gotta head over to the house," Sam said, his deep baritone rousting Gibb from his racing thoughts for a moment. "Boil starts soon."

Gibb nodded. "I'm sorry I wasn't able to be there today to help set up," he apologized. "I guess it was kind of a lot to think I could do that and be there for Leo, too."

"All good. Nobody can do everything. You comin' back to the house with me now or you need some time for yourself? Folks gonna show up around three – we start playin' at four. Cool?"

"Sam," Gibb said his voice apologetic now, "I'm real sorry for the way I've been talking to you here. I don't know what kind of weird magic happened to allow us to meet up there in the Finger Lakes, but I'm sure glad we did. I don't know how I'd deal with any of this crap if you weren't here to talk to. I'm sorry about all this. Just…thank you."

Sam raised a long-fingered hand and waved him off. "Stop, boy. I didn't do nothin'. Just listened. And I think you got this figured out already, just needed somebody to tell you that any decision you make is the right one."

He high-fived Gibb.

"Good luck," Sam said over his shoulder, disappearing into the dark shade further up Sixth Street.

Gibb turned around and headed in the opposite direction. For now, he had to keep walking, as far and as fast as he could, away from this miserable cemetery, its ghoulish laughing visitors, and those stone-grey monuments to the cruelest transitions people have to experience: the end of everything that love once was.

*Forever is not just time,* Leo had said in parting a few months ago. No, it is not, Gibb thought. It was much more than he could have ever imagined.

The rose-quartz crystal felt like a boulder in his pocket as he walked.

*Chapter 33*

# FRAGILE THUNDER

One short year. Twelve long months. Four full seasons, with one chance in history to change the world forever, all becoming the perfect mirror for the life cycle of a person's most cherished dream. First, the exhilaration and relief as it bursts into full bloom. The confusion about what to do next as the dream, still beautiful, matures but maybe changes into something different, something you didn't expect, maybe something you didn't even want. Then cold grief and mourning as the old dream dies and disappears. But somehow, miraculously, hope shows up. Hope in the dead of winter when a promise, born of a new understanding, revives the best part of something you may have thought was gone forever. And everything begins again.

That was Gibb's life and that was Gibb's dream with Leo. Exactly one year before, Gibb stood sick and anxious in front of Sam outside a New Orleans cemetery's gates, overwhelmed by the death of his ideals at the brutal hands of dark reality. But today, a whole year later, the twin blessings of time and distance allowed him the perspective to look back on those days with a lot less grief.

He'd learned something. Loving somebody was a lot more than infatuation with their looks, more than sex, more than laughter or companionship or being needed. Love's lessons actually came from the post-graduate school of life itself. And while his lessons happened to begin while he was young, it really didn't matter when a person enrolled in that school. They would be destined to a lifelong pursuit of knowledge because, in the curriculum of Love, not one human being ever, has ever been rumored to have ever earned their degree.

So here it was, whole year later, and it was summer in the Garden District again. And there he was, at Char and Sam's crawfish boil again. Thinking about Leo again. Everything the same, everything different. As he stood with Honey and Isabelle in the shade of the huge palm tree in the side yard of Char's Edward Street mansion, they talked about last summer. Even joked around about it a little bit.

"But when Isabelle pulled those two yarn voodoo dolls out of her purse…" Gibb said, almost doubled over in laughter out on the overcrowded lawn.

"I like to have died right in front of that lady doctor," Honey said, her own laugh self-conscious as she gave a sidelong glance to Isabelle who was standing right next to her, casually drinking a cup of sweet tea.

"Y'all knew I was serious, and that's all I'll say about that," Isabelle said, a smile in her eyes but not on her lips.

Tent-like canopies covered long picnic tables loaded with amazing New Orleans food: crawfish with corn and sausage, seafood gumbo, boiled shrimp, coolers full of drinks, and almost every spot around them taken by revelers who'd been invited to come "throw it down" (Sam's words) out in Char and Sam's amazing yard.

Gibb's attention shifted to the front gate.

"He's here," he said to Honey and Isabelle. "I'll go get him and bring him over here."

Cutting across the yard, Gibb could only shake his head. How was it already June again? He'd learned more in these past twelve months than he had in all the rest of his nineteen, now going on twenty, years. But last year, that troubled time when Gibb was facing the hardest decision of his young life, didn't really feel that long ago. Fortunately for him, though, he'd made the right choice, thanks to the sound and experienced mentoring of three individuals who'd now become the most trusted and loved people in Gibb's life.

The first, of course, was Sam. A year ago, Sam's wisdom had given Gibb new ways to think about life's entire set-up, from a completely different perspective than he'd ever been exposed to before. Gibb would never forget it and he would be Sam's friend forever.

The second person reminded Gibb of the practicality of life, the need to fulfill life's purpose not just for the physical and emotional joy of it, but also for the good of all the people in it. That person was Sam's sister Char.

When he'd arrived at the crawfish boil last year, it hadn't taken Gibb long to find out something very specific about Char Dreaux from other people in attendance. Char owned five different restaurants in New Orleans and had also opened successful places in Atlanta and Tampa. She also did a ton of work on behalf of the less fortunate and it got her a lot of attention in New Orleans. Quietly, the locals knew that if you were known to be poor and needed to eat, you could go to her restaurants and eat for free. There was a special table at the back of each one, out of view of the paying customers in front, to serve the needy and give those guests some much-welcomed privacy.

And it turned out that this event, her annual crawfish boil, was actually a big fundraiser for college scholarships for minority students living here in New Orleans, attracting many well-heeled locals and even some out-of-towners fortunate enough to receive an invitation.

At last year's boil, she had offered Gibb a part-time summer job at Zazzy's, her gumbo shop in the Tremé district of New Orleans. In private, she'd learned of Gibb's situation from Sam. Without mentioning his troubles, Char had only told Gibb that if he was planning to stay in New Orleans for the summer, she'd hire him. And once she realized he had landscaping experience, she started paying him to maintain the perfect lawn currently being torn up by all of her crawfish boil guests.

For a while that June afternoon last year, Gibb had convinced himself he was leaving New Orleans, leaving Leo, his struggles, and their whole relationship behind. Char's job offer had taken some of the certainty out of Gibb's tortured self-proclamation. If he could somehow make some money in New Orleans, he could work, help take care of Leo, then go back to Eislertown at the end of the summer. He just needed a place to stay.

When he brought up that possibility to Isabelle, she interrupted him mid-sentence.

"Stay as long as you want, baby. Honey doesn't ever want you to leave – at least not while that baby is in such bad shape."

So, he stayed. And over those hell-hot, long months of last summer in New Orleans, it was Isabelle who'd become Gibb's most deeply trusted friend. She was there every day to experience the challenges of Leo's physical and emotional rehabilitation. Like Gibb, she was connected to the Davion family but she wasn't truly part of it. That common thread linked the two of them, but it was their similar, resolute approach to dealing with the challenge of Leo's rehabilitation and his wildly emotional family, that bonded them.

Gibb could describe Isabelle's approach in three simple phrases: No airs. No attitudes. No nonsense. She had a quiet, steady presence. Where Gibb had been emotional and vulnerable last year, Isabelle was straightforward and level-headed. She became a sort of mother-figure to a young man who had always needed one.

"You stay with something only for as long as it makes sense," Isabelle told him last June, "but that doesn't mean you're gonna be able to leave tonight, baby. You won't get away clean. You wanna know why? It's because every ghost that has ever been has come fluttering out of a mess that somebody left behind, and it will haunt them every day until they fix that mess or die running from it. But once you make your peace with everything, you're free. Free to make any choice you want, and then that new choice commits you.

"From what I can see, you've only made one choice that commits you. That choice isn't Leo. You know what it is, don't you?"

Gibb had stared at her in confusion.

Isabelle smiled. "It's college. You love Leo and you want to help him. That's good. But you have your own life, too, and you need to live it. Stay down here with us for as long as it makes sense, but then you go on home and go to school at the end of the summer. Leo will understand. It's the only way, really."

And that was it. Looking back on it a year later the decision seemed so obvious, but in his own turmoil, Gibb had been thinking of this as a decision based on one of two extremes. Forego college and stay here to take care of Leo. Figure the rest out later. Or head back to Eislertown that night without saying goodbye and no further contact, disappearing exactly the way Leo did. Give him a taste of his own terrible medicine.

Seeing things only in extremes and absolutes, impulse and compulsion, Gibb hadn't really thought of how to find a solid middle. Loving Leo had been all or nothing, and now Gibb knew that his approach had come out of his own wounded need to be loved as deeply. And as desperately.

But that night last June, Isabelle was able to give words to a scenario Gibb should easily have been able to see for himself. And she had it right. Gibb could still keep a relationship with Leo and be there for him all summer, work for Char, and then he could head back home for school.

Three weeks after that heart-to-heart with Isabelle, Leo was released from the hospital to recuperate at Honey and Isabelle's house in their spare bedroom. And it wasn't only physical rehabilitation that Leo had to endure. There were police interviews and reports, denied insurance claims, and threats of lawsuits from Marie Guidry's family adding to the sometimes-overwhelming stress of last summer, but Leo weathered them with humility and courage. He really was sorry for what he'd put everyone through, often vowing to Gibb that he would try to make things right, somehow, when he was able to walk again.

Gibb slept in Leo's room on an air mattress and on the nights Sissie came to help and visit, he'd sleep on the couch in the front room so she could be close to her brother. Sissie and Honey continued splitting their time between Bache and New Orleans, tending to both Leo and Mrs. Davion at the same time until Mrs. Davion was discharged from the hospital a few weeks later. Mrs. Davion was able to live independently at home in Bache, but Sissie and Honey still made sure she had their frequent companionship.

Through it all, Isabelle was everybody's calm and solid rock, a positive and supportive presence for each of them as they dealt with the emotional and physical challenges facing them the rest of last summer.

Somehow, miraculously, Sissie and Honey finally made themselves get along. There were no more screaming matches or angry words. They weren't exactly best friends, but they weren't threatening to cut each other or snatch each other bald or talking behind the other's back, either. Progress.

On the day Gibb left to go back up to Eislertown late last August, on a plane this time, he promised Leo he'd come back at Christmas break. And when he did return, Leo had been able to walk to him on a walker, the event heartbreaking and amazing at the same time, another fine example of the two conjoined and opposite sides of Sam's coin of *being*. Just like everything else in the world.

They got to celebrate an anniversary of sorts on that visit, the anniversary of their first kiss, exactly one year before on Christmas Eve. Gibb brought the rose quartz crystal and placed it on the table between them, a silent symbol of all they'd felt and experienced since that night. There was a somberness to their observance, considering the dizzying and awful events of the last year. They raised glasses of iced tea to the memory of Leo's father and also to Marie Guidry and they cried. Leo would never again drink alcohol.

And now it was summer again. In the last year, Gibb had graduated high school, taken his legendary (in his mind anyway) ride to New Orleans with Sam, helped Leo recuperate for three months after almost ditching him and his family entirely, met a whole new group of people in New Orleans working at Zazzy's, finished his first year of college back in New York state where he'd also met many new people, and finally came out to his mother. Her reaction had been as awkward and muted as he'd expected it to be, but it felt good to tell her what she needed to know. Jack could still kiss his ass. He would always be a clown and Gibb didn't give a damn what he thought, especially now that he didn't have to spend any time at their house.

And there was one other, even more delicate, issue that Gibb had to address. He hadn't exactly been faithful to Leo in the time they'd been apart this past year. He struggled with the idea, but he was honest enough to tell Leo the truth about those encounters. Leo had been honest enough to say that he didn't like it, but that he understood and wanted, needed, Gibb to be careful.

Their lives depended on it now. A new disease called AIDS, caused by a terrible virus and transmitted sexually, was killing gay men by completely shutting down their immune systems. And once you had it, there was no stopping it. It killed everyone it infected.

The disease was being brushed off by "good people" as something gay guys deserved for their "wickedness" or "sinfulness", but now that some heterosexual people were also testing positive for it, AIDS had finally begun to get at least a little more attention from the federal government as a real health crisis. Leo wasn't being dramatic when he told Gibb that sex was a matter of life and death now and to remember that it wasn't just Gibb's own life at stake. Gibb made that promise and kept it.

Still, in the face of all they'd experienced in their young lives over the past year, the love between Gibb and Leo remained strong. Strong enough to bring Gibb back down to New Orleans for another hot, hellish summer. Strong enough for them to plan a road trip over to Texas at the end of August to finally see the Grateful Dead play a couple of shows if Leo could manage it. And tough enough for them to stare down the reality that, as powerfully as they loved each other, life would do with them whatever it wanted.

Whatever this relationship was, they both now knew that it may not last forever, no matter how hard they tried. But for today, anyway, all was well. A year ago, Gibb had hitchhiked down to New Orleans because, for the first time in his life, there was somewhere he truly needed to be. This whole experience with Leo and his family had finally given him the chance to connect with something bigger than his own thoughts, fantasies, and wishes. He was finally able to live outside of his head and in that two-sided world of *being* that Sam had mentioned, a world full of dysfunction but, as he'd also discovered, a world full of love for him and what he brought to it. There would be no going back to the old, grey Eislertown life, even if he did decide to stay in New York after college.

Gibb hustled over to the front gate. And there he was, Leopold James Davion - still the most important person in the world with the handsomest smile - sporting some shades and resting on his cane as he tried to get the gate open. He'd insisted on walking over here by himself today, even though he knew it was going to be slow, especially in the heat and sun. But he'd made it, New Orleans summer weather be damned.

Gibb wiped the sweat off Leo's brow with his own, now ever-present handkerchief. He'd learned last year that you can't get through a New Orleans summer afternoon without one.

"I did pretty good. Didn't take me as long as I thought," Leo said as Gibb wrapped him in a hug. "But we better all go and take cover under one of those tarps. It looks like there's another little storm comin'."

They both heard a low rumble as Gibb looked up into the quickly darkening sky.

"Oh, that's pretty unusual," he said with a laugh, taking Leo's free arm and escorting him to the table, both of them chuckling as they made their way over to the rest of the family.

## THE END

# ABOUT THE AUTHOR

Joe McKinstry is a musician and writer living on the amazing Olympic Peninsula of Washington State with his husband, Paul, and their fur babies: a beautiful Golden Retriever named Scout and a handsome one-eyed Catman named Jack. After Joe retires from his career in the Seattle biotech industry in a few years, he hopes to write more novels and short stories and get back to writing and performing his music on a more regular schedule.

# ACKNOWLEDGEMENTS

To my beloved father, mother, and four sisters: We will always be seven strong, no matter how life tries to contradict that notion. Love is forever.

For long-ago believing and instilling in me a sense of confidence in my ability to write, here's to my favorite English teachers and professors: Pat (Mrs.) McDonald, Irene Recuber, Fran Kline, Dom Guagliardo, Pat Stillwell, and Dr. Catherine Dibello.

Thanks to a great and encouraging editor, Don White.

Thanks, Jeanne and Mike Donsbach for your awesome NOLA hospitality as I worked on this story in your Lower Garden home for weeks at a time.

Love and Gold Stars for reading every version of this five-times-revised manuscript over the last five years: Joanne Prine Krüttli and Karen Manthey. Thank you both!

For my friends and family who encouraged me and believed in me this whole time, thank you. Not always easy to believe it when a middle-aged old coot says, "Yeah, I'm going to write a novel." But look, it finally happened! And you encouraged me. Thanks!

Finally, for my beloved husband Paul's unwavering love and support throughout this ongoing process of lessons and setbacks, he gets all of that love back, from my heart to his, always.

Joe McKinstry
April, 2022

Made in the USA
Middletown, DE
03 May 2022

65189308R00149